FRISKY INTENTIONS

THE FRISKY BEAN
BOOK 1

MICHELLE MARS

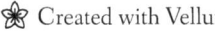

To the many people who have touched my life and there are so many of you. Thank you. 🤍

AUTHOR'S NOTE

I was five when we moved to the United States, to a Midwest city, with a language I didn't know. There were many times I struggled to fit in with my peers as they made fun of what I ate, how I talked, what I wore, and my religion. Is it any wonder that one of my closest friends in elementary school was a Black girl experiencing bullying as well.

Throughout my early years I became a competitive dancer. This became my world. Every instructor I had and many of my friends in my dance group were also from the Black community. Moving into my teens, I loved nothing more than to make up routines to the newest jams and take them to the dance club to show them off. That club was a hip hop club with a diverse group of teens sharing their love of music and dance.

Summer from this book isn't me, but the basis for her history is an ode for the way this awkward Jewish girl, fish-out-of-water finding her way in the Midwest, found herself and was so completely loved and embraced by the Black community I grew up with.

There are other characters in this story that are ode's to other friends I had along the way. The community around me has always been a rich one of various cultures and experiences coming together and that is what I try to incorporate into every book I write.

If I ever fail to do any group justice, I preemptively apologize, please let me know, and I will rectify it.

With love, respect, and an immense amount of gratitude.

P.S. You might wonder later about the Goddess cards... I've never believed in anything beyond until I met my Goddess cards. They aren't identical to the ones in the book, but they can be eerily accurate. Who can't use a little extra divine feminine power?

1

KEYS, PART ONE

Summer

"Oh my god. That's so good." I moaned, swiping at the cream escaping my mouth. "You gave me a mouthgasm."

"Don't I always?"

"Yes, yes, you do."

"Yes, I do, now get your ass in gear, because we only have time for a quickie this morning."

I took one more bite of the decadent new confection, pointedly ignoring my best friend and co-owner of our café, Kevin Johnson. Unlike what my mama taught me, I spoke around my mouthful of sweet, delectable mana.

"If you wanted me to be quick, you shouldn't have handed me such taste-bud-stroking goodness as soon as I walked in the kitchen."

I cringed at his downright insulted look.

"Summer Palmer, it's like you don't even know me. When have I ever done anything less than a full, sensual enticement of the senses? I'm not risking the wrath of your nana Winnie. That woman taught us well, and there's no way I'd insult her by doing anything 'just good.' You know she always said—"

I joined in with him, reciting what Nana Winnie had taught us. I couldn't resist. "Food is love, and baked food is love with a kiss." Nana was so right. I felt it every time I got to baking. That special connection between me and the person enjoying my efforts filled me with all the best feels. I knew Kevin felt the exact same way. It's why we worked so well together.

Annnnnd... since he had a point, I tipped my head in agreement and apology. This was our dream, after all. Each day that I stepped into the kitchen with Kevin and was enveloped by the scent of warm baked goodness, I was transported back to when we were kids. We'd spent endless hours learning from Nana Winnie. That quality and diligence showed in our relatively new café doing as well as it was. Uncontrollably moaning—again—around the last bite of our new pastry, the Pucker Cream Puff, nicknamed PCP, because it was life-altering, I washed my hands and set myself to doing some actual work.

As I chopped, I attempted to stay on task, but my mind kept wandering. Utterly unacceptable. Uneven fruit bits in the Feisty Fruit Cups would not pass my quality inspection, but despite my best efforts, I continued struggling to stay focused. I kept thinking back to the Goddess card I'd pulled that morning and what it could mean for my day.

I have this ritual, you see. Every morning, while getting ready, I pull a Goddess card for daily spiritual guidance. It's been an important part of my routine for years. The cards never let me down. In fact, I credited them with helping me manifest the café.

That day, six months earlier, Kevin and I had gone to lunch for a preliminary discussion about our mutual dream. On the way back to the car, we'd walked past a storefront with a lease sign. My card from that morning, which had given me the push to jump in, was the Greek goddess Eos. Eos represents new beginnings, lust, and adventure. Since I'd learned to listen to my cards—and so had Kevin—we'd called and started the process to lease, on the spot. A short time later, The Frisky Bean went from dream to reality. And here we were.

That same oh-so-powerful card was the one causing me so much emotional turmoil. Last time, I'd already been thinking about a transition so all I'd felt was excitement. But, getting such a powerful, life-altering card on a random day? I wasn't prepared for any more life-altering. I was still too busy with my previously altered life as it was. In the deep recesses of my mind, a new idea was poking at me, but no way was I ready for *that*. Life was good. I wouldn't want anything to risk destabilizing it. Goosebumps rose on my arms even as butterflies played in my stomach. Was I ready? I really didn't—

"Oh, shit! Motherfucker!"

I booked it to the nearest sink, threw the knife in, and quickly engulfed my finger in cold water.

Kevin rushed over, concern clear on his face and in his tone. "What the hell happened?"

"I won the lottery. What do you think happened? I cut my finger off."

"Don't take that tone with me, you big baby. Now let me see it."

I held out my hand for his inspection as I looked, away sure that part of my finger was going to be dangling there like some mob boss movie. "Is it bad? Am I losing a finger? Dammit! I'm losing a finger, aren't I?"

I felt the eye roll coming off of Kevin's tone. "Hon, you're clearly losing something, but it isn't your finger. It's barely worse than a paper cut. You'll survive."

I dared to look at my mortal wound, and yeah, okay, it wasn't *that* bad. Losing a finger would have definitely been a change, but clearly this wasn't what the goddess's guidance had been referring to. While I stared, transfixed, at the thin line of blood that appeared just at the tip of my index finger on my left hand, Kevin disappeared and reappeared with a Band-Aid from the medical kit in the office. He gently wrapped it around and I watched as my not-so-mortal wound disappeared.

"Wanna tell me why you're so distracted that you're cutting yourself? It isn't like you to be careless or graceless while we bake. Other times, absolutely. But here? No way. You look—" He gave me a once-over. "—anxious."

I considered his question and my answer as he turned away, washed his hands, and wandered back to his own workspace. He continued his earlier preparations, scooping mounds of "Sultry" Snickerdoodles onto a baking sheet because nothing but a lost limb would distract him from a smooth-running kitchen. When it came to baking and business, Kevin was all schedules, game plans, and potentially baked-goodness-world-domination. Nothing would come between him and our success.

Also, as my childhood best friend, he knew when I needed my space, like right then. So, instead of pressing me for answers he went back to work and waited patiently.

I took the silent space he provided and continued to consider my answer while doing mindless tasks. I washed the knife twice in scorching water and carefully set it aside. Then, I cleaned up the whole station, sanitizing it and tossing potentially contaminated fruit away. Finally, after covering my injured hand with a glove, I kept on working. Seeing as how distraction got me injured in the first place, I wasn't ready to handle the knife just yet, so I grabbed some mandarin oranges, peeled and put a few slices into each cup. A safe part of my routine.

Thoughts collected, I started to explain in a rush of words, "I don't think anxious is quite right, but I'm not sure if I have a better word. I'm feeling... restless? Or maybe uncertain?"

Ugh! This was *sooo* not like me. *Get your shit together and stop being such a Nervous Nellie!* I took a slow, deep, calming breath and tried again.

"It's probably nothing. I'm not sure why I'm so weirded out, but do you remember that Goddess card I got the day we leased this place? Well, I got her today and I guess since I don't feel ready for any major upheavals right now," though my mind briefly alighted on that one new idea I'd been flirting with, "I'm all out of sorts. It's probably nothing."

There. That sounded almost coherent and like I was back to making sense.

I picked up the knife again, ready to tackle the rest of the fruit, when Kevin scolded from across the kitchen, "If you're handling that knife again, you better fucking relax or you'll end up chopping the fruit into varying sizes or actually losing a finger. You know the first shit don't fly and the second will throw my baking schedule off for the whole day and that don't fly either. Anyway, you're probably right."

Kevin smirked while saying this, which had me narrowing my eyes at him. Before I could inquire about that smirk, though, he continued, "Of course, maybe some hot guy will sweep you off your feet today. That would be a life change you could use. Hell, that would be a life change I could use. Could I get that card next?" His smirk turned wicked. "Maybe we could have a good ol' cat fight over today's hot lover?"

"Uh-huh." I gave him my unamused face. Truth was, Kevin was a beautiful Black man. His arm muscles bunched beneath his tight t-shirt as he put the trays in the oven, taking out others that were ready. He looked like the love child of Blair Underwood and the Black Panther himself, Chadwick Boseman. Of medium height, dark, beautiful soulful eyes, and a smile for days. I would never want to compete with him for a man. No way would I win that battle.

Still, what kind of friend would I be if I let him throw down like that without dishing it right back? "You know I'd totally take you in that fight, right? I got my ninja skills on lockdown."

"Girl, you wouldn't even be able to get into a ninja outfit without falling down. I'm not even sure I'd have to fight you. You'd take two steps my way and knock yourself out on a counter."

Warmth suffused me, surely blotching my pale cheeks. Bantering with Kevin was one of my favorite pastimes. I lamented to him, while returning to my chopping, "Damn. It sucks when your friends know walking is your Achilles' heel."

"Tabling the hot men for now—"

"Yes. Tables of hot men. I'll take that, please."

"Quiet down, hussy. As I was saying, all I have left after the cookies, is to cool the 3B and then work on some more muffins and scones. I made extra 3B since we've been running out of it lately. Who knew it would be our best seller? I guess after that *Fifty Shades* book everyone thinks they're into BDSM."

"Oh! That reminds me. I came up with a name for the almond coconut balls we've been planning. What do you think of Sweet Hairy Balls?" I waggled my eyebrows at him.

"I don't think I want to know how you came up with that. Or maybe I do. Either way, it's perfection. Who doesn't like some Sweet Hairy Balls?" He snorted. "I'll add those into the baking rotation starting tomorrow morning. Now back to business, lazy bones."

We settled into a companionable silence working side by side. Our morning prep was like a perfected ballet. All movement efficient, effective, and creating beauty. In our case, edible beauty. Baking was the only place that I ever felt graceful. I was usually tripping over my own feet—and had the bruises to prove it—but when I baked, somehow my mind shut down, the world receded, and I flowed. That was the best way I could describe it, and I craved the high it gave me regularly.

An hour later, I gazed at the tempting tray of completed 3B—or Bondage Banana Bread—our signature baked good. After the bread cooled, I'd sliced it and laid the pieces out in a single layer. Then, I wrapped thin strips of sugared banana around them and brûléed the banana onto the bread. I couldn't help the fact that my mouth watered every single time, and this time had been no different. They could be classified as a dessert, they were so decadently delicious.

I picked up the finished tray and notified Kevin I was going to open. Pushing through the swinging kitchen door with my hip, I set the tray in the display case. With one last review of my comfortably small, beloved café, I made sure everything was ready to go. Warm and inviting as usual. The five rectangle-shaped tables with seating for two were all clean and orderly. In the two far corners, the comfy couches and chairs around low wood and metal tables were also neat and organized. All was in place.

I loved the ambiance we'd created with the warm mustard color we had chosen for the walls and even more so loved the pictures hanging there. They were provided by a local photographer, who preferred to remain anonymous, to showcase their work and sell them.

The images were black and white and suggestive. An obscure body part here, a rounded body part there. I found them evocative, classy, and also sexy as hell. Perfect for our theme and for my inner sex kitten, assuming I actually had one of those that is. I was no novice with my sexuality, but none of the guys I'd dated or slept with so far had ever fully done it for me. Sex was... mmm... okay, but I wanted so much more. I wanted fireworks. Maybe throw in some kink. Something. My toys had more game than the men I'd been dating lately.

In many ways, the theme of the café was my and Kevin's way of sending out into the universe a request for passion, since he felt much the same as I did. I hoped some someones out there were listening. Maybe the Goddess card was, like Kevin predicted, about a new relationship. Part of me was excited by the prospect and part of me didn't have time for anything else. After having a brief reprieve, finishing up my part of prepping, I was right back to distraction like I'd been earlier. With a wistful sigh, I made my way around the counter of the display case and unlocked the door, flipping the sign to *Open*.

I turned to walk back and, "Dang it!" dropped my keys, because of course I did. In my frustration, I let out a low scream from between my teeth, as the keys loudly clattered to the floor. There was nothing for it. I leaned over to grab them and, of course, that's when I heard the door open behind me. Still bent over, realization that I'd given our first customer of the day quite the backside view struck me much like puberty did... embarrassingly. Mortified, I startled into action. Unfortunately, I swung up too fast and fell backward into whoever had come in. Strong arms wound around me and my breath caught even

as my heart raced at the feel of muscles. Lots of yummy muscles and
—*oh* my—heat. Heat that radiated from those arms straight into my
torso, osmosis style. Somehow, that heat traveled south at warp speed.

"Oh, shit!" The words escaped before I could professionally
temper them. So, of course, I stumbled over my words too, "I'm so, so
sorry. I... I..." I grudgingly stepped out of the arms and spun. I
planned to offer my apologies for the ass view, the falling, and the bad
language. I planned to be a good store owner and make it up to
whoever was there. I planned, and I failed, because when I got my
first sight of the stranger, my jaw dropped low and the only thing that
fell out was, "Holy fuck!"

What. The. Hell? Summer!

Yes. That's right. That's what I said. And, clearly following the
path paved in regrets I was on, I blushed, my blood rushing through
my veins at an all too familiar pace, turning my face warm and
blotchy, while a coppery taste entered my mouth. *Fuckity, fuck, fuck!*
If I hadn't been wearing clothes, we'd both see the flush covering me,
head to toe. Every redhead's bane.

The handsome Norse godlike creature who stood there, amusement clear in his face, had butterflies hitting my stomach in full
migration. His absolutely lickable lips curled up on one side, and his
eyes were crinkled at the corners. And now that I had licking on the
mind, really, his whole body looked as lickable as a giant lollipop of
male proportions.

Why was I pooling drool in my mouth instead of forming words?
Only the goddess would know, but words continued to fail me. *Those
bastards!* I needed some goddamn words. Words that didn't amount
to cussing at my customer. I tried, again, to remind myself that I had a
business to run, but geez, his way-taller-than-me muscular build
—*Was he six feet?*—had shut my brain right down.

So I did the only thing I could do.

Absolutely nothing.

Priceless.

I just stood there gaping. Gaping and watching as his hazel—of course, they had to be hazel—eyes crinkled even more. Since I had nothing better to do with my brain cells in hibernation, I pondered the universe. More specifically why the universe saw fit to throw gods in the way of mere mortals and then, insult to injury, wrap all that perfection in a sexy business suit of dark gray, with a crisp white shirt unbuttoned at his throat. That was just downright mean. I was calling foul!

With my search for words being absolutely useless, I remembered I still had my damn keys to get, so I bent down to grab them because, why not?

His groan above alerted me to my miscalculation. You see, we'd still been standing relatively close together when I reached down. With that brilliant move, I found my head in dangerous proximity to his groin. His now slightly bulging groin. Or was that my imagination?

It took a moment, because it really was a lovely view, but I came back to my senses. I'd been caught ogling his groin. *Yikes!* I averted my eyes and swiftly grabbed for the slippery-as-fuck keys. That's when I heard Kevin, who must have come in from the kitchen, say, "Oh, honey. If you want to do that, you may want to turn that sign back to *Closed*. I don't blame you, though. Welcome to The Frisky Bean. Coffee? Tea? Me? Please tell me it's me."

All I wanted was for the ground to open and swallow me whole. Thinking about opening and swallowing, with my head where it was, proved a really bad idea that left me damp and dying all at once. I finally had the keys in my grasp and somehow made it to a standing position without falling over, and glared at Kevin. Finding my voice—hallelujah—I growled out, "Kevin Dwayne Johnson! That is *not* an appropriate way to greet a customer!"

Of course, neither was yours. Whatever.

I turned toward said customer, only to find him still silently sporting a sexy-as-sin grin. His eyes, though... *Damn*, his eyes held a warm heat I was pretty sure was directed my way, and my insides liquified. I thought I heard Kevin snort and mumble under his breath,

"Pot, kettle, black, sister." Then there was silence as the door to the kitchen swooshed and I assumed Kevin left.

"I... am... so... incredibly... sorry... for everything that has happened in the last few minutes. Can we please pretend none of this ever happened? None of it. Ever."

2

WHO'S ON WHAT?

Jason

I knew three things in that moment. First, I needed to hurry up and get what I came for. Second, I should focus on that and that alone. Third, there was no way that was happening.

Every inch of me bristled to take control of the whirlwind of chaos in front of me. My fingers itched to grab onto her curly, red hair that gave the impression of an attempted jailbreak from her messy bun. Meanwhile, my lips wanted to taste her cherry-tinged lips as they curved in a tentative smile. I'd been afforded a chance to study her as she'd fumbled through our first encounter, and I liked what I saw. A lot. My semi-hard state concurred.

I'd always thought I liked an orderly woman, but this woman was definitely someone I could have a thing for. Images replayed in fast-forward through my mind. First her well-rounded, delectable ass sticking up in the air hugged in tight black leggings, the way her lush body covered only by a tank top and sheer top felt in my arms, her deep blush, and then, the coup d'état, her head bent so close to my straining cock. Yep. My body was currently on full alert and wanted to get closer to her body as soon as possible.

It took me a moment to realize she was waiting for a response. It took me another moment to remember the question as my eyes drifted over her medium frame and full curves. I finally gazed back up into her eyes and answered her query. "I'm sorry to disappoint, but I'm afraid that nothing about the last few minutes is forgettable."

My enjoyment of the situation continued as she gasped in response and her cheeks continued to broadcast her embarrassment with the most beautiful shade of pink. I wondered if other body parts of hers would flush a similarly nice hue. I barely contained another groan and avoided adjusting myself.

"Um... How can I help you today?" she haltingly asked me as she turned and regrettably made her way behind the counter.

Once her perfect butt was out of sight, I walked up to the case with renewed intention. I had a client to please, which meant staying focused. Keeping my eyes on the prize was always my top priority and today that prize was not in getting laid, but in acquiring a hard-fought, exceedingly desirable client. I'd worked hard to make Jason Winter a name that others respected in my industry and that wasn't by losing focus on what was important. The client.

I maneuvered things back on track. "I've heard you have the best pastries and coffee in town."

It took her a minute to reply, and she must have found some calm in that time, because her voice sounded sure and steady when she finally replied. "You've heard right. What can I get you?"

"I need one vanilla latte."

"One Virginal Vanilla Latte. What size?"

"I'm sorry, what?"

She looked up at me in confusion, and here I thought I was the one confused.

"What size?"

I must have heard her wrong. "A medium vanilla latte."

"Okay. One medium Virginal Vanilla Latte. Whole milk okay?"

"What?"

"Whole milk okay?" She said this really slow.

That grated. I was done with this "who's on first" conversation. "Why do you keep saying virginal vanilla latte?"

She really looked confused now, and maybe even a little agitated. "Because that's what you're ordering?" She said it as a question. Her expression and voice changed as she continued. "Oh." Her mouth formed that perfect symbol of the letter itself. "I see. I'm guessing that whoever told you we were the best forgot to mention one of our defining characteristics. Did you notice the name of the café?"

"Yeah. The Frisky Bean. Why?"

To that, she gave me a saucy grin. I had to acknowledge I enjoyed her expressive face even as exasperation at our conversation grew.

"Because everything here is a bit... frisky. For instance, we have the Moaning Mocha, Hot and Heavy Chocolate, and the Cappuccin-Oh-Oh-Oh." Her voice drifted quieter on each successive "oh" as she looked up into my face. The lust she ignited on each subsequent drink order must have shown.

Before I could stop myself, I blurted, "You said everything here is frisky... does that include you?"

I did *not* ask her that. I wasn't in the practice of saying overly seductive things to random women. I was a fucking feminist. I had female friends. I was all for #allmen and #mybodymychoice. What in the ever-loving hell made me say that? Even as I berated myself, though, I couldn't bring myself to regret it, because that beautiful pink blush was splashed across her features again and not one note of disapproval was there. Still, it was inappropriate.

"I'm sorry, that was wrong of me to say."

She cleared her throat and reached to a stack of menus at the front of the counter I'd ignored up until then. She handed me one. "Yes. True. Accepted. Perhaps this will help? Now, back to your order. Um... Whole milk okay?" She smiled warmly my way.

I was glad she accepted my apology, but also disappointed at not getting an answer. It was probably for the best that she brought us back to my purpose there. Internally, though, frustration clawed at me to push. I ignored it. "Actually, skim milk."

"Got it. Anything else you need?" Her eyes danced.

Ignoring my inappropriate side didn't mean she wasn't still game to flirt, so I purposely ignored the menu in my hand, wanting to hear her repeat back my order. "Yes. I need a medium coffee, black."

She hesitated, briefly, but with a mischievous glint in her eyes she replied, "One medium French Kiss Coffee..." She paused and looked up at me and now her eyes danced with mirth. "Naked." She blushed again but held my gaze. "Anything else?"

Heat coursed through me everywhere at her willingness to play, but also her sense of humor was enticing as well. I smiled back, thoroughly enjoying the conversation. "Yes. A blueberry scone, two lemon breads, and a banana bread."

She looked down at the register, a loose curl caressing the side of her face, and tapped away. As she spoke, her voice grew huskier, and my dick grew heavier. "So, one Rock Your Socks Blueberry Scone, two Lickable Lemon Breads, and one 3B."

"3B? Dare I ask?"

Her nervous energy permeated the space between us as she looked up and met my eyes. Brave. Not backing down. "One of our most popular items," she said in a breathy voice, "Bondage Banana Bread."

I couldn't—didn't want to—say anything that could break our eye contact after that. Unintended time passed as we both studied each other. Heat rose like a bonfire. Thoughts I had no right to be having, being had.

Eye on the prize, Winter.

I broke the silence, my voice huskier than intended, "It's that good? I guess I'll need to try one of those myself. Make it two."

"Okay. Um... Anything else I can get you?" Her voice came out equally husky.

"No. That's all of it."

She rattled off a rather high price for coffee and pastries, but my client refused to get the stuff from anywhere else, and really, I didn't mind. My client could have asked me for a bunch more and I wouldn't have noticed or cared while transfixed with the barista. Transaction completed, the lightning rod for my electric response busied herself making and packaging my order. In an attempt to calm my libido, I looked around, hoping to discharge the current between us. On the wall closest to me, I studied a black-and-white print. It took me a moment to realize that I was intently staring at the curve of someone's well-rounded and lighted side boob.

Was it hers? Oh shit!

I looked away guiltily, afraid I might get caught ogling her breasts, or whosoever's breasts, instead of artistically appreciating the photo.

"It's for sale."

Before I could respond, the door behind me opened and I turned to see who was coming in just as she welcomed the two thirty-some-thing-year-old women, who were clearly regulars. Disappointed at losing the bubble of sexy one-on-one time but realizing it was just as well, since I had a schedule to keep, I turned my attention back to her and asked, "What?"

"The photo. All the photos. They're for sale."

"They are rather well-suited to your theme, but I'm not in the market for new art."

"We get new prints regularly. You never know, something might strike your fancy." Something had struck my fancy all right, but it wasn't framed on a wall.

She assembled the order into a special carrier with a box on one side and a drink carrier on the other. "Here you go. I hope you and your friend enjoy it."

Was she fishing? Well, I was more than fine with that. "I'm sure my client and I will."

Her sunshine smile was back and enthralled me all over again. "Come back anytime."

I repeated, "I'm sure I will."

I casually greeted the women behind me as I walked out of my new favorite coffee shop. It wasn't until I was halfway to the movie set, where my client waited, that I slammed my palm into the steering wheel with the realization that I'd never even gotten her name.

3

GOSSIP, FOOD, AND BOOKS

Summer

"Wow! If that's your new clientele, I'm going to be in here even more often than I already am." Camila with short, wavy brown hair and expressive brown eyes was also the speaker currently slow-fanning herself with her perfectly manicured hand. Her smooth light-brown complexion and perfect cheekbones along with her sweet personality and casual elegance made her a stunner.

Lisa was slow-nodding her head in coordination and apparent support of what Camila, her girlfriend, had said. She was a blonde with a shoulder-length bob and blue eyes. Always seemingly sporting the perfect tan as though she lived at the beach, her tall, full-figured frame was perpetually perfectly styled. Confidence oozed from her every pore.

They were regulars with a capital R. Lisa high-fived Camila saying, "We could definitely add a third if he looked like that."

"It's like a hall pass, or whatever they call them these days."

"Exactly."

I could hear them talking, but I was still staring out the door thinking how broad his shoulders looked in his fine-tailored suit.

Camila waved her hand in front of my face, "Earth to Summer. Are you with us, or did your brain walk out the door with Mr. Hottie McHotpants?"

My tension, sexual and otherwise, released in a burst of laughter, breaking whatever spell I'd been under. Balance reestablished for the first time since I opened the café that morning, I smiled at Camila. "You have no idea how bad I needed to laugh. Thanks, and I have no idea if—what did you call him? Oh yeah, Mr. Hottie McHotpants—will be coming back here or not. Of course, if it would drive business, an entrepreneurial girl can dream. On the other hand, considering how I reacted to him, maybe I should hope he never comes back. I made such a fool of myself!" I dropped my head in my hand and shook it in disgust.

"Who wouldn't make a fool of herself? Can I have the opportunity to make a fool of myself, too?" Lisa winked.

"I'm sorry, but I call dibs on fool making with Mr. McHotpants. You'll have to find some other hottie to be a fool for. Hmm. I'm not sure all of that came out right. Ignore me. English, sentence structures, and hospitality exited as soon as my libido held a breath it didn't know it was holding like a romance heroine from a spicy book." I paused, tilting my head and tapping a finger on my lip as a thought struck me. "You know, this gives me a great idea for the café. I'll have to run it by Kev, of course, but considering his own reading collection, I can't imagine he won't like it."

"Like what? You haven't actually shared with the class yet," Camila grumped.

"Oooo, hot girl and guy dance reviews here at The Frisky Bean? Tell me you're implementing Magic Mike and Michaela nights!" Lisa looked all too excited by her wild idea.

I couldn't contain my laughter again. This was what made these ladies some of my favorite customers. "No. Though I do get the appeal of that. But nothing quite *that* wild. I was thinking I could add a bookshelf to that corner near the pleather couches and under the butt shot—" I indicated the somewhat open area near the far couches.

"—and I could fill the shelves with super-hot romance novels. Maybe eventually even have author signings or something. Oh! I could even try to work out a joint effort with The Ripped Bodice up Venice Boulevard. What do you think?" The more I described the addition, the more excited I became for all the possibilities. It energized me. I loved my café. It filled something in me to be able to create a place for community and belonging. Somewhere where I belonged, too.

Both Camila's and Lisa's eyes grew big and their faces broke into broad grins. They exclaimed at the same time.

"Yes!"

"Love it!"

Camila excitedly gestured, "Isn't The Ripped Bodice that bookstore that carries only romance novels?"

"Exactly! Step one, I need to get Kev to okay the bookshelf. I might even be able to make that happen later today. Now, what can I get you both? The usual? I'll throw in a Two-O Scone for each of you for the great inspiration. I know it's your favorite. And I'm not talking about the 'orange' part." I winked at them conspiratorially as Camila and Lisa gave each other another high-five for the "orgasmic" part.

A few tiring but fun hours of service later, I stood alongside Kevin, studying our newly installed shelves with our swiftly pieced-together romantic library. It had been a simple thing to order the shelves for same-day delivery and an even easier thing to "convince" Kevin to take an hour to go grab us some books from The Ripped Bodice.

Kevin spoke up first, "Girl, I love this idea and I know our customers will love it too. I see one problem, though." He sounded really concerned, which in turn made *me* really concerned.

"What? Is it too much?"

"Hell no. The problem is keeping me working instead of sitting out here reading."

"Tell me about it. I've been wanting to read the newest book from Lexi Blake for a few days now, but I've been working too hard to get to it. Now, I'll have to watch as others get to read it before me." I sighed ever so tragically. "But, let's be real. There is no way you'd ever drop the ball on your business, good book or not."

"You know that's right."

"Well, it was still a great idea even if it's pure torture. And not the good kind." I waggled my brows.

"Speaking of torture, you've been torturing me all morning. You never did tell me what happened with that gorgeous man. Did he get your number? Did you get his name? Did your panties melt off? Do tell."

I nudged my friend playfully but knew exactly what he meant. It had been equally hard on me not finding an opportunity to gossip with him about Mr. McHotpants. Not that I was complaining. Nope. As a new business owner, busy was always a good thing. Still, I was quite excited to finally have a chance to gab with Kevin during our brief pre-lunch lull. "I am such a butthead. In all the things we said to each other, somehow, we never exchanged names. I honestly can't believe the way I behaved around him. I'm mortified. Like, change my name and move to a new location mortified. Like, *There's Something About Mary* hair gel mortified."

Kevin chuckled. "Sweetie, you are many things, but graceful, especially around someone like that, is not one of them. Don't be so dramatic and tell me what *did* happen. Do feel free to describe it in great detail."

I slapped him on his insensitive jerk arm. "Meanie. Well, after my performance of what-not-to-do-when-handling-a-customer, he placed his order, right?" I continued, relaying all of the events of that morning's encounter. Upon reflection I added, "I wonder if he might be a bit prudish." I bit my lip like I often did when in thought. "He was conservatively dressed and was clearly embarrassed when I caught him looking at the photos." I found myself frowning at the possibility of my dream man being a prude. I was most definitely not interested in being with anyone, anymore, who couldn't match my sexually adventurous nature.

Talk about putting the cart before the horse. You'll probably never even see him again, and that would probably be for the best.

I realized I'd gotten lost in my own thoughts and tuned into Kevin again as he was saying, "Now you have me picturing that tall, blond, heartthrob in a whole new way." He changed his voice to something that sounded prim and proper. "Excuse me. But if you don't mind, would you please pull up your skirt? And if it isn't too much trouble, lean over this table where I've laid out a tablecloth to keep things clean. Oh! Nicely done. Now I'll take a quick minute, dear."

And this, THIS, is why I loved my friend. He got me in ways no one else did. I laughed so hard I snorted. My hand flew up to cover my mouth, but that made me laugh even harder and the snorts kept coming. The sound of the door startled me back to sober. I straightened and took a few deep breaths, hissing at Kevin as I walked by, "You are so *bad*!"

More hours later, when Revi Stanfield, one of our small family of employees, walked in, I was caught off guard. How was it three o'clock already? Time had flown by, and I was ready to hand over the register reins and move to the back office for a couple of hours of bookkeeping.

"Hey, Revi. Nice shirt."

Revi was a big-hearted, green-haired, tattoo-sleeved, and metal-detector-nightmare pierced, mad scientist. I'd always felt amusement at those people who judged Revi based solely on their appearance. At the age of twenty-three, they were one of the youngest and most brilliant students working to receive a PhD in biotech and were being courted by various drug R&D teams upon their graduation this semester. Like a maternal older sister, I couldn't be prouder.

"Thanks! Found it at Re-New, that thrift store a couple of blocks over."

I thought the shirt, which read, 'Let's heal each other. One world,' fit them perfectly. I had no doubt that one day they'd achieve their lofty goals of finding cures and reducing the cost of medicine.

I pointed at our new bookshelf. "We have a new addition."

"Let me guess, theories on quantum mechanics? No, wait. Evolutionary biological defenses? Hold on. I got this. Systemic misogyny on the Oregon trail?"

Caught off guard, my funny bone tickled into snorts for the second time that day. "I like that last one."

"So, romance novels then?"

"Ah, you know us well." I patted them on the back, and then indicated the register. "She's all yours."

"Sounds good. Have you seen the couple of punks with signs on the corner?"

"No. Are they dancing advertisers?"

"Only if they're advertising their sensitive uptightness. They're protesting the café because, apparently, they don't like sexy things."

"Shit. I know it's not for everyone, but, come on, this is LA between Hollywood and Venice Beach. Give me a break."

"They're probably just bored jerks. I'm happy to have words with bored jerks."

I knew Revi meant well, but I didn't need anyone else fighting my battles or getting hurt. "Nah. Just ignore it and we'll see what happens."

They were washing their hands as they answered, "Ignore assholes. Easy as pie."

"Thanks, Revi."

They gave me a two-finger salute as I went through the door to the kitchen. Kevin snagged a hug as he was leaving, and I continued into the back office.

By five o'clock, I was beyond ready to go home. I was often staying after my shift ended, but tonight, I *needed* to gossip with my roommate, Jessica, about Mr. Hottie McHotpants. With a wave to Revi who was set to close the café at nine, I walked back home.

En route, I stopped to talk with some of my homeless friends and gave them some coffee, water, and baked goods. I'd gotten to know most of them by name since moving to the area. Benny, in particular, was the acting leader that made sure everyone was provided for as best he could. In our interactions, I'd learned that they had their own community, a found family, and I'd grown to love our time together as we shared our stories with each other.

It hurt to see them without homes. I didn't have enough to help get them all off the streets, but I could provide them something to make their life a little bit better, so that's what I did. It was the least I could do. We all needed to take care of each other. This lesson was taught to me from my youngest age. First by my mom based on tikkun olam from our Jewish religion and later by my adopted family, the Palmers, from their episcopalian church. Kevin and I often tossed around ideas on how we might help more. Until then, we did what we could.

I continued on my way, and for the rest of my walk, I wavered between fantasies of what if. What if he came back? What if we got frisky? What if I took the café earnings we'd seen recently and expanded into catering? What if I stopped trying to rock my happy world and just enjoyed it? What if I shut down all thinking because all this waffling was getting me nowhere?

I'd worked myself into quite the frustrated corner by the time I made it home and it wasn't even a long walk. I found Jessica Lin, my roommate and other bestie, busy prepping dinner listening to Beyoncé's "Lemonade" loudly in the background. She wore gray leggings, a pink tank top, and her favorite apron that read, "Books and wine and everything's fine," and had her black, straight hair pulled back into a high ponytail. I took a moment to jam out before turning down the volume so we could talk.

"Hey, Jess, what're we having tonight?" Jess was a waitress at a local diner, an aspiring romance writer, and most importantly as a roommate, also a phenomenal home chef. I appreciated the hell out of that last one, regularly.

"Oh, hey. Well, I was working on my book that we talked about this morning, you know, the *Jurassic Park* meets *When Harry Met Sally* dinosaur shifter one? So, I started writing about prehistoric flora. That had me remembering the plants I've killed over the years with my black thumb. That reminded me that one of those plants was a basil plant, you know, because I thought it would be neat to have fresh herbs to use while cooking. Well, anyway, one thought led to another, as they do, and we're having stir-fry chicken tonight."

"Uh-huh. Makes perfect sense." Jessica was the queen of "one thought led to another," but sometimes those thoughts were harder to follow than others. I knew, KNEW, I shouldn't say what I was about to say next, but I did anyway. "What can I help with?"

Jessica's horrified face as she spun to face me, ponytail slapping her in the chin, she whipped around so fast, was answer enough. But, for emphasis, she snapped, "You are *not* to touch this dish."

I very dramatically reenacted being stabbed. "Why ever not?" Obviously, I knew why not, but I also enjoyed poking the beast. What else were friends for?

"Oh. Please. You know exactly why not. You want to bake something or brew something, this kitchen is open to you, but I won't let you anywhere near here when there is cooking to be done and you know it. So stop poking me—"

Called out! Drats.

And yeah, we both knew the score. That was Jessica's very pristine kitchen even though both our names were on the lease. It had been true in our last apartment, as well. In fact, it was one of the things that had been evergreen since we met three years ago when I'd answered Jessica's roommate ad off of Roomie Times. If I ever tried, tried being the operative word here, to cook, inevitably it would go horribly wrong and it would make Jessica's eyes twitch. Inflicting regular eye twitches was definitely against our roommate code and since we were living in a two-bedroom, one-bathroom, shoebox apartment, a solid roommate code could be the difference between best friends and tabloid-worthy jail time.

"I cook, you talk. Tell me about your day," Jessica said as she walked back into the kitchen.

"Fine!" I flopped down on Elvis, lovingly named this because we had the most decadent blue suede couch, with a humph as I stubbed my toe on the coffee table. To comfort myself I tossed my beloved rainbow quilt over my lap, a gift from Nana Winnie, and lazily caressed my hand up and down the top of the couch. I took great satisfaction in watching the way the soft suede would get lighter and darker depending on the direction my hand went. Inevitably, Midnight, our cat, would come to investigate and catch me petting the couch, causing him great distress and jealousy. As expected, he jumped up and sat squarely where my hand had been with a loud, "Meow," and a judgmental glare. Giving him his due, I stroked the feline-in-charge, which was fine, because I also loved the feel of his silky black fur. As he began to purr, I began to talk. "So, I met a guy this morning. And really, by met, I mean embarrassed myself completely in front of the most gorgeous man I've ever seen. It was a complete and utter disaster. I may need to change my name and move to a new state type of situation."

While Jessica worked in the kitchen, I filled her in on what went down with the stranger who'd occupied my thoughts the rest of the damn day.

Jessica finally responded, "I wish I could've been there for that. Of all the days that I didn't come with you to the café... it's simply not acceptable. You are only allowed to have such interactions on the days I'm there from now on."

"It's not like I can plan for something like that. Excuse me, universe, do you mind scheduling Summer's embarrassing playlist according to my friend's schedule? No? *And*, it's not like you're ever going to be there that early. I believe it was you I found asleep on the couch this morning."

"True. But you know me, once I get an idea in my head, I either write until the laptop slides from my lap or I'm drooling on my keys. Between my shifts at the diner and my writing, who has time for early mornings? Not this night owl. We weren't talking about me, though. When do you see him again? What's his name?"

"Um... I don't know." I concentrated on petting Midnight, trying *very* hard not to blush. I failed. *Dang it!* If I never blushed again, it would be too soon. I tried for nonchalance but was pretty sure I failed at that too. "With the one percent of my brain that was functioning, I forgot to get his name. Though, really, he didn't get mine either so perhaps he wasn't interested. I probably won't even see him again."

"If you do see him, you have to let me come and drool with you."

"I don't think it's very hygienic to allow you to drool in the café. Anyway, I can try to reach you, but it's not like I can keep him in the store until you get there if he's in a hurry, like he seemed this morning. *But...* let's say you are there, can you promise me that you won't be obvious?"

"Me? Obvious? I don't know what you mean." Jessica's innocent act had me giving her my unamused look.

"Really?" Sarcasm dripped from my now three-syllable word. "What would you call your approach the last time we went dancing? You know, when you went up to the guy I was dancing with and told me, 'He'll do, but make him lose the shoes. Those are some god-awful shoes,' right to his face. Subtlety is a lost art for you."

"I find it's overrated. Anyway, I promise to try to be on my best behavior." Jessica came out of the kitchen, wiping her hands dry on a towel. "I've finished the prep. It shouldn't take too long to cook, so I'll start in a few minutes." Switching topics like a tennis match, she continued with the earlier one. "Do you think he was your—" said with an overly dramatic flair, so I knew what was coming, "—new beginning from this morning's Goddess business?"

Yes, please!

"Ye of little belief. You know, I can't be sure, but I can hope so." I gave her a saucy wink, so she threw a pillow at me.

"Hopefully some wickedly good endings too. I'll live vicariously through you and my books." She sighed with another dramatic flourish.

I was all on board for some happy endings. Realistically, I didn't know his name, and if we did get to know each other, there may not be any wild passion to speak of, but the thrill I'd felt that morning, well, I'd never felt that before. That had to mean that at the very least we had potential. Right? Would he come back? Well... I really hoped so.

"Is it an Elvis dinner and a movie night or should we set the table?" *Elvis! Elvis!* I may have had a preference.

"Definitely an Elvis night."

"Agreed. And before I forget, let me tell you about the new installation in the café. It's right up your alley."

Later, food in hand, my mind refused to concentrate on the movie even though Ryan Reynolds was in it. That right there said a lot. I started wondering if my sexy customer was Mr. McHotpants or if he was more a Mr. McProper. And, would I ever get the chance to find out? I couldn't wait to see what the Goddess cards had to say tomorrow.

4

WELCOME TO THE FRISKY BEAN

Jason

I seethed with irritation. Living in LA was the best, don't get me wrong, but on days like the one I was experiencing right then? When I made sure I left early, and still arrived late because of traffic? Well, no place was perfect. It still royally sucked. Fortunately, the actress I was courting to sign a contract with me wanted coffee and snacks from only one place, which actually worked toward my own goals, since I wanted to see the beautiful café owner again. Unfortunately, she also made it clear that she couldn't stand tardiness. Also, unfortunately, there had been an accident on the Pacific Coast Highway, which made tardiness an inevitability since I wasn't going to show up empty-handed.

It was especially frustrating because I'd hoped to have some time to get to know the café owner, hence the leaving early, but now, well, now I was already a few minutes behind schedule and time was a commodity I didn't have to spend. If I stayed on course, though, I could at least charm her name and number to be served along with my order. Considering the night I'd had, it was near the top of my priorities list.

I still couldn't believe that all of my dreams featured a curvaceous redhead, and were so hot, I woke up aroused to the point of coming within seconds of palming myself. The last time I'd come that fast was probably my first time, and even that may not be true. One thing I knew for sure was that I would have to behave better than I had the day before if I was going to stand a chance.

No stupid questions about friskiness this time, asshole. She'll think you're a creep.

Fortified with my game plan to be swift and a gentleman, I opened the door and stepped inside. She wasn't at the counter, nor bent over in front of me. I heard a noise to my right and came face to ass with her bite-worthy butt in formfitting, embroidered-pocket-on-the-ass jeans. I was rock hard in an instant. *Damn!* I was screwed. She was standing on a short ladder placing a picture high on the wall near the door. Then she wasn't. She gasped and fell.

Reacting on instinct, before I could even fully register what was happening, I found my face mere inches from hers. She was cradled in my arms, one behind her back and the other under her legs. Her messy bun was askew and somehow messier, like someone had pulled on it, and her lips were parted in a perfect O of surprise and all my previous intentions disappeared in a foggy haze. My gaze lingered on her plump lips and when I saw her white teeth bite into her bottom one, I groaned. I believe I also whispered, "Je-sus, you're killing me."

In an attempt at self-preservation, I moved my gaze from her lips to her eyes. I admit freely how wrong I was to think that would somehow help me control my lust-fogged brain. Dead wrong. Her eyes were a hot green, glazed and dilated with anticipation. My body thrummed with restrained action. Coiled like a spring. I froze. I couldn't move. I knew what I wanted to do. I knew what I should do. Indecision left me unable to fucking move. There was a good chance that if I moved, *want* was going to override *should* by a long shot, and that would be bad. So I stood there, like a statue, and stared, lusted, ached. *Motherfucking damn.*

She, apparently, didn't suffer from such indecisive problems. I felt as she pushed up in my arms, her head coming closer to mine. So, I met her part way. Her lips on mine. Just like that. If she had kissed me gently, things might have stayed on this side of sane, but she didn't. No. She kissed me with wild abandon and set my blood racing south. One taste of the soft sweetness of her mouth and my tongue surged forward ready to plunder. Frozen no more, I took all that her mouth offered. This wild creature took from me as well. No passivity. All action. I was lost, which might explain why I wasn't able to react with my usual reflexes when she pulled back on another gasp. Her swift, jerky movement almost sent her tumbling out of my arms. As I scrambled to grab her more firmly so she wouldn't fall, she flung her arms to encircle my neck, which threw all of her body weight into mine and, well, I lost my balance. A dull pain shot up my back and all of my air escaped in an audible *oomph*, as I slammed back into the door. Honestly, I was struggling to keep up with what the hell was going on, because... What the hell was going on?

She buried her face in my neck, and her body trembled. After taking a moment to catch my breath, I tried to reassure her, by holding her even more tightly and whispering in her ear, "It's okay. I've got you."

She made some incomprehensible sounds and concern lanced through me that she might actually be crying. What was I going to do with a sobbing woman? And why would she be sobbing? Was she scared? Did she hurt herself, after all? Damn it all! What the hell was happening?

When she finally lifted her face, I realized how wrong I'd been in my panicking. Snort-inducing giggles racked her body and every time she snorted it sent her into another fit of that adorable laughter. The beautiful blush, I loved so much the day before, was staining her cheeks and running down her neck, and one of her hands released its hold on me as she tried to cover her mouth. I was utterly entranced. Turned to stone, again, for a whole other reason.

"Seriously, girlfriend! You should take that man-sicle to your place and get it over with so you can stop throwing yourself at him

every morning. You're developing a bad, bad, baaad girl habit here."
The man from the day before, I thought I remembered his name was
Kevin, stood just beyond the kitchen door.

I looked back at the bundle of humor in my arms. She had streaks
of tears running down her cheeks. She was glowing and I was hard.
Very, very hard. She looked toward the other man and said, "Don't
you have some Sweet Hairy Balls to finish up?" *What?* I couldn't help
snorting myself. That made her turn an even deeper shade of red, as
realization of what she'd said sank in. She avoided looking directly at
me after that. "Perhaps you should put me down so I can go drown
myself in a bowl of cookie batter in the back. Kevin, you need a new
partner."

I relaxed my hold, letting her legs drop down first. Once I'd
assured she'd found her balance, I reluctantly released her, but not
before I felt her hard nipples press against my chest. *This woman.*
Jesus. My body filed its protest in triplicate when she stepped back
and away from me. Then I realized she had to have felt my erection
too. I inwardly groaned. *Smooth. Real smooth. Real gentlemanly.*
Dumbass.

"I'm afraid you don't have an out clause for being a harlot, honey,
so you'll have to stay my partner. If we had that clause, neither of us
would have made it a day. Now, don't do anything I would do out
here." Kevin swooshed back into the kitchen, but all of my attention
was for her.

She still refused to meet my eyes as she said, "I'm guessing there
is no forgetting this incident either? So, um, I promise I don't usually
—literally—throw myself at the customers. Since I'm not allowed to
die on my batter-made sword, I guess I'm left with saying, thank you
for catching me, and, um, sorry for kissing you, and what can I get
you today?" She finally looked up and hesitantly smiled at me. The
blush I adored was still in full bloom. I wanted to rub my finger over
her pink cheek. Over her soft lips. Across her straight brows.

It took me a few good moments to stop imagining all those things
and reconnect my brain with my earlier intentions. When I was

finally prepared to speak again and give her my order, I said, "I liked kissing you." *What was he, thirteen?* I cleared my throat and tried again. "A lot."

What the fuck? Ask her for what you want already.

I cleared my throat, again—*Third time's the charm, right?*—ready to order some pastries and coffee. What came out, was, "Your name." This time I groaned audibly. "What I meant to say was, if you don't mind telling me, I would like to know your name and I need the same order as yesterday, today." That was better. Since when was I awkward with a woman? But damn, she was so unpredictable and mouthwatering. Mouthwatering. Yeah. I didn't really want the coffee or pastries, I wanted a treat of another kind. Her lips.

5

MY NAME IS... MY NAME IS...

Summer

My lips still tingled from the earlier feel of his. I couldn't believe the last few minutes. Sure, I'd gotten the Roman goddess Empanada's card of hospitality and welcome, but there was welcoming and then there was... yeah, I wasn't sure what that had been. Could that really have been what the goddess meant to happen? If so, yowza. My spiritual self was biting a knuckle, I was sure of it. Could they give a better warning next time? Which Goddess card meant, "You're about to get your boat rocked?" or "Attacking customers with kisses up ahead?" or "You're about to fall head over heels, hold on?" Because, sure enough, I'd fallen, and was still falling, hard and fast, and I didn't even know his name yet, which reminded me that I was standing there staring at him instead of answering his question. I was doing that a lot lately. My voice sounded rather breathless when I said, "Summer."

"Summer?"

"My name."

Unprepared was going to be the word of the day, apparently, because surely I was unprepared for him to break out in laughter and blinked a few times in surprised response. *What the hell?* Sure my name was not the most popular, but last I checked, it wasn't something to laugh at. He was lucky that he was so beautiful to look at and that hearing his deep throaty laughter did funny things to my insides, because it went a long way to minimize my overall perturbedness. I didn't even care if that wasn't a word. With one hand on my hip in a fist, I proceeded to glare at him. He was being downright rude. Given a few more moments, I probably would have begun tapping my foot, too.

I could tell the instant he registered my annoyance because he sobered quickly. "I'm sorry. I didn't mean to laugh, and I promise, I'm not laughing at you."

"Riigghhtt." I dragged the word out with all the sarcasm I fostered in my soul.

"No. Really. Let me introduce myself and we'll see if you can keep a straight face. I'm Jason Winter."

"No joke?" *Come on. He had to be joking. What were the chances?*

"Nope."

My lips twitched. I tried, so very hard, not to laugh but there was no containing it. I burst out laughing too. "Oh lord. Could you imagine if we were to get married and I took your name?" I laughed harder until finally feeling all the awkwardness drain away. "No way."

He smirked. "Are you saying no to the marriage proposal I haven't issued on the second day we've met?"

Embarrassment warred with my natural enjoyment of the absurd and absurdity won out. Of course. "Yeah. I guess I am. Haven't had that happen before?"

"I can't say that I have."

"Huh. Weird. Well, Mr. Winter, I'm sorry I can't marry you, but I can take care of that order for you." I went behind the counter and started organizing the order I remembered from the day before.

"Call me Jason."

"Okay. Jason. How did you enjoy your 3B yesterday?" I winked at him and then inwardly cringed. Had I really just winked at him? Apparently, awkward was back to play.

"It was one of the best banana breads I've ever had, though I think it left me with rope burn on my tongue."

I looked up in confusion, saw the smirk on his gorgeous face, and snorted. "Good one."

"Thanks."

"Tell you what, stay right there. Be right back." I headed back into the kitchen area and before Kevin could say a word, I held up my hand. "Not yet." Kevin gave me one of his 'uh-huh' looks and continued working. I grabbed a couple of the new confections we were working on and headed back out. Jason was staring at one of the pictures on the wall on the far side of the counter. This one had a shot of some rounded skin taken at such an angle and with the edges fuzzed out that it takes a moment to realize that you're staring at the upper part of someone's butt. Imagining him staring as fixedly at my own backside had me heating up all over again. And, a part of me thought I should probably stop picturing it, but why? It was such a delicious image.

When the door between the kitchen and the front of the house made a slight sound from closing, Jason jumped and I could swear he was blushing. About time I wasn't the only one blushing. Apparently, he was as embarrassed today as yesterday to be caught staring. I considered smoothing it over for him, but... nah. "See something you like? As I mentioned, all the photos are for sale."

"Uh. They're really—" he looked like he was having a hard time finding the right word to use and then continued with, "—nice, but no. Not looking to buy a butt right now." He gave me a rueful grin. "That did not come out right."

I giggled. Like a schoolgirl. Who was I? Beavis and Butt-head? 'Har, har, you said butt!' Gathering my composure, or what was left of it, I said, "Well, you may not want to buy a butt right now, but I'm throwing in a couple of our new product, the Sweet Hairy Balls, for you and whoever else this food is for, to try." I threw them into the box with the rest of his order and rang him up.

"You were serious that you have a product called Sweet Hairy Balls? You guys don't play here."

"Oh... I wouldn't say that." What the hell did I just say? And with that tone?

"Good to know. Summer?"

"Yes?"

"I know you've already said you won't marry me," he paused and, yep, once again, I was the one blushing. At this rate, I may as well consider it my new skin tone around this man. Sometimes, I really hated being a redhead with such annoyingly expressive pale skin. Then he continued, "but do you think you might want to go out to dinner with me?"

I froze. Did he ask me out? Oh shit! *Yes! Yes! Yes!*

"That will be $24.75." Why must I be soooo weird? All I had to do was say yes and I would get to eat dinner with the Greek god. Attempt number two. I cleared my throat and tried again. "Ehem. What I meant was, yes, I would love to go out to dinner sometime."

He handed me his credit card while saying, "Great. How about you give me your number and we can text about a time and day."

"Okay."

After giving him his card back, I wondered why he was looking at me expectantly. I ran over the conversation again and that damn blush returned, oh wait, never mind, it probably just never went away. "Right. It probably helps if I actually tell you the number instead of assuming you can divine it from the great beyond." I pulled my phone out. "Why don't you tell me your number, I'll call, and you'll have it on your phone."

"Sure."

He did. I did. He answered, and the number exchange was complete. I stared at him because, now what?

"Think I can get that box from you?"

"Of course." *Of course he needs the food! Gah!* I handed it to him. "Enjoy!" *Well, that came out awfully chipper.*

"It can't beat my enjoyment of our kiss, but I'm sure I will. You'll hear from me soon."

"Okay." *Okay?*

"Have a good day, Summer."

"You too, Jason." We were both immobile and smiling for a heartbeat and then he turned and headed toward the exit. As he opened the door, one of our regulars, a mother with a toddler on her hip, was on her way in. He pushed the stepladder over a little more, making room, and held the door for her. Once the mom and child safely cleared the door area, he headed out. Warmth flooded my heart instead of my cheeks or body for once. Nice to know he could be kind to strangers. Sometimes it really was all about the small things. Once again, I was reminded of the lessons of kindness I'd gained from all of my parents. They also taught me that it could be a key indicator for kindness in a relationship, and that was an essential trait I was looking for in a partner. And right then, I was definitely looking and liking, and something in my heart area skipped.

6

NOT AN ASSHOLE

Jason

My blood pressure rose as I approached the trailers on set. As much as I enjoyed my time with Summer and was thrilled that she gave me her number, I was thoroughly frustrated with my tardiness. I doubted the actress I was trying to impress would understand if I told her I was late because I had to ask a girl out. It wasn't like me to risk my work for my personal life and it put me on edge. You couldn't make it as an agent in Hollywood if you didn't work your butt off to make a name for yourself and I had definitely been making a name for myself for the past few years. At this point, I had a few B-list and even some A-list clients, but if I got Vanessa Daring to sign with me, it would be a giant coup. I couldn't believe I'd put that at risk for a woman. Even an amazing one.

The Hollywood icon was looking for a new agent because her last agent died from an unexpected heart attack a few months back. Well, most heart attacks are unexpected, but really, with the stress the last agent carried around, it was not that surprising. I had met the man a few times and he was constantly a prickly asshole. Sure, the guy got the job done, evidenced by Vanessa's career, but you didn't have to treat people like shit to be a good agent. That was not my approach. I preferred to use charm and persistence, for my clients, to always get them what they wanted.

The fact that I was walking in twenty minutes late with Vanessa's latte and baked goods was not a good example of my usual success rate and ability to deliver. Well, damn! I flashed my ID at the movie set guards and made my way to Vanessa's trailer, hoping to find her in a good mood.

I nodded at the couple of bodyguards milling around outside as I knocked on her door. Her voice reached me, telling me it was open, and to come on in. Inside, I found Vanessa reclining on a couch petting her mini-poodle, Doodle, and reading a book. I thought it might be a romance novel, since I caught sight of a bare male chest on the cover. It made me wonder if Summer read them as well. I had spied the bookshelves filled with them today, at the café, and could have sworn it hadn't been there the day before. *Focus! Stop thinking about her.*

Vanessa was a middle-aged woman, by Hollywood standards, but she was still a stunning figure at forty-one. Her blonde hair was pulled back in a low ponytail and her tall womanly body was clad in a red pantsuit. "You're late."

"I know. I apologize. No excuse, but I do have a surprise to go along with my apology." She finally looked up from her book and her eyes sparkled. Looked like I was going to have to find a way to thank Summer the next time I saw her. That had me considering a few different ways I'd like to 'thank' her. I quickly worked to divert myself away from those thoughts before my body responded and I'd have even more explaining to do. "Turns out they added a new menu item today and I have some samples for you."

Her mouth quirked up on one side. "And what is the name of this new item?" She held out her hand to take the container from me, so I gave it over.

I momentarily hesitated before answering, but then blurted, "Sweet Hairy Balls."

She looked mock horrified. "No!"

"Oh, yes."

And just like that, she proved why she was desired by everyone around the world as she threw her head back and laughed. Her smile transformed her from beautiful to a total bombshell. Age had not dulled this woman's appeal one bit. In fact, it enhanced it. What I couldn't understand was why I wasn't affected by her beauty at all. Yesterday had been our first meeting, and for a few days leading up to that meeting, I'd been concerned. How would I keep a professional distance in the face of any attraction to her. It wasn't totally out of the realm of possibility. She was stunning and I was attracted to women. I wasn't in the habit of behaving unprofessionally, though, so I would have made sure to tamp down any such thoughts.

It had been a complete non-issue. Not even a twinge. Instead, I'd appreciated her like one might appreciate a gorgeous statue or painting. I could understand the appeal, but it did nothing for me. Nothing. For a moment I wondered if everything was okay with me. I hadn't been sure how it was possible not to desire this woman, but then my mind briefly wandered to a certain redhead, and zing. So I'd kept Summer out of my mind and was totally professional the whole meeting.

New day, same result. The woman in front of me had it all, except she wasn't who I wanted. Really, I should thank Summer for more than the treats.

One concern vanquished left me with another. What did it mean that I only hardened for one woman right now? Surely, it was a temporary condition and would pass sooner than later? I didn't have the time right now to deal with the drama of a relationship, and from my experience, they always involved some drama.

That didn't mean I wasn't going to pursue my lustful obsession. Something fun, flirty, and for a limited time only, was definitely on the table. In fact, I could totally see having Summer on top of one of the tables in her café, on the floor, against the door. Okay... Now I was going to have to cover up my hard-on near Vanessa. *Damn!* I swiftly sat down in the seat opposite from her.

Vanessa picked up the round confections covered in coconut shreds, brought it to her nose, sniffed, and then took a bite. Apparently, they were really fucking good. She looked like she did when she faked an orgasm in one of her movies, only she didn't look like she was faking anything. "That good?"

"You have no idea. Mmmm—"

"I'll let Summer know you approve."

"Summer?" Vanessa raised a curious eyebrow at me and I realized my slip. Clearly something in the way I'd said her name gave me away.

With as even a tone as I could, I replied, "The woman who is part owner of The Frisky Bean. Her name is Summer. You hadn't met her the times you were there?"

"Are you talking about the sweet redheaded woman?"

"Yes." I went for total nonchalance.

I tasted success until Vanessa answered me simply, "I see."

And, I was quite worried she did. I kept my professional and private lives separate, yet in the space of a couple of days, a few sentences, and things were already feeling a bit tangled. We hadn't even gone on a date yet. Of course, we had kissed, and it had been hot. So fucking hot. I really didn't want the tangles, though. That way lay the very drama I was avoiding. This right here was a good example to keep in the forefront of my thoughts. I didn't want Vanessa to think I'd been late because I liked Summer, even if that was exactly what happened. She didn't need to know that.

Time to change the subject and take control of the situation. "Have you had a chance to look over the contract my assistant sent over? Are you ready to sign on with Avalanche so I can represent you? If not, what are the stumbling blocks I could address to make you comfortable in doing so?"

Vanessa seemed to take the change in subject in stride because she got right down to business. She straightened completely from her reclined position, gently moving Doodle to sit next to her instead of on her, and her demeanor transformed from bombshell to shrewd shark. I always knew not to underestimate her like some other agents had. At least, that's what I'd heard from the showbiz grapevine.

Her voice was all business when she spoke. "I looked over your contract and while there are a few small points I would like to fine tune, in truth, that isn't my main concern."

"No? What then?"

"For too many years, I've been signed with an asshole. Don't get me wrong, Norman did what he needed to do, which is why I kept signing on with him, and, of course, I wouldn't be where I am today without his help, *but* he was a total prick to everyone and that includes me. Now that he's gone, and I am where I am, I refuse to sign with anyone who's an asshole, again. So, are you an asshole, Mr. Winter?"

"I can assure you that I'm not an asshole. I am shrewd and I am definitely aggressive on behalf of my clients, but I'm sure you've seen by now that I am a schmooze and charm kind of guy most of the time?"

"And you don't think charming men can be assholes?" The some-what imperious look she gave me let me know I had to tread carefully with my answer.

"I'm sure there are all types of assholes out there including charming ones. All I'm saying is I'm not one of them." I gave her my most charming smile. The one that usually melted women's panties right off.

Shit. That was totally an asshole thought. Keep it together, Winter.

Once again, that inquiring-minds-want-to-know eyebrow shot up on Vanessa's face. "Time will tell. I'll tell you what, Mr. Winter, I'll give you a couple of months temporary representation rights to prove to me that you're both good at your job and not an asshole. If you can prove those two things, I'll gladly sign with you a long-term contract."

This time my smile was completely genuine. "I look forward to working with you for years to come." Cocky, but I knew I could prove to her that she wanted to sign with me. It would be my topmost priority. "For now, why don't you send over those changes you mentioned? I'll make the revisions, assuming I agree to them, and have it returned to you, but with an end date for four months from now."

"You seem to have purposely misunderstood the word 'couple.' Last I checked that would be two months. I'll give you two and a half."

"Just wanted to make sure you had a taste for the kind of negotiating I can do on your behalf. Three and a half and I'll throw in a temporary reduction in my service fee."

"Three and I'll take the reduction as well."

"You have a deal but only if at the end of it, assuming you are happy with our arrangement, which I have no doubt you will be, you sign for a full three-year contract."

"Deal." She held out her hand and I took it in my own. She had a firm no-nonsense handshake I could appreciate since it was one of the first business lessons my father had drummed into me. That lesson came at an early age alongside learning to read. Business lessons were the closest I'd ever felt to my father. Another lesson... now that the ball was in my court, I was in control and I needed to make a win happen because losing was never an option. This was going to be a total breeze.

7

JESSICA'S TWITCHY EYE

Summer

This was a total disaster! I scanned the kitchen in dawning horror. What had I done? Jessica was going to kill me. *Kill me!* After Jason left that morning, I'd spent the rest of the day with my libido abuzz and my lips tingling. Maybe I could claim insanity. I could call it the buzzy bee plea. I snorted. Then, I scanned again and groaned. Jessica would never accept my plea. I looked down at Midnight and queried, "Any chance you'd be willing to cover for me? I think Jessica likes you better anyway." Midnight was too busy licking at the spilled milk, I refused to cry over, to respond.

What seemed a brilliant fucking idea an hour ago, when I first arrived home, left me filled with regrets. Despite all evidence pointing to my attempting to cook dinner as being a really bad idea, I couldn't help the attempt. After all, Jessica wasn't due to arrive today until it would be too late for her to cook and, well... I did run a successful coffee and bakery shop, dammit! I had to be able to make my way through one fucking dinner.

It was one fucking dinner too much. I even went in for something I couldn't possibly fuck up. Chicken pot pie should have been right up my alley. You *baked* it. It even had a pie crust on top and pie in the name.

How had this gone so wrong? Somewhere between burning the chicken and trying to make a cream sauce all hell broke loose. Fallout was not pretty and was likely to cause Jessica, the clean kitchen stickler, a twitchy eye. Luckily, what Jessica didn't know couldn't hurt her and she wasn't due for another thirty minutes. Time for operation deep clean, but first, I phoned our favorite local Mexican delivery place. Dinner would arrive in forty-five minutes. I shooed Midnight out of the kitchen, well, bribed him, because really, he wouldn't leave until he'd lapped up all the milk and eaten all the chicken. Yep. Some of the chicken had somehow ended up on the floor when I tried to shred it.

A bowl of the non-burned shredded chicken in the family room took care of him, and now I needed to get my ass in gear before Jessica arrived. Except, of course, of all the days, Jessica arrived home twenty-three minutes early. I stood completely still. Like, if I didn't move, I would stay hidden. As though Jessica was a fucking T-Rex.

Jessica's eyes went wide. She resembled one of those manga characters as she absorbed the mess, all of the mess, every little misplaced molecule. "What! The! Hell! If you hated me, you had kinder ways to tell me... You know... like stab me in the back or sleep with a guy I like, but this... Why? For all that's holy, what did this poor kitchen do to you? Did you get the Goddess card of mass destruction this morning?"

"There's a perfectly good explanation?" I hadn't meant for that to come out as a question, but yeah... it totally did.

"Really? Was there a six-point-eight earthquake that took place in our kitchen?"

"Hmm... Well, that would be a much better explanation than the one I was trying to come up with, but even that sounds lame. I was going to go with possession but then I'd have to go through with the whole exorcism and I'm not keen on that and really, I'm not sure I could do the whole head turning three hundred and sixty degrees and—"

My speech was halted by Jessica's hand covering my mouth. "Stop. Just. Stop. I'm going to hop into the shower to clean the greasy diner smell off of me. I'm also going to pretend that I'm arriving home when I come back out here after getting clean. We'll consider this the kitchen massacre of the year and we'll pretend it never happened." Jessica turned on her heels and strode away muttering to herself, "I love her. I love her. I love her."

"Please remember that and take your time," I yelled after her retreating back. Great. Sweet reprieve. Whew.

Twenty minutes later, kitchen sparkling like a Food Network show, Jessica made her appearance. I spoke before Jessica had the chance. "Casa de Salsa will be here in about twenty-two minutes and seventeen seconds."

"Thank you for trying to do what we shall never mention again. I do appreciate your attempt, if we can call it that, to provide dinner when I'm arriving late, but maybe stick to takeout or delivery? Or even cake for dinner."

"I know. My failings dumbfound me. It's heat applied to food items to make something edible. I am such a great baker. What is wrong with me and meals? It's ridiculous!"

"And you seem to need to re-prove that about once or twice a year. Still true, babe, ridiculous or not."

"I know. I just hate it."

"What made you choose today to sacrifice some poor unfortunate bird on the bonfire of your kitchen skills?"

"Ha. Ha. Very funny." Not that funny. "I saw him again."

Only a best friend could follow that logic with so little to go on. "And you didn't call me? We'll address that later. So, what happened?"

"I told him I wouldn't marry him."

"What? Okay. Back up and start at the beginning."

I energetically and with great flair recounted from ladder drop, to kissing, to name issues, and back to the kissing in detail.

"Nice, especially the very detailed description of his lips. Buuuttt... I still don't hear a reason in there for why you destroyed my kitchen."

"*He asked me out to dinner and looks like a Hemsworth!* Nuff said. You *know* me. There was no way I was going to be able to sit here until you got back from work. I was going mad! Mad I tell you! It's been hours and still no text."

"Drama much? Okay. I get it. You were a bundle of live wires tossed into a bathtub and my kitchen got the short circuit of the situation. We need to get you a hobby. How about scrapbooking. I hear good things."

"You're such a comedi—" The doorbell rang. "—oh, that will be our food! Let's have some tacos and some game plans! What do I do if he's there again tomorrow morning? Not sure how to top falling into his arms and kissing him."

"Drag him into your office?"

"Don't think I haven't thought of that."

We spent the rest of the night eating and formulating different game plays like a football team before the Super Bowl. I was going to be prepared this time. Mr. McHotpants would not get an ounce of crazy from me tomorrow. Properly armed, I would be cool, calm, and collected.

I WAS A MESS. Not even a hot mess. No. I was an anxious, don't have my shit together, why the hell didn't he come in today or text, mess. I would have been so well prepared this time. Instead, I was Cinderella without a ball. Sleeping Beauty without a kiss. Snow White with a locked casket. I grimaced at that last thought. A locked casket was getting a bit morbid. Maybe Jessica was right and I did need to lay off the drama.

But really, Jessica had even showed up that morning when we first opened and she absolutely detested mornings. *He* didn't show up. Now "the plan" was a big fat, what the hell? He came in two mornings in a row right when I opened, with every hint that he might enjoy becoming a regular amongst other things, and now, no Jason and no text message. Just radio silence. Maybe he changed his mind? What if he changed his mind? Shit! He totally changed his mind! And who could blame him after our first two cray-cray interactions.

"Girl. You need to relax. Should I get the Xanax?" Kevin stood in front of me, concern splashed like a Pollock painting across his face. "Want me to chase him down and tie him up? Oh. Please say you want me to tie him up."

How could I possibly keep a straight face with Kevin's humor warming me? I couldn't. "I love you, and thanks. You're right. I'm being ridiculous."

"Of course you do, and I know you well enough to know you're going to continue to obsess about this. Just remember what your pop always said…"

Together we recited, "No one ever got what they wanted by wanting it. Take action."

"He is a wise man, your pop. Now, if you need me, you know where I'll be." He winked. "Just call first because, honey, I met someone, and I hope we hit it off."

"Someone you want to introduce me to? I haven't heard you mention anyone in a while."

"Not yet, but you never know. He seems really nice and he's geek cute. He works in customer service for a game company during their middle of the night, early morning shift. That's how we met. We were both grabbing a super early dinner to go and ended up eating together on a bench outside the restaurant. It's nice to have someone whose wake and sleep schedule so closely mimics mine. You know how hard it's been for me to meet people since we opened the café. I regret nothing, mind you, dating can take a back seat for now, but this is convenient, and he's lovely. Of course, you'll be the first to know if it advances to meet-the-friends territory."

"Can I at least get a name?"

"Shawn."

"Well, have fun! I'll look forward to hearing more about Shawn soon."

With a hug and a kiss on the cheek, Kevin was off until Monday morning.

I spent the next hour in the office finishing up the books and reviewing some of the details of the plan I was cooking up. None of it went well. For the books, I reviewed my numbers over and over again because, while my eyes saw numbers, my brain saw firm arms, blond hair, and a killer smile. After finally completing the things that could not wait, I gave up the fight and closed my office. My business was too important for me to do such important work while distracted. I was thinking that if Mr. McHotpants ever called, I would need us to bang it out like in the books so I could get him out of my system. That never worked in the books, but I thought it was worth a try either way.

"You have any big plans for the weekend, Revi?" I asked as I walked out into the café.

"Solving the world's ailments. Same old, same old. You?"

"I'll be drowning in ice cream. A giant tub of Ben & Jerry's Caramel Core."

"Sounds like a good plan." They smirked. "Maybe I need to test the efficacy of healing through frozen milk products?"

I laughed and, of course, snorted. "Now that's a medical treatment I could totally get behind. Can I be your first test subject?"

"Will do. See ya, boss lady!"

"You too! Cure the world!"

"That's the plan."

As I walked out of the café, I thought about the two things I *had* resolved as I sat in my office. First, as tempting as my new idea for expansion was, I wasn't ready to risk what we'd already built. I needed to run it by Kevin but I wanted to make sure it was a viable secondary path before doing so. Second, my pop was right. If I didn't hear from Jason in the next couple of days, I would act. I wasn't some wallflower. Just like I always had, I would go after what I wanted. I may not feel ready to pursue my business plan, but ready or not, I'd already started falling for Mr. McHotpants and I wasn't letting an opportunity like him pass me by. My resolve grew as I brushed my fingers along my lips, remembering how hot, firm, and demanding his kiss had been. That kiss was anything but Mr. McProper. He had a couple of days, and then, I was going to act.

8

WHO'S THIS?

Jason

I hadn't moved in what felt like forever. The last two days had *not* gone as planned. I liked my life organized. I had my schedule on my phone calendar. I had my to-do lists. I knew where I was supposed to be, when, what deals I was working on, and how to get them closed. I also had my assistant to manage any changes and details I didn't take care of myself. Usually, things flowed like clockwork and that was the way I liked it.

That was all true until two days ago. That was when the world came to an end. At least that was how it felt. That was how it felt to me. I was a man of action and waking up the other day with a really bad cold left me a lump of inert misery and it was not something I handled well. I knew it. All my well-laid plans were knocked off my timeline and grumpy didn't begin to cover my mood as it flipped back and forth between wishing to end it all and wishing to jump back into it all.

I looked over at my phone so I could torture myself with the schedule my assistant was in the process of cancelling for yet another day. It was now ten-thirty on Friday morning. I was supposed to have had another meeting with Vanessa today to go over the revisions and sign on our temporary contract. This was *not* the way to start our working relationship. Damn it all to hell.

I miserably crunched over to the side, struck by a coughing fit lasting for a good couple of minutes. I grimaced and popped a honey lemon lozenge in my mouth. One day I'd make it up to my soon-to-be client when I didn't look like the victim of a zombie apocalypse. No one should have to see or deal with my ass right now.

I was in the process of swinging toward wishing for an early demise again when my phone dinged. I flung my arm out and almost hit it off of the nightstand. Quickly grabbing it, I flopped back on the bed dizzy but triumphant with my phone in hand. I looked at the screen at my incoming text message. I thought perhaps I was sicker than I thought because I didn't recognize the number and the message left my already foggy brain even more confused.

UNIDENTIFIED NUMBER:
  Hey. Was the naked French Kiss not to your liking?

WHAT? Was this a woman from my past? I hadn't been naked with anyone for a while now and, as far as I knew, none were waiting for me to contact them. Wrong number? I was about to respond, figuring that had to be the case, when my phone dinged again.

UNIDENTIFIED NUMBER:
  Jason?

NOT A WRONG NUMBER, but who could it be? I did not have the bandwidth to be dealing with an old hookup trying to reconnect. I finally responded.

. . .

JASON:

Listen. I'm sorry if you were expecting me to contact you, but I'm laying here on my deathbed and can't deal with anything right now.

I REALIZED I was probably too harsh and I should have let whoever it was down more gently. So... I began typing again, *"Can I contact you in a few days?"* but before I could hit Send another message came in.

UNIDENTIFIED NUMBER:

What?! Your deathbed? What's wrong? What have the doctors said? Please tell me you're joking. I'm sorry for all the bad thoughts I've had about you the last few days. Oh shit! Please tell me you're okay.

I LET all of that process through the sludge that was my brain. A few days? Naked? French kisses? Oh damn! It all made sense now. I had meant to text her. Why hadn't I done it that day before I got sick? Deleting the previously typed-out message, with great trepidation and no small amount of embarrassment, I sent one word.

JASON:

Summer?

UNIDENTIFIED NUMBER:

Um... Yes?

. . .

I SLAMMED my head back into my pillow. Definitely ready to end it all.

JASON:

Sorry for being weird and for not contacting you. I forgot to go back and enter your name with your number and I've been sick for the last couple of days. I'm not really dying. I just feel like I want to. So. You've thought bad things about me the last couple of days?

SUMMER:

Blush emoji Yeah... Sorry. I may be texting you with a wine filter right now. I admit I was disappointed that I hadn't heard from you nor seen you for the last few days. You can't trust me with fermented grapes. Clearly.

JASON:

Wait. You're drunk at 10:40AM?

SUMMER:

Heh... Was hoping you were too sick to notice the time. I guess claiming drunk texting when making a fool of yourself only works after 3 o'clock. Sigh. Anyway, its 3 o'clock somewhere and I've moved specifically for this conversation.

JASON:

LOL. Not buying it. I'm on to your faux drunkenly ways. Now, if you were thinking bad things about me, I guess that means that you were thinking of me?

. . .

SUMMER:

Let me step away and faux sober up. Wait... Okay... Good to go. Yes. I was hoping you'd text.

SUMMER:

Well, actually, I was kind of hoping to see you again in the mornings. *Blush emoji* Confession time. I lack patience. I'm pretty sure patience is one of the seven deadly sins instead of a virtue. I much prefer instant gratification.

SUMMER:

Oh Shit! I didn't mean that how it sounded.

JASON:

Oh no. You don't get to take that back. I'm taking notes. Well, I would be if I had a pen, pencil, or crayon and some paper. I'm unable to get beyond my bed right now, except for water. Speaking of beds, where are you texting me from?

SUMMER:

Oh no, back at you! We are NOT sexting before we even go on a date, sick or not.

JASON:

So, you're open to sexting after our first date. Duly noted.

SUMMER:

Oh god! That's not what I meant. But does that mean we are having a first date?

JASON:

Absolutely. Let me get better and we'll make it happen.

SUMMER:

Can I get you anything? Do you have someone taking care of you?

MY HEART CLENCHED at her words. It had been such a long time since anyone had taken "care" of me. My parents died when I was eighteen and about to head off to college. But even before then, my family had never been close, not with each other and not with any of our extended branches. I could remember being close to both of my grandmothers, but I'd lost all of my grandparents when I was still a kid and I'd been left with my distant parents. When they died, it was the last sliver of connection I'd really had to anyone. I'd never felt comfortable forming close ties to my childhood friends. When I'd buried my parents, I embraced my lone wolf existence and vowed to forge a way for myself, by myself. I didn't *need* anyone. Still... Her words touched something I usually kept far from the surface.

SUMMER:

Jason? You still there?

JASON:

Yeah. Sorry. Dropped my phone.

.   .   .

A WHITE LIE.

JASON:

I don't have anyone coming here. I'm more of the lay here and let fate decide the outcome kind of guy. *Smiley face emoji*

SUMMER:

Give me your address.

JASON:

What? No. Really. You don't want to see me this way. I'm pretty sure my neighbors are about to call the cops from the smell emanating from my home.

SUMMER:

Give. Me. Your. Address. Patience I don't have, but stubbornness I have in spades. Do you really want me knocking on the door of every Jason Winter located in Los Angeles? I looked it up... at least six options if I include the spelling Jayson because maybe you didn't want to correct me. Should I start knocking?

JASON:

Fine, but don't blame me when we miss out on our first date because you walk in and run away screaming. Are you always so pushy in text messages? 1010 Topanga Crest, Topanga, CA. Bring a face mask. No joke. Maybe a hazmat suit.

SUMMER:

Whatever. You're only making my case for me. I'll be there in about 2 hours. Try to survive until I get there. And I'm always this pushy, period.

JASON:

I see. Well, pushy can be such a turn on.

SUMMER:

*Uh. Huh. I'm taking my own notes. *Winky face emoji* See you soon!*

I FLUNG MY ARM OUT, not so gently placing my phone back on my nightstand, wondering how I could maneuver myself into a shower. By my estimation, I had approximately two hours to figure out how to make myself and my place look and smell marginally better. It should be easy, but nothing was easy right now. This... was going to take effort. I didn't have the strength to panic, though. Instead, I did what I always did, made a mental list of action items, a plan to tackle them, and proceeded with implementation.

Step one, I rolled to my side with my feet dangling off the bed. *Okay, Winter, time to sit up.* I slowly leveled myself into a sitting position and my head instantly began to swim. This... this would be hard. *Suck it up, buttercup.* I recognized my dad's voice with that thought. He was right, though. No way was I letting Summer see me like this. I was going to get clean one way or another. The sheets would be a whole other problem. I was a smart, resourceful guy and I would figure it out.

9

DON'T TRY THIS AT HOME

Summer

I wondered when exactly I'd been hit with the stupid stick. I didn't know where I'd gotten the audacity to invite myself over to a total stranger's home. I wasn't actually this pushy, it was just one of those things that fell out of my mouth. Like asking a stranger for their address. Well, maybe not a total stranger, but geez, close enough. As soon as I finished texting with Jason, I started to doubt my own sanity. Deciding I couldn't back out on a sick person in need, I proceeded with my dating without borders agenda, anyway.

Hopefully, the fact that I'd gotten the Egyptian goddess Sakhmet, the goddess of healing and medicine, that morning meant I was doing the right thing. Originally, the goddess had been the reason I texted him thinking to heal my own frustrations about his lack of communication, but lately the cards have seemed quite straightforward. Sick guy, curative goddess. Even Jessica couldn't miss that message. Of course, Sakhmet was also a goddess of war, but I was going to ignore that possibility for the one that made me feel better about my life choices.

First stop, a soup stand near our home where I grabbed a few pints of chicken soup. I then stopped by The Frisky Bean, which had been opened today by our weekend bakers, Linda Carter and Benny Frankel, two baking students from the local culinary school, and Revi. I was due to switch with them in a few hours and stay until closing at eight. While there, I picked up two teas made with lemon and honey and some treats. A part of me recognized that there was a well-known blonde actress that Revi was busy helping, but I was too distracted to take note of who the actress was and since Revi seemed to have everything under control, I moved along.

Oft times left unused, I hopped into my navy blue, older Prius whose custody I shared with Jessica, who didn't need it today. I checked. Last stop was a drug store, where I threw together a get-well gift bag filled with medicines, tissues, and chocolates, oh my. Thrilled at the speed with which I acquired all my loot, I made my way toward the sick hottie's house. Would he really be hot while on his 'death bed,' though? That would be so very unfair since I usually looked like a mouse-shaped, cat toy after Midnight had his way with it when I was unwell.

I followed the map direction as given to me by my British-voiced map boyfriend. I kinda loved when he told me what to do. Kinda bossy. Kinda hot. Kinda ridiculous that I got such a kick out of it. When his directions pissed me off, I'd switch to Aussie-voiced map boyfriend for a while and felt ridiculously better, briefly. Then I would feel like I was cheating on my map boyfriend and always went back. Then I felt I might need therapy and a real boyfriend and switched to a different map app entirely. Today, I was happy to have British-voiced map boyfriend along for the ride, because clearly today's theme was sanity be damned.

I slowly and carefully drove up the winding roads into the Topanga Canyon area. The farther I went, the more I thought that Jason's house was looking like a great place for me to have made my fatal mistake. The roads became rougher as I climbed the mountain and the house was more remote than I had expected. *What were you thinking?* Jessica would easily label me the heroine too stupid to live. When I chose to be the main character in my own life, I hadn't meant a thriller but here I was. I would have facepalmed if I dared take my hands off the wheel. *I'm going to be an after-school special of what not to do. There's still time to abort. True. True. But I can't leave him all sick and alone. Gah!*

Drawing closer to my destination, I turned onto what couldn't possibly be called a real road. More like a wide dirt path full of car damaging dips that ultimately led me to a driveway. I checked my phone and realized that Jason must have been using his Wi-Fi earlier, because I had zero reception. Shit... Shit. Shit. Shit! It would serve me right if no one ever heard from me again. *No. Really. What are you thinking?* Obviously, I must have been thinking with my kitten part. I knew sometimes men were led by their dicks, but I hadn't known I could be led so easily by my pussy. *Bad cat!*

I once again considered turning around, because clearly that would be the smarter move. I deeply considered it. But, then I remembered how Jason had mentioned he had no one taking care of him, and it got to me all over again. I liked to take care of people. My old therapist boss would probably tell me it was some deeply seeded need stemming from my childhood when I took care of my mom in the hospital, or perhaps from my need to try to fit into a new family, but it didn't really matter where it came from because the end result was the same. I was who I was and I couldn't leave without making sure he was okay. At least I'd texted his address to both Jessica and Kevin before heading up. I wasn't *totally* too stupid to live, thank you very much. Studying his house, all I saw was a simple entry gate. That was about all that was visible from the driveway. *Please, please don't be the hottest axe murderer ever.*

I gathered all the things I'd brought with me and went through the gate. There was a comfortable sitting area to my left and a path around the house to my right as, with trepidation, I walked up to the door. There was a note stuck to it that read "Come in." *Okay. Walk in, drop the food, make sure he's okay, and leave. Simple.*

I opened the green door. Ahead of me was a stairway leading up to what I assumed were bedrooms. *I would not think about his bedroom. The man was sick.* I decided to leave looking for him in his bedroom until last. Hopefully, that wouldn't be where I found him.

Continuing with the lower area, a warm honey-toned, hmm, bamboo maybe, covered all the floors I could see. Another set of stairs led down to my right into a comfortable sitting area with a stylish dark gray leather couch and a few forest-green leather, cushioned chairs. It looked like a perfect place to curl up and read. There were some bookshelves and a TV across from those along with a dark wood coffee table in the center. Nice. I continued down toward the room while nervously calling out softly, "Jason?" No answer. I walked farther in.

Beyond the sitting area to my right there was a stainless steel and dark wood kitchen with a white-and-tan marbled countertop. The oven was perfect for baking and if Jessica saw the rest of the kitchen, she'd try to move in. I dropped my bags of food items and drugs on the counter and looked beyond. There was another sitting area with a dark gray suede couch and another dark wood coffee table. This couch while still stylish, looked even more inviting. Next to that was a long dark wood dining table that could seat ten with matching wood and dark green cushioned dining chairs. My mama would love this dining area. My impressions as I surveyed the space were of comfort, class, and masculinity. I loved decorating and couldn't help my mind from inventorying a few things I would like to add to the space.

A sound from the suede couch surprised me out of my musings, and I made my way toward it. As I drew nearer, though, I ended up walking right past it, because that was when I registered what lay beyond the gray couch and dining table. A whole wall of windows and a set of sliding glass doors overlooked a slice of heaven on earth. Momentarily distracted, I walked to the screen open doors in awe. The breeze felt amazing as I took it all in.

Outside, was a huge deck that looked out over the canyon. It was absolutely breathtaking. Rolling hills of trees and far-off homes in every direction. It was one of the most beautiful views I'd seen since moving to California. A beach view is gorgeous and I absolutely loved living near a beach, but I grew up in Colorado and sometimes missed the mountain views a person could get from almost anywhere. I pictured what it would be like to wake up each day and have my morning coffee on the deck. Heaven. I imagined that the canyon would get covered in the morning mist before it burnt away and longing filled my soul. Absolute heaven.

I heard another soft sound coming from behind me this time and swiftly turned, letting out a very feminine and inappropriately infatuated sigh. Jason Winter was lying on the couch with a fluffy brown-and-cream throw blanket covering him from feet to just under his arms. He was asleep and he looked like he *might* be nude. At least, the top half visible part of him was and he was fucking gorgeous. His hair was damp like he had recently taken a shower and it flopped over his head at all angles. Totally unfair. Nothing looked sick about him. He was all virile, muscular male.

I quietly tiptoed over to him and hesitantly reached out to touch the back of my hand to his forehead to check for a fever. Relief flooded me when he felt cool to the touch. I startled and yanked my hand back when his eyes opened. He silently stared at me for a few long moments. I forgot how to breathe for that same span of time. When he finally spoke, his voice came out gravelly and I was finally capable of inhaling some oxygen, which left me mildly light-headed.

"Summer. You came."

"I told you I would. Why are you down here and not in bed? You should really be in bed."

"Unintentional. I showered, wrote the note you saw on the front door, opened the back door to get some fresh air, and then I ran out of energy. I laid down to rest before tackling my sheets, but I must have fallen asleep."

"When's the last time you had anything to eat? Drink?"

"I've been drinking plenty of water, but only snacking here and there for a couple of days. I haven't really had the energy to cook."

I shook my head. That wouldn't do. Scoldingly, I said, "You need to eat to keep up your strength."

"Like I said, I haven't had the energy to make anything and I can't order anything this far into Topanga."

He sounded like he was getting a little frustrated with my scolding, but I ignored his tone and continued on. "Why didn't you ask someone to drop off some food?"

Now he sounded defensive and irritated when he replied, "I guess I'm not used to asking for hel—" Unfortunately, it was one thing too much for him to say, because his body shook with a coughing fit as a result. I supported him as he leaned up in an attempt to stop coughing. When he did stop, and my attention was less focused on his face, I saw the throw blanket had fallen to his navel and my mouth went desert dry even as my pulse sped up. His chest was a freaking sculpted masterpiece. Every ridge, dip, and ripple made me want to beg for a lick.

Get it together, pussy parts! Stop ogling the sick hottie!

Needing a distraction or a healthy dose of a morality check, I abruptly said, "Don't speak. Let me get you some soup and tea," and shuffled away. On the way to the kitchen, I mouthed silently to myself, holy fucking hotballs Batman. I searched around the kitchen cabinets and it didn't take long before I found a spoon and a bowl, into which I poured out some of the soup. I then brought the bowl, a paper towel, a box of tissues, along with the tea back to Jason. I placed the tea in his hand and said in my sternest voice, "Drink."

His eyes narrowed, but he complied. It would be a "him" problem if he didn't like my take-charge side. My mama taught me at a young age how to deal with overbearing men like my pop and brother, and I was almost a hundred percent sure that Jason would fall into the same group. He would have to learn that I was no pushover.

"Mmm... Tastes good. Feels even better." He sighed with his eyes closed in contentment.

"Good. Now it's soup time. Do you think you have the energy to feed yourself or—um—do you need me to feed you?" His mouth tilted up on one side, which made something clench inside my stomach. Devastating.

"I definitely think you should feed me. I'm feeling rather faint still."

I was not a fool, traveling to a stranger's home notwithstanding, so of course I pondered the possibility that he was lying and messing with me, but I didn't have any evidence to contradict him. He *had* fallen asleep on his couch from overexerting himself and hadn't eaten in a couple of days. Soooo...

I surveyed the surrounding area attempting to figure out how I would best accomplish feeding him, but there was really only one way to make it work. And that way, made me genuinely hot *and* bothered. "I'll need to sit next to you, so skootch your legs over a bit." I indicated the middle cushion and Jason adjusted his body, making room for me near his legs. I sat down slowly, my back ramrod straight, and my breathing became erratic from his proximity. From his bare chest, which was right there. *Once again, the man is sick, you pervert! Get a hold of yourself!* That was so much easier said than done, though. It had been a long dry spell for me and he was right fucking there. Sans shirt. And, sans who knows what other clothing items.

I worked to keep my hand steady, and mostly, surprisingly, succeeded, as I spooned some of the broth with vegetables and chicken. Chicken soup was the cure-all for my people, after all, and Mama had made sure I grew up knowing all about my heritage along with learning that of my adopted family's. It was important to Mama since she and my mom had been best friends. That's how I ended up adopted by the Palmers when she passed. And now, since this was a home cure that had science behind it, I hoped it would help make Jason feel better.

Hoping the soup wouldn't be too hot, because I felt awkward blowing on a grown man's food, I prepared myself to feed him. I looked up and was caught in his intense gaze. *What was he thinking?*

I brought the spoon to his lips and he opened, took it in his mouth, and then swallowed it. I watched as his Adam's apple moved with his swallow and my eyes dropped to his chest again. I quickly raised them back up to his face so he wouldn't catch my inappropriate perusal. *Was it hot in here?* Just then, I felt the breeze from the open door, mocking me.

Damn you, pussy parts!

He closed his eyes again, briefly, and his face suffused with satisfaction. "That tastes fucking amazing." His stomach made his hunger known, now that it was being addressed, and his embarrassment was evident.

In an attempt to smooth it over for him, I tackled it head-on. "Clearly you've not been taking good care of yourself. You really should reach out next time."

"I'll remember that. I rarely get sick, so—" when I saw my opportunity, I stuffed his mouth with another spoonful of soup. He grimaced at me even as he finished the mouthful. "Like I started to say, I rarely get sick, so I don't have a good plan in place for when I do. I'll make sure to get some frozen meals and canned food for next time."

"Ooorrrr, you can reach out and ask for help. Is that really such a hard thing?"

"Yes." And, apparently, that was all he was going to say on the subject. Well, okay then. I tried to do the waiting him out thing so he would talk, but he kept eating the soup I brought to his lips and just stared at me. I grew quite uncomfortable under his scrutiny, his proximity, and his ability to be silent and lost this round. I squinted my full displeasure even as I capitulated and spoke to break the tension.

"There's enough soup for you to eat it a few times a day for the next couple of days. On top of that, I also brought you some baked goods from my café. I hope it'll be enough, but if not, I can bring you some more food, if you let me know what you need."

"Thank you. Did you make the soup?"

I laughed and a snort escaped. Of course. "Oh no! I'm not

allowed in the kitchen to cook. I recently tried a chicken pot pie, which ended in disaster and Mexican delivery."

He chuckled but his expression was one of surprise. "How is that possible? I was under the impression you baked alongside Kevin."

"Oh, I do. If it has to do with baking, I somehow work through it like a master, but for some reason, if I need to cook something, well, it's like I'm possessed, really. Things end up on the floor, the walls, I get injured, and things get burned. I don't cook. Ever."

Now he laughed in earnest. "I would never have guessed. It's a good thing I know how to cook. I'll invite you over for dinner one day. That assumes I survive this cold, but I'd say my chances of survival are now greatly improved. Thank you."

"Speaking of which—you big baby—you scared the shit out of me earlier. You do realize you have a cold, not a plague, and it doesn't seem to have landed you in the hospital, meaning, you *will* survive. And, don't worry about me, I'm all up on my vitamin C." He reached out and touched my face. I wasn't prepared and feeling his warm hand along my cheek, after holding myself so rigidly, made me jump in surprise. I splashed the nearly finished, luckily cooled, soup over his lap. "Oh, no! I'm so sorry. Let me..." I quickly set the bowl down, picked up the paper towel, and began dabbing at the blanket where the soup had fallen. "I may need more paper towels. I'm so sorry." It took me a full minute dabbing and babbling, but eventually I realized that there was a hard length under my hands. I noticed as he let out a low, guttural moan.

His voice came out growly, "Jeeeezus. Summer. I can't decide if I want you to stop or keep going."

I was sure my blush had to be one of the deepest in my life. Beet red wouldn't even cover it. I scrambled to my feet and tried to walk away but moved too fast. In my agitation, I somehow tripped on the trailing end of the blanket at my feet. I fell right back down onto the couch, only now, I was lying across Jason's chest with his arms, once again, catching me. The air rushed out of my lungs from the impact to my body and my soul. I whispered, "I can't seem to be around you without literally falling into your arms."

"It's one of the things I've liked most about our interactions. You feel good in my arms." He took a deep breath and continued, helping me to sit up again next to him, "but I don't want to get you sick, so I really shouldn't have you this close right now."

10

INSTEAD OF SOUP

Jason

"I enjoy being in your arms, too." Summer smiled shyly, yet directly at me. She was such an interesting combination of sweet and seductress.

Heat simmered between us.

I couldn't help it. I knew what I was about to say was probably too much, too soon, but nothing about our interactions followed any traditional paths. Why start now? I dropped my voice lower and told her exactly what I was thinking.

"If I was well, Summer, I would have you under me so fast. That is if you wanted to be, of course. But if you wanted me like I want you, I would spread your thick thighs wide, get a good look at all the delectable parts of you, top to toe, and then make you the meal I'm craving instead of soup. Every inch of your delicious body would be a feast for my mouth."

I loved dirty talk, and I figured it was as good a time as any to test our compatibility with something I considered rather benign. Summer's blush was stunning against her pale skin with the sunlight coming in from my giant windows behind her red hair turning the edges into little flames. She was heat personified in form. Part of me wanted to do and say whatever I had to, to keep her blushing at all times. I pictured the fantasy I just painted for her and how splayed out before me, she might have a flush that would spread down over her breasts. I barely contained another groan. She didn't seem to notice as she seemed in her own head figuring out how she would react to all I said. I studied her face and waited patiently.

She seemed to come out of her momentary trance, took a few deep breaths, met my eyes, and responded in a breathy voice, "That sounds like a really good night and God, Jason, I want you too. I've never felt such instant sexual attraction to anyone before, it makes me nervous and needy all at once."

She was perfect. I put my hand to her cheek and pushed a lock of sun-kissed hair behind her ear. The silk of her skin and her hair made me itch to grab the back of her head and pull her to me. Not today, I had to remind myself. Instead, I figured, I could try to put her at ease that the intensity was mutual. I was just about to do that, when a coughing fit hit me, *again. Fuck!* I turned away, quickly, covering my mouth with my arm.

"Oh, shit! I'm overtaxing you!" She grabbed the tea and brought it and a tissue up to me.

I snatched the tissue first and wiped at my nose as all heat diffused under a wave of frigid shame. I firmed my jaw and attempted to cover my weakness. In a calm, distant tone, I told her, "For now, I think it's best that I get some rest." I didn't need a potentially hot new fling seeing me like this. That's what she was, right? And, flings don't take care of you, which was fine with me. I took care of myself fine and had for years. She needed to leave. *I* needed her to leave. Still stiff with embarrassment, I pushed her away even more. "Thank you, Summer. I do appreciate all this. Now, if you don't mind, I'll be in touch in a few days when I'm feeling better."

I saw her flinch and her expression turn to confusion at my abrupt dismissal, but I couldn't stand to appear weak in front of anyone, and especially not a woman I had an interest in. I also saw the moment her face hardened in anger. She stood up taking the bowl and dirty paper towel with her to the kitchen without another word. I heard her moving around, the sink going on and off, and the silence between us reached a deafening pitch. I hadn't realized how much someone's hurt feelings could echo sans sound. But, hers did. Then, there she was, standing at the side of my couch, with a gulf of my own making between us. *This was what I wanted, right?*

In a tone that seemed ill fitted, in stark contrast to all of our other interactions, she spoke. "I've left all the soup in the fridge. There's also an extra tea in there. Feel free to heat it or drink it cold. It's premade like the last one, and good either way. All the baked goods are in a Frisky Bean box on your counter and should be good for a couple of days. You also have Tylenol, some other meds, and a second box of tissues on the counter. I—" She paused and bit down on her bottom lip.

This distance I had created felt so wrong, so fast. *What had I done?* I was such an ass. Just a minute ago, we'd felt so close, so fast. I was about to apologize when she continued, "I hope you get well soon. Let me know if you need anything else. I'll talk to you later." She turned to leave and I couldn't let her go like that. Something told me that if I did, that would be it. We'd be over before we even started and embarrassed or not, I was not ready to accept that.

On instinct, I reached out and grabbed her hand. She turned to look at me and I wanted to kick my own ass. Her slightly glistening eyes did me in. I had to do some damage control and fast. "I'm sorry. I didn't mean to, to—"

"Be a jerk?" she added helpfully and pulled her hand out of my grasp. She crossed her arms in front of her in a protective stance and I rushed to express what I knew I had to say.

"I deserve that and probably more. I'm not used to needing help nor being weak and you saw both those things today and I guess... I guess I had a knee-jerk reaction to it. I instinctively needed to regain some distance and control." It came out stilted and awkward because I wasn't usually so open with anyone, but something pushed me on.

"I'm sorry. I didn't mean to hurt you or appear ungrateful. I can't thank you enough for your concern and care. You deserved better from me than what I said." The skin around her eyes had been pinched since I'd pulled away but now her whole expression relaxed and even softened.

"Thank you for explaining. I understand. I'll leave you to your grouching." She smirked—*Oh, thank God!*— "But please reach out if you need anything even if it's a conversation. Deal?"

My body relaxed back into the cushions. Somehow, I'd found the right words and she wasn't going to write me off. I ignored a small part of me that was reluctant to let her go. Keeping her healthy was more important. "Deal. Again, thank you. Drive safe, Summer."

"Out here? Definitely." She laughed and it felt really good to hear that from her again. I was actually proud of myself for opening up, even if just a little, and being able to fix what I'd broken. I was also filled with warmth toward her. It wouldn't have surprised me if she'd made me work harder for it, but she hadn't, and it made her that much more appealing. Just maybe, she could understand me.

She leaned down and kissed my forehead, her lips soft and warm and surprisingly comforting, and then, she walked away. Again, something in me wanted to revolt at watching her walk away, but that didn't make any sense, so I tamped it down. I heard my front door open and close and a car engine start outside. Then came the crunch of gravel as she drove off and after... quiet. Solitude. I'd never minded the solitude before, in fact, it was part of what I enjoyed most about my home, but today, something about it irked my calm.

I looked out the screen doors at my view, sipping tea, and revisiting my earlier imaginings of what I would like to do with Summer, with my mouth, perhaps outside in my hot tub. I did have total privacy on my deck. I tried to convince myself it was only her body I was craving right then, but another voice continued to notice the quiet around me in a newly negative way. It seemed as though she had taken all the warmth with her when she left.

11

UNDERCOVER THINGS

Summer

"Don't do it! Turn around! Go back!" Midnight jumped down off of Jessica's lap clearly agitated with his tail twitching and his cat-scowl deeper than usual. Jessica kept right on yelling at the TV screen. "This is such a bad idea! Seriously!"

I would be amused, but since I, too, was sitting on the edge of my seat, well, couch, tension live streaming through me as my gaze was super glued to the screen. "Maybe it'll be okay?"

"You really still an optimist? No one is ever really okay on this show. You know that."

"A girl can hope. No way they kill him. He is way too hot for death."

"And his brother? He was hot and he was a total goner!"

"Touché! Still..."

"Also, a girl has no hope." Jessica deadpanned that line and I snorted.

"Oh my god! What is about to happe..."

We both jumped as my phone dinged loudly between us, detonating our tension bomb, resulting in mutual shrieks, laughter, and scrambling. I grabbed at my phone as Jessica pushed Pause on the remote.

I couldn't stop my broad smile as I read the incoming text.

JASON:
Paging Nurse Summer. You available to talk?

JESSICA, her Summer-is-talking-to-a-man-dar still at peak performance, questioned me, "Is that him?"

"Yep."

"If you want to take it, I can entertain myself."

I looked between the paused screen and my friend. "Are you sure? It's pretty bad timing."

"Go on." She nudged me on my shoulder with her foot. "Get outta here."

I smiled warmly at her. "Thanks. You're the best! I'll try to be quick."

"Uh-huh. Take your time."

"I think I'll go to my room for a bit." I winked conspiratorially.

Jessica chuckled behind me as I left the room. "I'll expect a full rundown later."

I yelled back, "Of course," as I closed my door. I laid back and got comfortable in my bed before responding. It had been a full day and a half since I'd left Jason's house with not a peep, so of course I had to harass him. It's what I do. It's what I live for.

SUMMER:
He lives!

JASON:

It was touch and go, but I think the soup was the tipping point in my recovery. I feel almost human again.

SUMMER:

Good thing. I know there are a lot of romance novels about the undead, but I prefer the people I date in the real world to be one hundred percent living. *Wink emoji*

JASON:

I am definitely alive, though I may still bite. Forewarned and all that.

SUMMER:

I've added it to my notes. In the spirit of full disclosure, I might bite too.

JASON:

You sure you aren't interested in a little not so innocent sexting? Because right now, I think a little sexting might banish the cough I feel suddenly coming back.

SUMMER:

Well, that's one I haven't heard before! LOL

I WAS SO VERY TEMPTED. What could be wrong with a little flirting? It didn't have to go too far. Did it? Did I want it to? Remembering how he had made me feel with just his words last time, I rushed to reply.

. . .

SUMMER:
Are you still in bed, per the nurse's instructions?

I BIT MY BOTTOM LIP. *Too much? Oh shit. Maybe that was too much. Why can't you take back text messages?*

JASON:
Oh Summer. I would never dream of disobeying my nurse's instructions. I am most definitely in bed. And you?

SHOULD I ANSWER? I should answer. I found, surprisingly, I wanted to answer. Okay... So... I'm doing this. Here we go.

SUMMER:
I'm in bed too.

IT PROBABLY ONLY TOOK MOMENTS FOR him to respond, but my heart was racing. I hadn't noticed I'd even stopped breathing, while I watched the three dots at the bottom of the message, until I gasped at his next words. *Oh. Em. Gee.*

JASON:
Summer, tell me what you're wearing.

. . .

I COULD ALMOST HEAR his deep voice and see his sultry smile as I read the words. Holy smokes it was hot!

SUMMER:
Um... I'm in shorts and a tank top. You?

JASON:
I'm not wearing anything. Same as when you were here.

OH, lord. I'd speculated that he might have been completely nude under his throw blanket the other day, but to have it confirmed? Why did he confirm it? Had he noticed me wondering about the state of his undress? I'd been so very close to his perfectly sculpted nude body. And, his hard erection. And, the things that came out of his mouth. Shit, I was getting so wet thinking about him both then and now. Before I could get my thoughts together enough to reply, he continued.

JASON:
I know you said you weren't going to sext with me before our first date, but it feels like you might've changed your mind. Tell me to stop at any time, and I'll stop, but until you do, I don't want to stop. I want you. Now, take your shorts off for me. Not too fast. I want you to slowly slide them down your legs. Caress your skin with your hand as you do it. That's my hand.

SHOULD I DO IT? I could pretend, but I was so turned on and I had never actually done this before and somehow doing this with him, well, I really wanted to do this with him. Right now. Apparently, we *were* going to do this before our first date and I couldn't bring myself to care. I did as instructed and slowly pulled off my shorts imagining it was him. Once they were off, though, I silently laughed at myself. I kept trying to strike a casual pose on the bed, as if he could see me. Sure. I was totally cool doing this kind of thing. See? *Ugh. Oh. Right.* I better write back.

SUMMER:
   I pulled them off.

JASON:
   Good girl. Now your tank top. Remember... slowly. Caress your arms like I want to. Like they deserve all the attention for a moment. Like I'm thanking them for bringing me all the things they carried to make me well.

I TRIED. I really did, but I'm also ticklish and, well, impatient, so just between me and my room, I wasn't a good girl this time. I flung the sucker right off and went back to typing after an appropriately seductive amount of time.

SUMMER:
   Done.

JASON:
   Are you wearing panties? A bra?

SUMMER:

Just panties.

JASON:
Describe them to me.

HE WAS DEFINITELY BEING BOSSY, but I liked it. Really liked it. Getting wetter with each word, liked it.

SUMMER:
They're lace on top and along the butt and joined by a silky blue material.

I COULDN'T BELIEVE I had the chutzpah to do this.

JASON:
I want to pull those off of you with my teeth, slowly, very slowly. Might even need to take a few stops on the way down to nibble at those thighs of yours. Or maybe a bite of your mouthwatering ass.

SUMMER:
Oh god! I guess you did warn me you bite.

JASON:
Take them off like before. Slowly while imagining me doing it.

· · ·

I WAS GOING to die of either embarrassment or lust and maybe both and nope, I still wasn't stopping. No way. I did as he told me, again this time, and it kept me getting hotter. My nipples were so hard and I was starting to feel a coiled tension in the pit of my stomach. I took a very shaky breath and wrote back.

SUMMER:

Um... Okay. I did as you asked.

JASON:

I wish I could see you right now. Are your nipples hard for me? Are you wet for me, Summer? With one hand, grab your breast, and with the other, reach down and place one finger inside your pussy for me and tell me. Just one, though.

I CONSIDERED LYING and saying I did it without actually doing it for a full two seconds, but since my body was in full agreement with his demands, I enthusiastically complied. I was primed and had been for days, and I really wanted to come, for him, but also for myself. I wrapped one hand around my aching breast, feeling my pebbled nipple, while my other hand slid just one finger between my folds and into my very wet center. After giving myself a few minutes to enjoy the touch, the imaginings, I texted back with my breast hand.

SUMMER:

I'm wet, Jason. My nipples are hard and I'm so very wet.

JASON:

Jesus. I am so fucking hard for you right now. My cock hurts thinking about your wet pussy and what it would feel like to slide into you. I'm rubbing up and down my length imagining it's your hand instead of mine.

I PICTURED EVERY WORD. Even though I hadn't yet seen his dick, I had felt it briefly and my mind knew exactly what to do with that information.

JASON:

I want you to put the phone down now, Summer. While I rub my cock until I come, I want you to pleasure yourself. I'm going to picture you sliding your finger in and out of your pussy. Do it and then flick at your clit for me. Use your other hand to pinch your nipple, hard, do it hard for me and then rub your clit until you come. Do it, now. Come for me, Summer, while I come for you.

HIS FUCKING words were too much. I was already wound up but they were so hot, it was like they played my clit on their own. I, of course, did just as he directed. How could I not? I placed my phone to the side and imagined Jason's big hand instead of my own small one. I pictured him pinching and massaging my breast as he pushed me over the edge of ecstasy. My other hand, his other hand, fucking into me and then rubbing my clit in just the way I liked, the way I needed, the way that made my orgasm crest and shatter, leaving me trembling. My body was swimming with the sensations that even just thinking about him had evoked. I released my lip, realizing I had bitten down on it, at some point, in an attempt to stay quiet with my roommate right beyond the door.

As I was still coming down from my pleasure, my phone rang. This once again startled me, and I figuratively tripped out of my euphoric state. I reached over to grab it, but my hand pushed it off the side of the bed. "Oh shit!" In my effort to snatch it up before it fell, I, not so figuratively, toppled over and landed in a tangled mess with my sheet, next to my phone. "Shit!"

There was now an insistent knocking at my door. Jessica's concerned voice said, "Are you okay in there?"

Ugh! I yelled back, "I'm fine! I just fell out of my bed. You know me." I fake laughed as best I could, while scrambling through my sheet for my phone.

"Okay. Let me know if you need help. Though I refuse to help you with your orgasm."

"Oh god! You heard?"

"Sister, we have a really small place. Good luck in there."

I groaned and facepalmed myself a little too hard. Finally finding my phone, I only then realized that in my scrambling, I'd answered the call and, of course, it was from Jason. I put it up to my ear. "Jason?"

Sexy male laughter came back at me over the line. "And I thought my orgasm was good. Mine didn't knock me right off my bed, though. You have no idea how much I look forward to seeing you come in person one day if that's the result. I promise to catch you."

"Oh god. I need the earth to swallow me, right now."

"No way. In all seriousness, are you okay?"

"Bruised ego and maybe backside aside? Yes. You may have noticed I'm constantly falling into things, or in your case, people. It's become a lifestyle."

His voice came over the line deeper. "But, did you orgasm for me? It sounded from your roommate's comments that you did."

"You heard that, too? What do you have, bionic hearing? Sheesh. But. Um. Yes. I did and, Jason…"

"Yes?"

"It felt so damn good," I admitted.

"Me too. Just thinking about you coming is making me hard all over again. You're killing me. We've got to have a date. Soon. I want to get to know you. All of you. What I know of you so far, only intrigues me more. I don't want you to think I'll expect anything, but if things go well, when you're ready, I will want to fuck you so hard, Summer."

"I guess we'll have to see how it goes."

"Are you available some evening this week? Thursday?"

"I have Thursday evening free."

"Thursday it is. Can I come pick you up?"

"How about I meet you in front of the café? I don't usually give my address out before I get to know someone. Of course, I don't usually go to someone's house or sext with them before I get to know them, but we're going to ignore that for now."

"It's smart of you to keep your address safe. I get it. I'll meet you at the café at six-thirty on Thursday?"

"It's a date. Will you text me details so I know what to wear?"

"Sure. And, Summer?"

"Yes, Jason?"

"Wear a pair of sexy underwear or none at all. I know it's unlikely that I'll see them that night, but it'll be fun to let my imagination run wild wondering what you chose."

"You know you can be rather controlling?"

"Yes. Will it be a problem?"

"Hmm. I guess not. I appear to like it. Just wanted to make sure you were self-aware."

"I'm fully aware of what I want, and I have a tendency to pursue what I want relentlessly."

I was momentarily too stunned to speak. Normally, I was at the other end of the spectrum personality-wise. Most people thought of me as laid-back and easygoing. I wasn't sure why this man's intense personality was driving me to do and like things I hadn't before, but I also knew that there was no explaining chemistry and attraction, and I was definitely experiencing both. "Noted. I'll see you Thursday, Jason."

"See you then, Summer, and thank you for today. It was—" He

paused and I held my breath waiting to see what he would say. When he continued, so did my breathing. "—a revelation."

I could barely find my voice. Had he said revelation? Yeah. I supposed it was. "I enjoyed it too." *Wow... ringing endorsement. Way to match his energy. Why don't you just tell him how pleasant it was? That it was downright fine. A good time had by all.*

"Goodnight. I'm off to dream of all the things I'd like to do to and with you."

This is your chance to get in there and be all sultry. You got this. And... Go. "I will look forward to learning what those are. Goodnight." *Yeah, okay. There's always next time.*

I hit the button to hang up and just sat there. I needed a minute to compose myself. After some time, I slowly got dressed and crossed over to the bathroom, cleaned up, and made my way into the sitting room. Jessica was reclining on Elvis with Midnight curled in her lap. She was reading on her Kindle but looked up as soon as I stepped into the room.

She took me in with one swoop of her gaze and grinned. "Well, damn. Does he have a friend? Brother? Sister? Because if he can do all that—" She waved her hand as though to indicate all of me. "—then I need me one of those."

Just like that, my tension and embarrassment dissolved. A best friend always knew all the right things to say. "You have no idea! Holy hell, Jessica. I am so out of my league but I really, really don't mind one bit."

"Sit down and tell me everything."

Before I did, I grabbed two refilled bottles of water and a couple of apple and honey cookies I'd brought home from the café. They were from a unique Jewish recipe book I'd found from a place called Bear-y Good Bakery and we were thinking to add our version of them to our menu. I handed Jessica one of the waters, a cookie, and then collapsed onto the other end of the couch. Then, well, what else could be next but that I shared every salacious detail, because girl talk is sacred.

When I finished, Jessica fanned herself and said, "I'm now in dire need of a cold shower. You may have to sleep with him for all of womankind at this point."

"Right? It's like a public service. If a man like that pops into your life, you don't let the opportunity go without taking one for the team." We both laughed.

"Yeah. Let me know when I can—" Jessica flashed air quotes. "—take one for the team. Oh! Oh! Oh!"

"What now?"

"I want to be a fly on the wall as you tell Kevin all about what just went down. He'll have the same question, about a friend or brother, as I did."

"Actually, Kev had a hot date this weekend, so maybe he already has his own hot distraction and I can send you to him to ask about available siblings."

"That's so good to hear. He deserves some good love coming his way."

"I know. I keep crossing my fingers he finds someone worthy of him. He plays like he likes playing the field, but I know what he really, really wants is someone to love. He's a bigger softy than me and I'm a freaking marshmallow."

"Same. Well. Same on wanting him to find love, not on being a marshmallow. I may love writing romance but you can keep that shit away from me with a ten-mile track. Now... we need to figure out what you should wear for your date Thursday."

"As soon as I know what the plans are, I'll let you know and we can invite Kevin over for a consultation meeting."

"Sounds like we have a Wednesday night pre-date dinner. Make sure to give Kevin the heads-up."

"Will do. I miss hanging out with him. It's been so hard to catch him in the evenings because of his schedule at the café, but hopefully, since he doesn't work Thursday morning, he'll join us."

"Summer?"

Jessica sounded serious all of a sudden, which had me answering with some trepidation. "Yes, Jess?"

"I've never seen you this invested, this fast, before. If he hurts you, I'll cut off that dick you like so much."

We both guffawed, but I knew there was a kernel of truth there. "Thanks. Love you."

"Love you, too. Now, can we finish watching our show? I'm all tense about what happens next. You left in the middle of a wild scene!"

"Aren't they all wild?"

"Too true!" Jessica pushed Play and we snuggled in. Midnight, who wasn't going to be left out, ever, negotiated his way in-between.

12

AND SO IT BEGINS

Jason

"You'd be crazy to let my client go because of a couple hundred thousand. You know that she can carry a movie to financial success based on her name alone, imagine what she could do with your show." I'd spent the last few days playing catch up. I worked twelve-hour days, laid out my plans, ate at my desk, negotiated, and then went to sleep only to head right back into work. At the moment, I was making my bid to show Vanessa, who signed the temporary contract a couple of days before, that I could be the best agent she ever had and the only one she would need moving forward. She'd hinted at wanting something more constant in her life in our last conversation, and I'd heard through my connections about a great new WebShowz series. It had a versatile, intensive, and gritty lead role written by Beth Bell and made for an older actress. It was perfect for her and would show the world a new side of Vanessa Daring.

When I visited her trailer the previous afternoon and showed her the script for the pilot, she'd loved it and gave me the go-ahead to negotiate for the role. That was all I'd needed to hear. The group working to put together the cast for the show had jumped on the chance to get Vanessa, but the offer they sent was totally unacceptable to me. I refused to even bring it to her attention.

"Listen, Mr. Winter. You and I both know that this will be a great role for Vanessa. She's been pigeonholed into a particular character and she could use a project like this to really branch her out into other opportunities." Brad Danvers, network executive, and as far as Jason was concerned, hard ass, retorted.

"Clearly, you're correct, but since Vanessa is also considering another career changing character role in an Aubrey Haggarty film, that she would have to turn down, it's only right that compensation be worth her sacrifice." I wasn't going to let this opportunity slip through my fingers, which meant showing Vanessa I understood her career aspirations and could make them happen for her. I turned my charm to full blast and said, "How about I throw in an appearance on one episode of another show, with Vanessa's approval, of course."

Silence as Brad considered his options, but I could be patient. Brad eventually replied, "You've got a deal. I'll have the lawyers send over a contract tomorrow and we'll expect a response by Monday."

"You'll have it by then."

"Good." Danvers hung up without so much as a "see ya." I was used to that, though. Many of the wheelers and dealers in Hollywood thought of time as money and wasting it was not a part of our culture. I tended to like a little schmoozing but I was also adaptable and not easily offended. Anyway, with the rush of triumph running through my veins, I couldn't care less.

I pressed the intercom button and exclaimed, "We got it, Janet!" I heard her loud cheer through the door and the intercom, both. I'd hired Janet Sterling a few years back when I first chose to open Avalanche Talent Agency. An assistant had been crucial to making the business run smoothly while freeing me up to do what I needed to do, gather clients, find amazing projects, and matchmake clients to those projects. She was a single mom who wasn't the most qualified for the position but when she came in for the interview, I saw the hunger for the work in her eyes and decided to take a chance on her.

In this business, sometimes all you have to rely on is your drive and determination and Janet looked like hers could match mine.

I'd been right about her potential a thousand times over. She was organized, persistent, and amazingly efficient. If there was something she didn't know, it took her little to no time to look it up and self-educate. Anything I threw at her, anything she chose to tackle, I trusted her to come through. She was probably the closest I had ever come to counting on another person. "Thanks again for handling all the details leading up to this while I was out of commission. I couldn't have come through with this deal without you. You truly are the best!"

Janet's happy voice came over the intercom, "It was my pleasure! Is it bonus time yet?"

"What's this bonus thing you mention? I haven't heard of it," I joked back. She was definitely getting a big bonus this year if all went as planned.

I heard her mocking sigh loud and clear. "It's a travesty your education is so sorely lacking, but I'll set you straight eventually. This time, I'll accept getting to meet Vanessa Daring as a bonus. I'm so excited. I've loved her since she played the teen Clara in *Jesse's Treehouse*."

I chuckled. I couldn't remember ever hearing Janet get excited about something so frivolous. She was usually too busy working and taking care of her kid. "I'll make sure to let you know when plans are in place for her to come to the office for a visit."

"Please do. I want to make sure I'm on my game that day."

"You're always on your game. That's why I hired you. In other news, I don't see anything else listed on my to-do list. Are you telling me we've successfully caught up?"

"Yep. I have nothing here either."

"Perfect. I'm going to take off in thirty minutes. Please feel free to leave."

"I'll leave in five. Let me know if you need anything until then."

"Will do. See you tomorrow."

"Have fun tonight."

"Tonight?" What was tonight? I rechecked the calendar on my desk and there was nothing listed.

Instead of a response, my door opened and Janet stood in the doorway rolling her eyes at me. Her brown hair, tied back in her customary tight bun, she shook her head in disappointment and that hurt more than I would have thought. I hadn't worried about disappointing someone in a long time. Still in the dark, though, I just stared back confused. With an arched brow, she asked, "Your date? Remember? I can't believe you forgot. Poor woman."

Damn! Damn! I dreamt of Summer every night. We even casually texted a couple of times, so how could I have forgotten our date? "I didn't forget my date," I defended and lied. "It's Thursday?"

"It sure is," she assured me, but looked unconvinced with my inquiry.

"Apparently, I've forgotten my days of the week, *not* my date. I'm leaving right now." I quickly stowed my laptop in its case and hustled out of the office calling back over my shoulder, "Thanks again, Janet. Lifesaver." I needed to hurry if I was going to successfully meet Summer in front of her café at six-thirty. Luckily, I'd planned our date shortly after our unintentional sexting, before I dived into my hellish schedule for this week. Despite nearly forgetting it, it was going to be a great night. I'd make sure of it.

Summer

TONIGHT...WAS going to be... a disaster. I was sure of it. I was a nervous wreck. Why had I sexted with him? Now I was going to be blushing and anxious the whole date. Perhaps we shouldn't date. We could just stick to text messages. I was so much bolder in text, anyway. *What makes you think that?* More eloquent. *Sure you are.*

Less falling. *If you say so.* Yep. I should totally stick to texting with Jason. Maybe I could text him right now and stop him from coming. That seemed like an excellent plan.

"Would you stop? I can see your brain frying from all the way over here." Jessica was standing in the doorway to her bedroom, brushing out her long hair.

"You're a whole three feet away. That's not an achievement." My brain *was* frying, though. I looked down to remind myself of what I was wearing. Again. For, like, the thirtieth time. On Monday night, Jason had texted me with a dress code for our date. He'd refused to divulge what we were going to be doing, but said "dress comfortable but for a nice dinner." How the fuck are you supposed to dress for a nice dinner and be comfortable? That's not how nice dinner fashion worked, dammit.

Wednesday night had been spent with Jessica and Kevin figuring out the answer to that very question. They'd scoured my closet over Chinese food, wine, chocolate, and laughter. It ended up a game of who could come up with the most inappropriate outfit for my date. There were many good contenders but then Kevin found a well-hidden back of the closet t-shirt with the words 'I like to roll a twenty-sided dice.' from my Dungeons and Dragons days. Jessica decided to pair it with a pair of, also forgotten, sequined blue short shorts from my rave days. To top it off, Kevin found my cowgirl boots I'd brought with me from Colorado. So, what? I was multifaceted, but what I hadn't been in that ridiculous outfit, was ready for a comfortable nice dinner. Really, that outfit just gave them a reason to roll around tipsy and hysterical. Worth it.

Somehow instead of making everyone more obnoxious, a few glasses of wine, each, finally mellowed us all out and we'd finally focused on finding the right outfit. We settled on what I was wearing now.

Cute black ballet slippers paired with my shin-length, lace and cotton, A-line black skirt, along with my emerald green, scoop-necked, formfitting, cotton shirt fit the bill. To make it a little more formal, they added my beaded, multilayered, multicolored strand necklace. It started with a strand like a choker and had four successive strands each longer and drooping farther down. The last skimmed the top of the scoop in the shirt. I had matching chandelier earrings which I was currently fidgeting with. As outfits went, I thought I looked pretty nice. With any regular date, I'd feel quite happy with it, but with Jason, hot as hell, get her off with a text, Jason, nope. I was raw nerves.

Jessica had helped me dry my hair so my curls were cascading red waves down my back. I'd only applied a light smattering of makeup because I really wasn't into it. A little black liner, some mascara, a little blush, and lip gloss. Done.

"Maybe I should be wearing pants? What if by comfortable he meant we're going bowling after dinner? Honestly! Mr. Bossy McHotpants can't just tell me what to wear? Oh wait. He did tell me what to wear, for undergarments. He couldn't extend that to the rest of the wardrobe, which would have actually been useful? I—"

"Summer! Stop! Seriously. Why are you so nervous? And what did he say about the undergarments? You never mentioned that." It seemed my friend's curiosity required good posture because Jessica suddenly sat up straighter on Elvis.

Great! And there goes my blush again. I was going to be utterly blotchy by the time I met him. I answered the easier question. "He might have told me to wear sexy underwear or none at all so he could speculate on what was under my outfit all night."

"You know I hate you right now, right?"

Just like that, once again, Jessica diffused bomb Summer. I took a deep breath, released it. Then did it again for good measure. I finally relaxed. My shoulders stopped keeping my ears company, and my hands stopped moving. I really was being ridiculous and totally out of character, so I went ahead and answered Jessica's first question, too. "I think I could really like this one, and yet, I have no concrete evidence of why. I sold him sexy baked goods, twice, and apparently that was enough for me to act like a person I don't recognize. Who goes to a total stranger's house with soup when they're sick? Who sexts with someone they don't really know? Not me. That's for sure."

"Actually, I beg to differ. It's exactly you, now that you actually like someone. You're exactly the kind of person who hears that someone you have feelings for is in pain or sick without anyone to take care of them, and you go out of your way to provide them comfort. You're the kind of person who feels things deeply and now that someone has triggered your switch, double entendre for your clit is on purpose, you're following your heart instead of your head and..."

I felt Jessica's scrutiny on me as she left her last sentence dangling. Opening up had been a challenge for Jessica for as long as I knew her. What was she thinking? Wanting to say? Jessica came over to me and held one of my hands. This odd behavior had some of my nerves itch back to life. What was Jessica going to say? She finally spoke. "It's one of the most beautiful things about you, you know. When you came into my life, I was ready to make sure my life and your life wouldn't interfere with each other as roommates. For some reason, you cared about me instantly, despite me being rather aloof. You bulldozed through any of my more standoffish behaviors with all the small ways you made me feel cared for. It's why Kevin and I are so protective of you. We both love that you follow your heart so fully, but we both want to protect you from anyone who wouldn't appreciate it for the gift it is. The gift you are. Anyone who would accept all you have to give but won't give you all that you need will be hearing from all of us who love you."

My eyes burned with tears. I was *not* going to cry. No crying! No. Crying. Period. I sobbed. Dang it. I had the best of friends. I gently wiped at the drops that made their way to my cheeks and blinked rapidly to clear my eyes and regain my voice.

"None of that. You're going to ruin the little bit of makeup you allowed me to talk you into." Jessica put her arms around me and I lost the fight.

My throat, still clogged with emotion, had me whispering, "You're the best. You know that? Thank you. I think the three of us have all had stumbling blocks in our life to overcome, but being white has meant that I've never had to deal with some of the ones that you, Kev, or the rest of my family have. I've witnessed. I've supported. I've allied. I've marched and called. But none of that means I fully grasp what you've dealt with. The closest I get is being Jewish, but I know I can hide any signs of that considering my coloring. It's not the same. If I'd had to experience what you have I'm sure I'd be more guarded with who I trusted too. Throw in some of your exes..." She got the side eye with that. "And you both are so much more loving and giving and just plain wonderful than the world deserves. I hope you know that. Did I mention how much I love you?"

"Yes. But I do so love to hear it." She gave me a big hug, and when we were both in charge of all our feels again, she pulled away and said, "So. We have a few minutes to get you under control and fix your makeup. I think we need some *Will & Grace*. Sit and I'll go grab the artist's tools for your face."

"Yeah. Sounds good."

We sat together on Elvis and between petting Midnight, makeup reapplication, and Karen and Jack, clearly the best characters on the show, making us laugh, I finally felt ready to take on whatever Jason Winter had planned for the night. I took one more fortifying breath and then grabbed my black clutch, a light, black knit sweater, and proceeded to follow my heart over to the café.

13

OF DATES AND FUCKERS

Jason

I sighed in relief even as my heart rate evened out. The dating gods had clearly been looking out for me, as I made it through one green light after another, and miraculously arrived a few minutes before six-thirty. Those same gods continued looking out for me as I found a parking spot just a few spaces down from the front of the café. That put me in the perfect position to see Summer as she walked down the sidewalk toward The Frisky Bean. Toward our date. Toward me.

I grew even more thankful for those unobserved minutes, because seeing her again did some weird things to multiple regions of my body. My heart began racing, again, my breath caught, and my dick instantly went on full alert. I needed these moments to get my shit together.

I'd been attracted to her from the get-go, but tonight, well, tonight, she was absolutely stunning and in such a natural, unexpected way. Spending most of my time immersed in Hollywood, I was used to a controlled, made-up type of beauty. That was fine for some people, I wasn't here to judge what anyone liked, but having grown up around it, I was drawn to Summer's casual appearance more. It was clear that she had put in some effort for our date, but she still looked like herself. She wasn't racing toward the café, but her natural enthusiasm for life showed with the way her hair swayed with every step she took. All of her curves were highlighted by her tight shirt that drew my eyes.

Next, my gaze drifted down to appreciate the sway of her hips. Her hips triggered a visceral response and I wasn't sure how I was going to be a gentleman through the whole date. I still remembered how sexy she sounded breathless from her orgasm and subsequent fall. Damn. Pretty much everything about her drove me crazy. I was going to have to keep it on lockdown, though, because I never wanted her to feel like all I was interested in was sex with her. I was definitely interested in sex, clearly, but it just wasn't *all* I was interested in. I may not do long-term commitments but that didn't mean I treated women like they were just a good lay. No. I treated them well, we enjoyed each other's company, and when the relationship ran its course, like they all do, we moved on. Nobody had to be treated ill or to get hurt if done right. Sex was definitely on the table, it just wasn't the only thing.

Of course, if that was the case, why had I asked her to wear something sexy or nothing at all under her clothes? What was I? A masochist? Even now, as I watched her skirt sway with her walk, I wondered at what I would find if my hand trailed over her legs inching up her skirt until I felt the inside of her thighs, and, ultimately, to the core of her. I was very stupid.

I continued to watch her as she drew closer. I was about to exit the car when I saw her reach the opening café door just as a man exited and greeted her. The man was tall, had long brown hair coiled into a ridiculous man-bun with a short beard, wearing a 'Save the Earth' t-shirt and jeans, and lots of muscles, emphasized by the tightness of the shirt. Could the fucker not find a shirt that fit? The man stopped and took in Summer with an overly appreciative look. That was my body to ogle, dammit. It was clear he was a regular, by the way they greeted each other, which only made me hate him even more. A part of me, I was trying to ignore, knew this guy looked like someone Summer would make sense with. Her coffee house was all about fair-trade beans and compostable packaging. They continued to talk and The Fucker, I decided it was the right name for him, kept eyeing *my* date. Enough. I stepped out of my car, the sound making the two of them turn my way.

I stepped around my navy blue BMW baby and walked directly toward Summer. She blushed, as I crossed to where they stood, which pleased me to no end. She hadn't blushed for The Fucker. I also saw and felt the excitement in her gaze and it fed my own. When I reached her, I ignored The Fucker completely and instead wrapped my hand around Summer's elbow, leaned in, and kissed her cheek. Then, I lingered cheek to cheek so I could whisper in her ear, quietly but loud enough to be overheard, "You look lovely tonight."

I leaned back in time to catch the red of her blush deepen. Only then, did I look toward The Fucker who was clearly sizing up the situation. Everyone was silent until Summer finally stammered, "Oh! I guess you probably don't know each other. Let me introduce you." She indicated The Fucker and said, "Shane Paxton, meet Jason Winter. Jason, Shane."

I was going to stick with The Fucker for a name, if only in my own mind. I held out my hand. "It's a pleasure to meet you." It was definitely not a pleasure and the look in the other guy's eyes indicated he didn't think so either.

Nevertheless, The Fucker responded, "Pleasure to meet you, too." The Fucker firmly shook my hand. Too bad his man-bun didn't come along with a weak handshake.

Summer, clearly oblivious to the tension, continued on, "Shane is one of our regular customers and works at some tech company around here."

Unease settled in my gut. "Paxton you said? Like Paxton Solutions?"

The Fucker got a self-satisfied, cocky look and nodded slightly.

"The very one. I guess you've heard of me."

The smug look on The Fucker's face made me want to go full caveman on him, but instead, I gave him a thin smile and said, "I've heard good things about your... company." I emphasized the company part because I was being a dick. Sue me.

"Hmm. I don't think I've heard your name before." Direct hit. "What do you do?"

"I am Avalanche Talent." I was quite proud of my career choice and my accomplishments, but knowing what I knew about The Fucker, everything in me felt scraped with sandpaper. My dad would have been so proud of me if I'd pursued a career path like Shane Paxton instead of the one I had. My dad wasn't around anymore, but his judgement lingered, always. Luckily, I'd had a lot of practice portraying a façade, so none of my discomfort showed in the smile I returned. Tired of making nice, though, I said, "If you'll excuse us," and pointedly turned to Summer and held out my arm. "Shall we go?"

Apparently, catching on to at least some of the tension in the air, Summer looked back and forth between us. I could tell the moment she chose to let it go, she stared into my eyes, gave me one of her sweet smiles and said, "Sure. Am I dressed okay? Surprises are hard to dress for, you know."

"You're absolutely perfect."

The Fucker spoke up, too. "I hadn't been aware you had a boyfriend."

"I don't."

"She does."

We spoke at the same time and I was agitated with her response even as she opened her mouth in surprise and blushed. I had no right to claim what I did and we both knew it. But, that blush was going to be my kryptonite. I had to remind himself that this was our first date. *What the fuck was wrong with me?* I had to salvage the moment before it spiraled in front of The Fucker. I tapped into my schmooze and said, "I guess boyfriend would not be the right term *yet*. We're dating, though." Close enough. The Fucker didn't need to know it was our first date. And really, in many ways, it didn't feel like a first date.

"I see." The other man's eyes narrowed in cold calculation.

Summer jumped in. "It was great running into you, Shane. Good luck with the surf tomorrow morning."

So he was a rich tech guru and a surfer? Clearly, I was going to have to be on my guard, because the man was also clearly interested in my Summer. My Summer? Yeah, my Summer. I never did like to share what was mine, being an only child and all, and until we were finished with each other, Summer was mine.

"Have a nice night," the other man said, which would have been a great end as far as I was concerned, but then The Fucker added, "I'll see you in the morning after I catch some waves." That statement was directed at Summer even as The Fucker stared right at me. I had a rival. Well, too bad. The guy had missed his chance with her and I was going to make sure he understood that fact.

I led Summer to the car, opened the door, and helped her in, all the while feeling The Fucker's eyes on us. It was utterly childish but I couldn't help looking The Fucker in the eyes just before entering my car and waving. Clearly, despite my reassurances to Vanessa Daring, sometimes, I could be a total asshole, and I didn't care. I actually gave myself props for not flashing him the finger. Something about Summer was different and I didn't plan to waste any time analyzing it.

Summer

I scrutinized Jason, wondering at this new side of him I'd just glimpsed. Up until tonight, he'd been lighthearted and funny, well, except for that one incident when he was feeling vulnerable and sick. Even that was different than what I just experienced. If I was reading his behavior correctly, and I was pretty sure I was, he'd been rude and territorial and I couldn't decide how annoyed that made me. I hoped it wasn't a bad sign, but I was worried that it was. My ponderings served me in one way, though, all my nervous energy from earlier was replaced with traditional first-date trepidation. What did I really know about Jason? Not much, but I wanted to rectify that by the end of the evening. I'd reserve judgment until then.

As usual, I couldn't stand the silent tension for long, so I figured I may as well jump right in. "I've never been confused with a bone before."

"A bone?" After pulling out into traffic, he looked over briefly, clearly confused.

"The way you were fighting over me back there, sure implied you had me confused with one."

Jason blushed. Now, that was a turn of events that I could totally get behind. It was high time I wasn't the only one blushing. He sheepishly returned, "I'm sorry. I don't usually behave that way, but when I saw the way Paxton was looking at you, I guess I did get a bit territorial."

Called it. Wait. What? "He wasn't looking at me as anything other than a friend. We've known each other for some time now. Actually, since shortly after the café opened."

Jason looked shocked. Full-on, mouth gaping open, shocked. Still sexy, though. Seriously, did he ever look bad? His voice even sounded shocked when he asked, "You thought he was looking at you like a friend?"

I hesitantly answered, "Um, yes?" because I felt like I must have missed something.

"Clearly you didn't look at the same man I did, because he was too busy undressing you as you spoke, to be a friend." Yep. I had missed something.

Just like that, his blush was gone and mine was in full bloom. *Shit!* I thought back to what Shane looked and acted like before Jason had shown up. Now that I thought about it, he'd definitely been friendlier and his gaze had seemed to linger more on my full C girls than when I was behind the counter. Still. I decided to switch to another part of the earlier interaction that had struck me. "Even if what you're saying is true, when did I acquire a boyfriend exactly? Usually there's some amount of conversation involved when people become exclusive where I come from. Are you telling me you do things differently in California, because if so, that would be a problem for me." He was back to being the one blushing and I was probably a total weirdo for getting so much delight from that fact. I didn't care. *Score one for the redhead!* I inwardly patted my own back.

"I may have gotten a tad bit carried away and perhaps a smidge possessive. I know it's our first date... did I mention how much it bothered me when he looked at you like that? After everything that's happened between us, this also doesn't exactly feel like a first date. No excuses, though. You're right. I owe you an apology." He paused, pensive, but then continued with a smirk, "Of course, I only said we were dating before we were. You turned down a marriage proposal before I issued it, so, perhaps we're both jumping the gun with whatever is happening between us?" His smirk turned into a full-blown smile full of mischief and sensuality, as he briefly turned to me. Devastating.

"So, we're evenly bad at misspeaking?"

"I'm willing to go with that explanation if you are."

"It's a deal. So. Where are you taking me tonight?"

"You'll see. Tell me about your week."

I got a thrill from the way he said that. Not a question, but a demand for information. It went along with the demanding side I'd briefly glimpsed before. Since I liked it, I began describing some of the funny customer situations from the last few days. My café, and its location, always drew an interesting crowd. "Since you're part of the Hollywood world, you might find it interesting to hear that, the day I brought you the soup, I think there was a well-known actress visiting the café. I can't remember who, because I was in such a hurry, and she was trying to be incognito, but I think I would have recognized her if I stopped to see. Revi, one of our family of employees, was helping her and I had the impression that maybe they'd helped her before. They both seemed comfortable with each other."

"Hmm. Do you know who Vanessa Daring is?"

"Of course. I'm a big fan. She has a movie coming out soon based on a book I loved reading. Why?"

"I think she might be your mystery actress. She's the reason I found out about your place. I had meetings scheduled with her the mornings I came by the café, and I asked if I could bring her anything to the meeting. She pointed me to The Frisky Bean and gave me her order. I'm really happy she did."

My heart melted at that. "Me too. Is she signed with you? You mentioned you run a talent agency to Shane."

"We have a temporary contract, for now. I'm hoping to convince her to sign something more long term."

"How exciting. Do you like what you do?"

"No. I love it. I assume about as much as you love your café."

"Then that would be a whole heck of a lot. Was getting sick a problem for your job?"

"It delayed some things, but I have an amazing assistant and for the last few days, I've been working my butt off catching up. I want to thank you, again, for coming out and taking care of me. Not many people would've done that for a virtual stranger, and it probably wasn't a very safe decision, but I'm sure you helped shorten my sick time."

"You're welcome. Now, where are we going?" I was dying to know and my frustration sounded in my voice. I was really bad with surprises. "Remember? No patience over here."

"I promise you that patience can be a good thing. A thing that can be rewarded. Give me your patience, Summer, and I promise it'll be worth it."

Patience. Rewarded. *Yikes!* I gulped even as my I grew warm and wet down below. I just barely resisted rubbing my thighs together. What I didn't resist was the thrill running through me at the idea of being rewarded by this clearly passionate man. Mr. McHotpants it is.

14

THE FIRST DATE

Jason

I started running figures for my various contracts through my head in an effort to distract my thoughts from the obvious effect my words were having on Summer. My libido was going to have to take a back seat for now, one way or another. This woman fascinated me even as she pulled at my sensuality stronger than any other woman had in the past. She was flirty and awkward, hot and quirky, kind and strong, and I wanted more. More of her mind and her body, but the body was going to have to wait until I understood the mind a little more. I ruthlessly clamped down on my need and went back to getting to know her.

"You mentioned that things were different where you came from versus California. I take it you're a transplant? Where from?"

"I moved from Denver. I lived there my whole life until I moved here three years ago."

"Why did you move?"

"I finished my master's and decided to move out shortly thereafter. I take it you're a local?"

I hadn't missed her change in focus to me without really

answering my question of why, but I decided to let it slide, for now. "Born and raised." I flashed her a quick smile and wink and went back to focusing on the road. "What was your master's in? Something to do with business?"

"That would probably have been smart, but I had no idea at the time that I would open a café with one of my best friends. That had always seemed a pipe dream. So, no. I have a dual master's in psychology and early education. I was planning a career as a therapist with a specialty in childhood traumas."

That intrigued me. "What happened?"

"While waiting to start my PhD, I got a job as a secretary, in the office of a child psychologist that I knew. I wasn't privy to the sessions, for obvious reasons, but some of the kids grew to like me and talked to me while waiting to go in or for their parent to come out. I quickly realized I wasn't able to separate myself from the children's problems. A good psychologist empathizes but also compartmentalizes. I don't compartmentalize well. I felt constantly on edge. I developed anxiety and depression. I began having sleep problems, my eating was off and, basically, I was a mess."

"That sounds tough."

"It was. One day my boss sat me down for a heart-to-heart. We both knew I wasn't cut out for the job. After that, I dropped my PhD program, packed my bags, and moved to LA. A new start, with a new life, full of new possibilities. Best decision I ever made. And wow, short story made longer. Sorry. I have a bad tendency toward rambling and over-sharing. Please feel free to interrupt if I go too long or too far afield."

I looked over in time to see her take note of her fidgeting fingers messing with the material of her skirt. She took a deep breath and then her fingers stilled. She calmly waited for my response. Apparently, whatever was going through her mind about that time, still agitated her, which made me want to do something I wasn't used to. I wanted to comfort her, which was a form of connection I wasn't used to sharing.

"Don't apologize." I reached over and took hold of one of her hands and gave it, what I hoped, was a reassuring squeeze. Then I tried to reassure her with words. "I enjoyed hearing all about your journey here. In fact, I'm curious why you first chose that profession." I moved my hand and focused back on my driving as I turned right onto the Pacific Coast Highway heading north along the coast towards the restaurant I'd chosen for our first date.

Summer

I was dying to know where we were heading. I also debated how much I should open up. It felt a little weird to start a date with such heavy information as my childhood. It wasn't a pretty story, it also wasn't all bad, just... heavy. Something about Jason made me want to share, well, all of me, and so, as I watched the homes on the hills to my right and the waves in the ocean to my left, I did.

"As a kid, I lived with my single mom who was pretty much everything to me. She was very busy trying to provide for us, but she always made sure that I knew I was loved. When I was ten—" I paused to calm myself, so I wouldn't cry as I continued. "—she was diagnosed with cancer. Since we had no money, no insurance, she ignored her fatigue and pain for too long, thinking it was just a result of long hours and poor eating. As it turned out, by the time she got to the ER she was suffering from severe pain, and there was nothing more they could do. She had stage four pancreatic cancer and a few weeks to live."

I paused again to get my feelings back under control. It didn't seem to matter how many years went by or how many times I told this story, the tears and pain always came too. Some things you never really recovered from, you just learned to endure them. Losing your only parent in such a short time and at such an early age, was one of those things.

Jason's hand grabbed mine, and he just held it as he continued driving. His silent support was a balm I hadn't expected. His kindness was worming its way into my heart. His silence allowed me the space to continue. Quietly, I concluded, "She was gone soon after."

"Did you end up living with another family member?"

"No. It was just us. My mom liked to call me her little sidekick. She used to say that we were like Batman and Robin and together, we would take on the whole world. I remember, when she passed, I used to wonder, what was Robin supposed to do without his hero?" A shudder ran down my spine and his squeezed my hand again, and his kindness wormed in a little deeper. Still, I wasn't ready to go on talking about her and probably shouldn't anyway. Things were definitely into the realm of uncomfortable now.

I took another calming breath and continued the story forward to better times. "Anyway, I would have gone into the foster care system if it weren't for my mom's best friend. They'd worked together as waitresses for years. Our families were super close. When my mom was in the hospital, she wrote out her will with her friend's agreement, and I was adopted into the other family within months of her passing. The Palmer family, Mama, Pop, Derek, and the rest, were like my second family already, which made the transition so much easier. I could never repay them for giving me a home, but I love them as much as I loved my mom. Even with the soft landing, it was a rather traumatic event in my life, as you can imagine. I grew up wanting to help other children who might have experienced a trauma in their lives. It's funny how some jobs seem great when they're all theory but then you get out in the field and you realize you're a very poor fit. Well, that was me."

I compelled my thoughts out of the past and back to the present and then looked over at him to see how he was taking my story. He briefly took his eyes off the road to look back and our gazes met. In that split second, for some reason, I felt understood. As though he really did understand, well, everything. What I said, and what I hadn't said, equally. It was both sweet and disturbing. Too intimate.

Too deep. It was definitely too much for a first date, so I changed the subject.

"That was more than enough about me, how did you end up an agent?"

He didn't answer right away. He did, however, move his hand back to the steering wheel. Disappointment surprised me at the loss of contact. I studied him and, even though it was subtle, I noticed that he was agitated and a new distance existed between us that hadn't been there the moment before. Was he uncomfortable with sharing his personal information? This was the second time I'd experienced him pulling away. I may not be a therapist in practice, but I was trained, and I recognized self-preservation when I saw it. I wondered if he would tell me where that instinct came from. If it hadn't been for the Palmers, I could have easily ended up reserved and with-drawn too. Would he share like I had?

He finally spoke, but it wasn't what I wanted to hear. "We've arrived, how about we postpone this until we're sitting down at the table."

Despite what I had told him in texts, I could be patient, up to a point. "Okay." Pushing someone to open up when they weren't ready was a poor way to build trust. So... I'd give him his space. On the other hand, I knew I could never be with someone who wasn't willing to open themselves to me at all. *Even if it feels like more, it's just a first date. Give it time.* I decided to do exactly that.

JASON

I needed some time. I needed some space. I *needed* to leave. I wasn't going to do that last one, but I *could* stall. All of Summer's revelations left me feeling sucker punched. I couldn't understand how she could be so open and share so easily the things that obviously pained her so much. How does someone do that? She was remark-able. It was clear that she was waiting for me to reciprocate, but it wasn't in my nature. Instead, I took the opportunity provided by my need to pull the car into the restaurant parking lot and hand it over to the valet to postpone and organize my thoughts. I spent the time reflecting on the last few minutes of our car ride and the one thing that stood out to me was how much I enjoyed holding her hand. Such a small thing, but I could still feel her in my palm, like a brand. I couldn't interpret all the feelings that had flooded me at being the one able to comfort her. I felt important, needed even, if briefly, by someone strong and lovely, and it filled some empty space inside me with something, well, I wasn't sure, but something.

As soon as she'd asked me about myself, though, all the good feelings had rushed right the fuck out. Instead, anxiety and irritation were left in their wake. I'd held her questions off, but I knew I had a decision ahead of me. There was no way she was going to drop it entirely. Was I going to honor her openness with my own, or leave her in the dark like every other woman I'd gone out with? What a good question. If only I had a solid answer.

15

THE SEAFOOD CABANA

Jason

After passing the keys to the attendant, I moved around to the other side to open Summer's door. My brain running through my options even as I reached down to offer her my hand. As soon as I had her hand in mine again, the contact soothed something inside of me. Her skin was not soft and overly pampered. They were the hands of a woman who worked with her hands, strong, and sure and—

I caught Summer as she tried, tried being the operative word, to step out of the car. Her hands may be sure, but her feet caught her skirt on their way out of the car and luckily my quick, instinctual reflexes saved the day once again. I silently thanked all those basketball games in college for my honed instincts. Being Summer's personal safety net was going to be a full-time job at this rate. Her laughter was husky and low and, following different instincts, I pulled her closer, briefly inhaling her scent, before setting her back, stable once again, on her own two feet. "Favorite. New. Pastime."

Her voice still husky, she answered for my ears only, "Mine too." She looked around and said with glee, "We're in Malibu at The Seafood Cabana. I remember seeing this place advertised recently, but I've never been." She gave me a suspicious look. "I heard it had a long wait list. How did we get a reservation?"

"I'm one of the investors. I hope it meets with your approval."

"Absolutely. I love seafood and I love the beach."

I'd been pretty cocky about my choice for our date, but it felt good to hear I'd planned well. A while back, I'd looked for something to invest in and when one of my friends brought this new restaurant venture to my attention, I invested straight away. I put my hand at Summer's lower back, and thoroughly enjoyed the arch there, as I led her in the shiny, silver-scaled metal door. The hostess greeted me by name and asked us to follow her to our table.

"It's so beautiful."

Yes. It was. I'd loved the concept from the very beginning. The restaurant was nicely appointed, if I said so myself. With floor-to-ceiling walls of windows overlooking the ocean on three sides, glass tables with a stainless-steel base and matching clear high-quality plastic chairs with navy cushions. The floor was covered in sand-colored bamboo wood slats. The overall effect was eating on the beach, instead of above it. It was a huge success.

I kept leading Summer as we followed the hostess out the back door. Summer looked at me quizzically, but I just nodded in the direction of the hostess and raised an eyebrow in challenge. She picked up the gauntlet and lifted her chin, moving forward, which was the perfect reaction as far as I was concerned. *Good girl.*

As soon as we walked out the back door, we were on the top landing of some stairs leading down to the ocean. I had a moment of panic thinking about Summer negotiating the stairs and sand, and wondered if maybe I should go first, but she started down, after the hostess, before I had a chance to implement operation 'save Summer from falling to the sand.' I mentally shrugged but made sure to stay close enough to grab her arm if she stumbled. As the stairs turned, we got our first glimpse of what was below.

Three individual cabanas with cream-colored cloth drapes and one side open towards the ocean were set up separate from each other along the sand. A glass wall was installed between the surf and the cabanas so that even during high tide, the splash coming off the surf would make quite a show, but not disturb the customers. The best part of the cabanas was that each allowed for a very private dining experience since the noise of the crashing surf and the distance between them didn't allow for very much sound to travel from one to the other. That was, of course, by design.

I watched Summer's face, when she paused mid-step, to gauge her reaction. She looked enthralled and so beautiful as the wind whipped her red curls around. I itched to wrap one of the red strands around my finger and tug her close. She turned her face up to mine and her enthusiasm and joy stole my breath. It would take so little to lean the short distance and capture her lips in a kiss. Luckily, her enticing lips began to move, releasing me from my mesmerized state. She said, "It's..." She looked back toward the beach and then back at me as I held my breath waiting to hear what she thought. "Magical." Yes, she was.

We continued down the stairs with no mishap. Summer's skirt wrapped around her legs, her hair tripped along my chest as I followed, and I sent a silent thank you to the wind. Our final destination was the most remote of the cabanas. I wanted Summer all to myself, so I'd made sure to get this cabana for tonight. The hostess placed our menus after we scooted in, sitting near each other to the back of the semi-circle cushioned seat, facing the water. The wind inside the cabana was mostly blocked leaving patrons able to eat in peace. Heaters were also set up along the inside, above the opening, in case of cool evenings. "I'm so glad you like it."

"Love it. I love it! I may just move in here. Are you kidding?"

I chuckled. "I'm not sure we're accepting rental applications, but you'll be the first to know if that changes."

"Oh good." She started perusing the menu even as she said, "What should I order? I figure since you've invested here, you would have a direct line into all the best things on the menu."

She was leaning her chin on her right hand curled up, supporting her head. Adorable. "I would be doing our chef, Bex, a disservice and pissing her off, if I didn't tell you that everything on the menu was fantastic. What's one of your favorite types of protein?"

"I love white flaky fish and also crab. Well, shredded or lumped crab. Don't give me crab legs and tools because that's a recipe for disaster, right there."

"Noted. Then let me recommend the opah. Would you like some wine?"

"Sure. I'd love wine."

"May I order for us, then?"

"Yes. That would be great. Do the waiters actually have to carry the food down those stairs to get it to us? That's a lot of work, and if you hire anyone like me, downright dangerous." She gave me a self-deprecating smile. Adorable.

"Nope. The kitchen has an elevator for the staff to use to get the food down here, as well as for handicap access. It's located just under the stairs."

"Handicap access to the sand?"

"Yes. We have paths we can lay down. It was important to all of us involved that every part of the restaurant provides full access." She had a loose curl flying around teasing me, so I gave into my urge to touch her. I reached over and slowly tucked the ruby strand behind her ear, loving the silky feel of it. My fingers lingered just at the edge of her chin for the briefest moment, but long enough for her cheeks to stain my new favorite shade of pink.

The next few minutes were spent placing our orders and enjoying the view, but I felt and saw when my reprieve from the car's conversation had come to an end. Her serene face tensed minutely, she took a breath, which I was coming to associate with her generally relaxed demeanor, and looked like she braced to speak. Yep, I had mere moments to figure out if I was going to reward her openness from the car with my own, or if I would proceed in my usual manner with deflection and partial truths. *Damn!* I hated either choice this time, which should inform my decision, since it had always been easy in the past.

Then she spoke. "Will you tell me about becoming a talent agent now?"

The way she phrased her question made me pause. She'd given me an out if I wanted to take it. I could say I wasn't ready to talk about it or even give her the most basic facts about what drew me to my chosen profession, but that route tasted of cowardice and with this open brave woman at my side, I found I didn't want the coward's way out. Still, I wasn't ready to go into everything on our first date, so I decided on the truth, but not all of it. Hopefully, it would be enough.

16

PANTING, SLACK-JAWED, AND HUNGRY

Summer

I waited, ready to give Jason the space he needed to come to me with whatever information he was ready to share. It was fascinating to see how the tension at first built in him, noticeable only because he went completely blank and still, and then, as he came to his decision, his shoulders relaxed and his face became animated again. This was why I was able to see the shadows that danced across his chiseled features, and was left wondering at what or who put them there.

His chin firmed, as he began to speak, "My parents always wanted me to become a business mogul and take over my father's business. When I was eighteen and about to head off to college, they both passed away in a car accident."

"I'm so sorry. That had to be so hard, losing them both in an instant like that." I reached out, just as he had for me, and held on to his hand. I only hoped that he would find it as comforting as I had. He must, because he turned his hand over and laced our fingers, staring at our joined hands for a moment before continuing. The rest of me was jealous of my fingers as he held on the whole time he spoke.

"I'd originally planned to follow the very career they wished me to have, but while part of me wanted to honor them and do just that, another part of me recognized how short life could be and I didn't want to wake up one day in a career I didn't want to have—my chance to live having passed me by. I'd always been good with people and couldn't imagine being closeted in an office most of my day, so I considered all the skills I had and of those, which I liked most."

"Seems like a solid plan."

"Yeah. Well, while I was contemplating all this, a friend of mine asked me to join him at a movie opening he'd been invited to. Being wealthy and connected in LA comes with benefits. While at the after-party, I met one of the agents who managed a lead actor from the premiere. I ended up watching her the whole night. She spoke with people, subtly made inquiries for future projects, casually dropped hints about some of the other actors she represented in someone's ear, and overall, schmoozed her way into more work and success. I was hooked. She was conducting business, but she was out and about and enjoying a party while doing it. I was confident that I could do exactly what she was doing, and my ego said I could do it better."

"Because she was a woman?" I glared. This was about to be the shortest date I'd been on.

"No! God no! My ego said I could do it better than anyone no matter who they were because I was raised a Winter. I was a prick but an equal opportunity prick."

"Oh good. Can't have you being a prick and a misogynist." My features went back to my resting happy face. Good save.

"Of course not." He whisked out a devastating smile for me before fading back into his story. "Now then, the more important thing was that I would enjoy the challenge and the social nature of the job. In doing so, I would most likely be disappointing my parents in their afterlife, but I did it anyway. I redirected my education toward a marketing and public relations dual degree. The rest is history, as they say. I've been very aggressively pursuing my career ever since. First by building up my skills, then with learning some humility, and finally by starting and growing Avalanche Talent Agency." He turned his head from staring off to the ocean for most of the time he spoke, to finally meeting my eyes.

Pain. I got a brief glimpse before he walled it away and I knew there was more to the story he wasn't ready to share. That's okay. This was enough for now. It showed me he was willing to try. "I always think it's amazing when someone can find the courage to pursue what makes them feel whole. What makes them roll out of bed happy each morning to go off to work. So many people fall into their occupations without ever asking if it's something that they want to be doing. Something that makes their soul sing. And I'm not talking about those families struggling to make ends meet. I've been there and done that. No... I'm talking about the ones who have a choice but don't ever try. I wish they would so they, too, could be happier. I'm glad you've found what makes your soul sing. That's the very reason Kev and I opened our coffee shop. We always joked as kids about one day doing that, but it was a big jump into the unknown to actually take the risk and pursue it. Looks like we both have big balls." I winked at him and was rewarded for my quip when he smiled back, eyes now dancing with humor. I felt rather proud helping him out of his dark thoughts.

He joked back, "No offense, but I hope not. What works for others works for them, but there's only room for one set of balls in this relationship."

"Hmm. Balls aren't really that strong anyway. I'll stick with my takes a licking, keeps on ticking pussy parts." I slammed my free hand over my mouth in horror. Had I really just said that? He was laughing, but I was ready to crawl under the table and hide. Dropping my hand, I said, "It's not funny! I don't know why I seem to do and say things around you that really shouldn't be done or said. My mama would be horrified and want to wash my mouth out with soap."

"I have other ways of stopping your mouth so your mama doesn't have to be horrified." With that warning, he leaned over and captured my lips in a kiss. I quite literally melted into him. *Yes! Yes! Yes!* My mama would still be horrified, seeing as how I had sexted and kissed this man before even eating a meal together, but I wasn't about to stop him and point it out. One of Jason's hands snaked around the nape of my neck and he applied just a touch of pressure to angle my head to one side. He also applied pressure from his mouth, nipping at my bottom lip lightly in question. Seeing as how I wanted to kiss this man something fierce, I opened for him, and he went in for a deep, hot, hungry kiss. His tongue licked at mine, playing. Teasing along my lips again, only to delve back in as he shifted my head to another angle. He was in full possession of me and I was happy to be possessed. The cool breeze off the ocean did nothing to cool my overly heated skin. I answered every sweep of his tongue with one of my own.

Just as fast as he rolled in, like the tide, he pulled back, leaving me panting, slack-jawed, and hungry. It was only then that the sounds getting closer to our cabana permeated my sexually-charged brain and I swiftly straightened just as our waitress arrived with a second waiter and they presented our meal to us. *Holy hotness hell.* I placed a friendly smile on my face even as I was internally still trying to recover. I also had to hope that neither waiter would be able to see how flushed I must have been. Jason thanked the staff and once again we were alone.

Only then, did I remember to look down and see my food and it was beautiful. A work of art. The opah was placed alongside a crab-stuffed smashed potato. There was a carrot and asparagus string slaw to the other side of the fish. Drizzled over the top of everything was a creamy dark yellow sauce. I looked over at Jason's plate and found he had a medium-rare steak, sliced in half, topped with lumped lobster and blue cheese. Accompanying that was a side of broccolini as well as a sweet potato hash. Everything looked divine. "If this food tastes as good as it looks, I really am moving in."

"Oh, trust me. It does. Please."

He indicated I should take a bite and so I did and my mouth went straight to heaven. If mouths could have orgasms, mine totally had. We spent the next thirty minutes slowly and decadently indulging in our mouthgasms talking about our day-to-day life. What his work entailed. Some of his current projects. How Kevin and I started the coffee shop. About my estranged grandparents who had abandoned my mom when she'd gotten pregnant, yet still left everything to their granddaughter, me, when they passed away. It hadn't been a lot, but it allowed for the initial investment it took to create the café and keep it running for a few months while we drummed up enough business for us to be in the black.

I told him about what it was like gaining a new family. I talked about how my good friend Derek became the most protective older brother. How Kevin came about being considered family as well. He told me about some of his antics from high school and college. Like the time he and his buddy skipped school to go skateboarding in Venice Beach, only to be caught because they both forgot it was a half-day due to parent-teacher conferences. I laughed so hard at that story and its fallout, I almost choked on a bite of the crabby potato. Jason gently patted me on the back and I'd narrowly avoided "Death by Potato" as my headline.

The sunset began to blaze pink, peach, flaming yellow, and orange just as we finished our meal. It was breathtaking and left me in awe of the beauty of life itself. It also grew cooler and I put my sweater on even as Jason wrapped an arm around my shoulders and pulled me into his side. "Better?" he questioned.

"Yes. Thank you. It's so beautiful here and the food, I mean, the food... my mouth is still thanking me for that meal. I can see why you invested in this place."

"I definitely don't regret it for a minute. I hope you left room for dessert."

I looked at him with full incredulitiousness, and didn't care if that wasn't a word. "You know you're talking to a pastry chef, right? I wouldn't dream of skipping dessert from a place like this."

"Good. I preordered our dessert."

We snuggled in to enjoy the sunset and once again thanked the staff as our plates were cleared and wine glasses were refilled. A few minutes later, the waitress reappeared with a long covered plate. She placed it between us and uncovered it to my utter delight. Under the lid was a selection of cakes and mini-cups of creams and a multi-colored mousse. Jason had known. He had known I would love to sample it all and he had instinctively made it happen. As soon as the waitress left I turned to him and cupped both of my hands around his face. I loved feeling his end-of-the-day stubble there. The same stubble I'd felt across my face when we'd kissed earlier. I stared directly into his eyes and said, "Thank you. It's perfect. The whole meal, but especially this." I leaned in and gently pressed my lips to his. I'd meant it to be a quick show of my gratitude but once our lips touched, my world shifted.

17

DESSERT, DRIVE, DESSERT

Jason

What could I say, I had no doubt that I'd planned the perfect evening for us. In my profession, reading the client's needs and more importantly, their wants, and providing both was my bread and butter. It was why I'd never lost a client. Once I reeled someone in, I made damn sure that I kept them happy. To create this date, I did what came naturally. I'd known exactly where to take Summer, the atmosphere I wanted to create, the mood I wanted her in, and so I made it happen. I'd also known that someone who worked with pastries would love to sample a little bit of everything. What I hadn't been prepared for, hadn't properly planned for, was just how much her joy, her pure enjoyment of the evening, would mean to me. How much every moan of pleasure and shining smile of delight would impact me.

I also hadn't planned to kiss her, quite so thoroughly, before our food had even arrived, but I hadn't been able to restrain my need to feel her. To feel close to her, physically, after all the emotional information we'd shared. And damn, had she felt good. My body had been completely tuned into hers all night after that. Hell, probably since we met. It was pure luck that I'd retained enough awareness to hear the waitstaff as they arrived or else we would have put on quite a show.

Now, with her hands framing my face, my arm dropping from her shoulders to her waist when she turned, and her mouth on mine, the inferno of desire I'd leashed throughout dinner exploded into action. Using the arm around her waist, I scooped her up, placing her across my lap. Meanwhile, I wrapped my other hand, once again, behind her neck. Summer made a slight 'oomph' sound from the adjustment, but her lips never left mine and then she opened for me. Her mouth was all warm welcome and shared desire. I jumped into the sensations of her tongue, lips, and moans. Some amount of time later, I wasn't sure exactly how long, I broke off the kiss before I did something totally inappropriate. Oh wait. Apparently it was too late for that. At some point my hand had slid down and was now cupping her right breast. I rubbed my thumb back and forth over the turgid peak of her nipple, wishing I could suck and bite it too. In a monumental effort to regain control, I dropped my forehead to hers, but couldn't seem to keep that damn thumb still. Her name came out as a reverent whisper. "Summer."

Her voice was a little shaky when she whispered back, "Jason."

We stayed in that moment, saying nothing. Forehead to forehead, thumb to nipple, and breaths mingling. God it felt good. She felt good. Words popped out of my mouth offering her my truth. "God, I want you. I've never felt this drawn to anyone before. Every part of me wants to understand, touch, taste, and know every part of you. It's killing me to be this close to you but not be inside you."

"If you keep touching my breast like that, and kissing me like that, I'm going to insist on it. I've lost all inhibitions with you, and maybe the wine has helped, but I'm pretty sure, considering past behaviors, it's just you."

It was past time to stop, but the devil in me couldn't stop without pushing just a little bit more. I pinched her nipple even as I bit at her lip and she gasped, "Oh god!" That was my notice to quit while we could. I dropped my hand to her thigh and squeezed just a little bit.

"Mmmm."

"That wasn't very nice." She sounded grumbly and unsatisfied. Good.

"I'm not always a nice man."

"You know I'm still taking notes."

"I'll make sure I continue to do and say noteworthy things then. May I feed you our dessert?"

"I can feed my—"

"I know you can, but I would like to. May I?"

"Oh. Um. Sure." She began to squirm in an attempt to get off my lap, but stilled as soon as her bottom rubbed against my rock-hard erection. Then, she squirmed again with a mischievous look in her eyes. Pure torture.

"Summer..." I groaned. "...stop squirming, or is this payback for the nipple?"

"Mmm. It wasn't meant as such, but yeah, it just might be." The minx purposefully squirmed her butt right up against me again and my head dropped to the back of the seat.

"Are we skipping dessert?" I was quite prepared to do so.

"Nope. Weren't you supposed to be feeding me?"

I popped my head up again. "Originally, I planned to leave you seated in my lap while I fed you, but I think at this point, we better seat you next to me." I gave her a rueful smile. "I don't think I can handle your version of revenge much longer."

She returned an impish smile. Pride enveloped me upon seeing how plump and red her lips looked from my kisses. She glowed and I had done that to her and it felt phenomenal. With the last rays of the glorious sunset to view, I lifted the tiny spoon, and gave Summer a bite of the mini chocolate lava cake. Her lips closed around the spoon and she moaned. Her eyes closed and I was ready to start kissing her all over again. I didn't, though. Mauling her had not been a part of the plan. *Get it together, Winter.* I took a bite of it myself, and yeah, I moaned a little too, because it was just that damn good.

Next, I chose a bite of the strawberry-lemon cheesecake, followed by a bite of the dark chocolate bacon layer cream cake, then a bite of caramel-banana panna cotta with candied walnuts on top, a few bites of a few more cakes later, and I finished with the three-layer chocolate mousse featuring a white chocolate layer infused with champagne, a milk chocolate layer infused with Chambord, and a dark chocolate layer infused with port. Summer looked like she had reached tantric level sustained oral pleasure from the flavorful assault. When we finished, she looked over at me with an odd expression and I felt unbalanced because I wasn't sure what was coming next.

She licked her lips, like she was savoring every flavor that still clung there, and God, I wanted to lick her lips too. "Jason."

My eyes remained transfixed to the last spot her tongue had caressed, and I distractedly answered, "Yes, Summer?"

She wasn't answering and so I finally drew my eyes up to meet hers in question. When we locked gazes, in one of the most serious voices I'd heard from her, she said, "Take me to your home."

My whole body was primed and ready to go, especially my cock, which, at her words, seemed to be strategizing a way to escape solitary confinement. I had no doubt that she meant it. She wanted to come over and not to check out my view. She wanted me as badly as I wanted her. And really, why not? This might be our first official date, but we hadn't exactly been running along traditional lines here. She'd taken care of me when I was sick. We'd sexted. We'd flirted a whole bunch before the date. "Yes." That was all that was needed to be said right then.

As swiftly as I could, I dropped sixty dollars on the table as a generous tip, because I could guess at what the bill would normally have been, if I wasn't a partial owner eating for free, and I also wanted to give extra for the excellent care we received from our waitress. I scooted out of the seat and then reached back to help Summer up to her feet. She grabbed her clutch and I shuffled her safely up the stairs and out of the restaurant. The waitress must have seen us getting up, because by the time we walked out the front door, the attendant had my car waiting for us. I very carefully helped Summer back into the passenger seat, handed the valet a twenty, and climbed in.

I wanted to bask in the heat coming off us both, but I knew I had to ask, "Are you sure? We could wait."

She rushed to answer and it came out dripping with sensuality, "No. I need more. Now. Tonight. Of you. Us. Please."

Summer's senses had clearly been overwhelmed with sensations because she sounded as on edge as I felt. Carefully weaving my car up the mountain, eyes trained on the road, hands maneuvering the wheel, my body was aware of only one thing and that was Summer. My girl, as I was starting to think of her, needed some relief, and I needed more of her. "Summer, inch up your skirt for me."

She was hesitant at first, and I was about to tell her it was okay if she didn't want to, but then both of her hands, that had been sitting inert on her thighs, began to bunch the material of her skirt. It was a slow sensual climb that first revealed the curves of her calves, her knees, her rounded thighs, and... that was it. She paused. My first priority had to be our safety so I had to keep paying attention to the road, but I also knew these roads like the back of my hand, and speaking of hands— "May I touch you?"

Her response was a breathy, "Yes."

I reached over with my free hand and ran it leisurely from her knee up the length of her thigh. When I reached mid-thigh, I cupped the inner curve, leaving my hand sandwiched between both of her thighs. She was on fire. Her skin burning my hand. I inched even more slowly up the inside of her thighs and felt the heat coming from her core before I even made contact. Damp heat that I felt through whatever underwear she had chosen to wear. Or perhaps there was no underwear and that was why I could feel her so easily? I yearned to find out. Now. "You okay? Can I keep going?"

Again, the reply was immediate and more a plea than an answer, "Yes."

I continued my climb until I found my answer.

Summer

I had never given much credence to the often-used line in romance novels about needing someone more than you needed your next breath, but I totally got it now. I needed Jason, not just wanted him, to touch me. I couldn't think. All I could do was feel. Every part of me had been awakened with our meal. The breeze that caressed my body and hair, the sunset that amazed my eyes and heart, the feel of Jason's mouth on mine, his hands on my neck, behind my back, teasing my breast, his firm cock beneath my ass, then, then, when I thought I was already drowning in sensation, he introduced my mouth to delight after delight until I was flooded both inside and out with a need to relieve the pleasure. A need for this man, who had known me so well, so quickly, that he planned the perfect date, the perfect seduction of all of me.

And now, in the car, his commanding nature once again ratcheting up a desire I didn't think could go any higher. Every time he took charge like that, I melted even more. His hand was so close to where I needed him to be. So fucking close. I was immobile in my need. Just sitting in a bonfire waiting to combust. Then he asked if he could keep going, if he could touch my pussy and, God, *yes*. Please!

His fingers moved up so slowly, leaving trails of longing on every inch of skin he touched, until he finally discovered what I'd kept to myself all evening. Commando. It was my first time going out in public without underwear, but I liked knowing that I wore nothing under my skirt throughout dinner while he didn't. Like a salacious secret only I was privy to. That in and of itself had turned me on. I originally hadn't planned for us to get to this point, but thinking about how easily we could, had driven my desire higher just like everything else tonight. My plan was to get turned on and go home to play with my wand friend. That plan was so two hours ago.

His deeply inhaled breath as his fingers met nothing but my arousal had been so worth it. "Fuck, Summer. All night. All night you've been hot and wet and bare for me. Waiting for my hand to find out your little secret. When you were on my lap earlier, I could have inched up your pretty little skirt and had you riding my cock while we watched the sun set and no one could have seen. Fuck me. It would have been so easy. I think we'll find ourselves there for another date soon. Hell, if you promise to come in a skirt with no underwear on, I'll take you there for every date." Even as he spoke, he was pulling the car into his secluded driveway all while the fingers of his other hand gently played with me. The image he put in my head of fucking him at the restaurant practically had me coming right there and then. So close, but no, I needed something more.

I really wanted to move my hips, needed to even, but I figured since we were parked, he would pull his hand away, so we could go inside. I should have remembered that pinch to my nipple at dinner. Jason had a mischievous side to go along with his commanding side when it came to sex, and I was going to have to keep that in mind. Assuming my mind ever worked again, because Jason's fingers didn't stop. No. As soon as he parked, he dove a finger inside of me and I couldn't help the gasp that escaped. "Oh god!"

"You feel so good Summer. All this wet heat just for me—" He paused and chuckled. "—and maybe dessert, but I can live with that."

I would have laughed, but his thumb started rubbing at my clit and I couldn't think straight. He rubbed and thrust but slowly, leisurely, and it took me a few minutes to come out of my sexual fog enough to realize he was keeping me on the precipice but had no plans it seemed to push me over. "Jason?"

"Yes, Summer." His voice was deep with desire, but he continued to just thrust and rub and dammit I needed more.

"What are you doing? Faster!"

"Do you need something, Summer?"

"Yes! Dammit!"

"What do you need, sweetheart?"

"I told you. Faster! More!"

"I didn't ask what you wanted me to do. I asked what you needed."

Was that hot? Why was that hot? "You're so bossy. Fine! I need to come. Please, Jason. I need to come."

"Yes. I think you do."

Finally! But a split second later, he pulled his hand away and climbed out of the car. I sat there glaring as he walked around to my side and opened my door. I was generally a pretty laid-back, go with the flow kinda girl, but I was about to throw either a full tantrum or hands, and only future me knew which it would be. I wasn't sure I could actually stand right then, but frustration might just help a girl out. I swung my legs out the door and was in the process of pushing my skirt back down when Jason knelt in front of me in the drive, pushed my hands out of the way, and used his body to spread my thighs wide. He pulled my hips gently to the edge of the seat, which had me reaching for the 'oh shit' handle, and then his breath blew over my overly heated and underappreciated pussy.

"Oh god, yes!" Frustration was burned away as my desire came flooding right back to the surface with Jason's mouth kissing me right where I needed him most. I leaned back, bracing myself on the middle console as his tongue licked at me.

His lips were against my labia as he growled, "I wanted a second dessert." He bent his head and devoured my pussy the way he had devoured my mouth earlier. Licking and nipping, sucking, and thrusting. His tongue and mouth learned every single inch of me as far as I could tell.

The coiling need in me got tighter and tighter, my body throbbed along with my pussy, and I kept needing just a little bit more. Just a little more. "Please!" As I begged for release, he closed his lips around my clit and sucked. At the same time, he thrust two fingers into my core and that was it. I exploded in sensation and the throbbing need became glorious satisfaction as I convulsed around his fingers. When the clenching of my orgasm waned, he withdrew his fingers and I looked up and saw he was looking back at me with eyes dark with need. He brought his fingers to his mouth and sucked, cleaning them, and then with obvious purpose, his other hand pulled me up by my neck to a sitting position even as he leaned over and kissed me deeply.

He was sharing the taste of me with me and, though a few seconds before I'd been coming down from my orgasm, I found my desire driving me once again. Once again, I wanted more. Who knew I was such a hedonist? Oh... wait. I did. I just had never had a chance to experience this side of myself in a sexual context. But now that I had, yeah, I wanted more. So I kissed him right back with all the passion he had elicited in me. When we finally pulled our lips apart, I leaned in close to his ear and told him the one word most true at that moment. "More."

18

KEYS, PART TWO

Jason

Listen, I had my fair share of sex. I enjoyed it quite a bit in fact, and yet, even though Summer and I hadn't actually had sex yet, nothing I'd done previously even compared. I could have luxuriated in Summer's orgasm and taste for hours except for the fact that I thought my dick might well detach soon if I didn't give it some relief as well. When she'd leaned in and told me she wanted "more", well... I had very "I'm Tarzan, You Jane" like feelings that drove me to swiftly pick her up into my arms, fumble with the gate, and then fumble with the keys as I tried to open my fucking door. All the while, Summer kept kissing and nibbling and licking my neck and ear and, "Fuck!" I dropped the keys.

She giggled. My tormentor actually giggled. "I fucking need to be inside of you and you laugh?" I growled at her as I dropped her legs so she could stand. Our bodies were pressed together and she got even more sadistic as her hand made its way between our bodies and cupped my erection. "What are you doing, Summer?"

"I'm checking to make sure you're okay. You feel a bit... constrained. Doesn't this hurt?"

"Yeah, it hurts. Hence the fucking keys. Can you stand?"

"Yes."

I checked to make sure she was steady when I let her go but she instantly dropped to the ground.

"Shit! Are you o— Fuck!"

"But why would I want to?" Summer had my slacks unbuttoned and my zipper down in a flash. Woman had to be magical, because I don't know how that happened so fas—then I wasn't thinking at all. She wrapped her hand around my cock and licked the tip. "Want me to find the keys while I'm down here?" I definitely heard mischief in her voice. Yep, misch—she licked me again and pumped her hand a few times.

"What?" I think she asked me a question but I wasn't tracking well with her tongue on me.

She moved her hand again, but this time she wrapped her lips gently over the tip of my cock and then swirled her tongue. And, holy hell it felt good. Then she lifted her mouth and said, "You know. The keys? To the door?" She licked all the way up my shaft and I thought I might have momentarily blacked out. She was still talking, though. "Did you want me to get the keys?"

"I don't know." Did she expect me to hold down a whole conversation while her mouth engulfed my dick.

Wait... was she giggling, I wasn't sure. I looked down to check but just as I did, she wrapped her mouth around my cock, taking him a little further this time. The sight was the hottest thing I'd ever seen since—um—well—her pussy a few minutes ago, but still. "Damn, that feels good!"

She moved up and down on me a few more times and then came off with a wet pop. "And about the keys?" She smiled innocently up at me.

Why was she smiling innocently? "The keys?" I repeated back, as my hand ran around to the back of her neck and tangled in her beautiful hair, which seemed darker in the moonlight. I vowed to myself that one day in the very near future, I'd get to see my fingers tangled in her red locks glowing in the sun. I gently urged her to take me in her mouth again. Beautiful lips. Wrapped around my cock. Yeah. I wanted more too. "More."

This time only lust shown back at me from her face as she looked up. "Yes. More." She took me fully into her mouth and her warm heat overwhelmed me and almost had me coming right there and then. I gripped a little harder in her hair, loving the feel of her soft, thick locks. In response, she moaned around my shaft and fuck it felt good.

My brain finally caught up to the surprise attack Summer had initiated and I knew I didn't want to come in her mouth tonight. At least not right then, the night was young, after all. I gently yanked her off of my cock and tilted her head so she was looking up at me. "Get the keys." It was clear that she understood I was taking control back, because she nodded, and as I eased my fingers from her hair, she eagerly jumped up with the keys in hand.

"Fuck!" I hissed out. Unfortunately, she'd jumped a little too fast and ended up nailing me in the chin with her head. We'd both yelped in pain. I was busy rubbing my abused chin and I saw Summer was doing the same with the top of her head.

"Ow! I'm. So. Sorry," she said slowly, haltingly.

Even in pain, I couldn't help but register how lovely she was. "It's okay. I'll know to bring multiple types of protection next time." I paused and saw when she realized what I'd said, because she giggled, and I felt ten feet tall for diffusing her embarrassment and hopefully getting us back on track. "Are you okay?"

"I have a very hard head. You sure I didn't damage your chin, though?"

"Nope. Chin is still good to go. So is my cock. Think we can finally move this inside?"

"Yes." She handed me the keys and I swiftly opened the door. She followed me inside, and in a split second, I closed the door and had her up against the wall, with her skirt the only barrier between us as her legs wound around my waist. I rubbed my erection against her skirt-covered pussy. Through the material, I could feel she was wet for me, all over again. Her voice was back to husky as she yelled, "Jason!"

I licked her neck up to her ear and whispered, "I want you naked. Come with me." Then I lifted her up and walked with her in my arms up the stairs to my bedroom, nuzzling her neck the whole way.

When we got there, I set her down so I could swiftly turn on both bedside lamps. Summer looked around and whatever she saw, she must have liked. She looked back at me and smiled warmly. Her desire still simmering, but on the back burner waiting to be stoked back to life. As for me, my cock felt like it wanted to take up permanent residence inside her. She was so damn beautiful every day, but slightly messed up from our foreplay, she was downright *hot*. I liked it. A lot. "Take your shirt off for me, Summer. I want to see you."

"Okay, but fair is fair. I want your shirt off too." She grinned. Our eyes stayed glued to each other as she pulled her sweater off first, and then her shirt up and over her head while I undid the buttons on my own shirt until I could throw it off, too. "Do you want my necklace off as well?"

"No. It's lovely against your skin. I kind of like you adorned with your necklace, your earrings, me, and nothing else."

"Okay." She reached behind and somehow one-handedly unsnapped her lacey black bra. No matter how many times I saw that move, I still couldn't accomplish it nearly as smoothly with two hands.

Her bra slid down her arms and I held my breath. Her breasts, as she finally revealed them, were perfect. Better than I imagined them and, yeah, in the couple of weeks I had known her, I'd imagined them a lot. A perfect handful for me with pink, pert nipples that were standing proud and firm almost begging for my mouth to ease them. Before I did, though, I said, "Ever since we sexted, I have tried to imagine what you looked like as you pleasured your breasts for me. Show me. I want to see."

"You know what I imagined?"

"No."

"You. Rubbing your cock. Why don't we have a visual exchange."

So I did. I slowly moved my hand up and down my engorged cock as Summer rubbed and pinched at her nipples. Neither of us stopped staring across the space between us. My cock twitched with every move of Summer's hands. When she pinched her nipples, my hand behaved as though it was pinching them and I had to wince, because it had clenched around my cock like a vise. "You are so fucking beautiful. I want to see all of you. Push the skirt and shoes off."

By now, I'd learned that she would ask for reciprocation, so I pushed my own pants down even as I watched her do the same. I strode over to her and using the same hand I had at dinner, on the same breast, I rubbed my thumb back and forth across the rigid peak. Summer's green eyes were hazy with lust almost instantly. "I enjoyed tormenting you at the table earlier."

"Yeah. I could tell." Her words came out husky.

"Summer. I think I've reached my limit. I need you. Need to be inside you. Are you still good with that?"

"Yes. Um. Do you have condoms?"

"Yes, I do." I smiled reassuringly at her.

"Then touch me all over, Jason. I want to feel you too. I know we've only known each other less than two weeks, but it feels like I've wanted to feel your touch for so damn long."

"I feel the same way." I pinched at her breast just as I brought my other hand to the nape of her neck again and pulled her in for another hungry kiss, swallowing her gasp of pleasure and pain. I switched hands and breasts, kissing my way down her throat, past her necklace, and licked at the nipple I'd been mildly torturing. It was fully distended and I heard her breath hitch with each rough lick. She tasted and smelled like honey and cinnamon and felt like silk. I sucked her nipple into my mouth and she inhaled sharply. Clearly, she enjoyed breast play as much as I did. I was going to enjoy her beauties for so, so long.

Well. At some point. Not now. Later. Later, I would lavish them with so much attention, she might just come from that alone. I pinched her other breast before switching my oral attention to it. This time I sucked her nipple in and then grazed it with my teeth on the way out. She moaned. My new favorite sound.

Actually, every sound she made was as perfect as her body. I loved hearing them all. Impatient, I lifted her up off her feet, carried her to the bed, and set her down gently even as I pressed her body into the mattress with my own. The full skin-to-skin contact was delicious. I truly did want to devour her from head to toe, but once again, my cock reminded me that it had been patient long enough. One thing I wasn't willing to bend on, though, was making sure that Summer would be ready to take me.

I reached between our bodies as I continued to suck and lick each of her breasts with my mouth. Rubbing the stubble on my cheek against her soft flesh hoping it left her just a little bit marked up. My fingers once again found her heat and I was excited to feel how wet she already was. Feeling the evidence of her need for me, the same as I was feeling for her, soothed something inside of me I didn't even know needed soothing. We were both ready. *Thank fuck!* I reached over to the nightstand, opened the drawer, and pulled out a packet from the pack there. Summer looked over and joked, "Convenient."

I joked back, "I have to be prepared in case I find myself attacked by a feral woman." I ripped open the packet and pulled out the condom. I pinched the tip and began rolling it on, my eyes never leaving Summer.

"You have a lot of feral females in these mountains?" She was still joking with me, but her eyes stayed transfixed to my cock as I finished rolling on the protection.

"I've found at least one. I was attacked even as I was trying to enter my home."

Now she looked up into my eyes with her impish grin. "Yes. I suppose you were. You should definitely do whatever it takes to subdue the wild creature. I suggest sex."

"That I can do." When had I ever enjoyed a witty conversation in the midst of sexual pleasure? Summer brought so much of her joy and passion into everything she did and now I wanted it all directed fully on me.

I leaned down for another long kiss, even as I settled my hips between her thighs and lined the head of my cock with her entrance. With one arm near her face, tangling my fingers into her hair again, and the other gripping her thigh and holding her wide open for me, I started to push in. *Damn!* Hot. Wet. Tight. I was thinking in single words and it was all good. "Summer! You feel so fucking good."

"You feel so fucking good yourself, but I want more!"

"Yes. Take me. All of me." I pushed further and further in until I was buried so deeply my balls hit her ass cheeks. I stayed there for a moment, letting her adjust to me and quite frankly, letting myself get a grip. I wanted it to be good, and if I didn't get a grip, I'd be coming within seconds.

"Jason. You feel amazing but I need you to move."

I gritted through my teeth. "Try again. Tell me what you *need*, Summer."

Summer apparently remembered my little lesson from the car because she said without faltering, "I need to come. Please, Jason! I need you."

"I need you, too. I need you to come all over my cock. Do you think you can do that for me?"

"Yes!"

I moved slowly at first, but I could tell that Summer was just as on edge as I was and so I picked up the pace. Harder. Faster. I was drowning in the feel of her but I wanted her to come first. Needed to give her what she wanted, so I moved my hand away from her thigh down to rub at her clitoris. There was nothing gentle or easygoing about it this time. I tried a couple of different methods I'd picked up over the years and when I saw the one she reacted to the most, I went hard and consistent. It wasn't but a few minutes later and Summer's whole body tensed and then flew apart in spasm after spasm as she gasped and screamed for me in ecstasy. And, that was it. I couldn't hold on any longer. I pumped a couple more hard thrusts as I felt her inner walls clamp on my cock and I joined her in passionate release. I came so hard it hurt a bit but in the best possible way. "Summer."

We lay there gasping for breath, sweaty and satiated. I moved to one side, so I wouldn't crush her under me, but I turned her body with me as well, pushing her leg over my hip, so our bodies stayed joined.

"That was..."

Summer didn't seem to be able to finish that sentence, so I just answered, "Yeah. It was."

19

DOWN WITH THE PATRIARCHY

Summer

I wasn't exactly sure how much time had passed, but I regained full awareness of my surroundings when I heard Jason returning from the bathroom. The bed dipped as he climbed in. He sprawled on his back and rolled me until I was laying along the full length of his side. I bent one leg across his firm thighs and placed one hand on his chest over his heart. His chest was sculpted from pure muscle, the lean kind, and had very little blond hairs across his pecs. My head fit perfectly under his chin and I sighed in full-body contentment. I had absolutely no regrets. None. Nada. Mama may have taught me better than to jump into bed with someone like I just had, but not one part of me had an iota of regret. Every rule had its exceptions and Jason, tonight, had exception written all over him.

His touch left goosebumps as he trailed his hand through my hair, down my back, and then lightly grazed his fingers all the way back up to do it all again, on repeat. I was boneless and happy. I was also unsure of what happened next. Somehow, bold Summer, who told this amazing man to take her home only a few hours ago, was wishing to transform into an escape artist post-orgasm. Maybe I should say something. But, what? Or, maybe I should lay here contented and leave any further conversation to him. Solid plan. I could totally do that.

I couldn't do that since he wasn't saying anything and now the silence was starting to feel weird. Something needed to be said and it looked like I was going to have to be the one to say it. But, what does one say to a man who just totally blew your mind? "Hey. You just totally blew my mind." *Um, no.* "Thanks!" *Thanks?* Next I'll be handing him a gold star and telling him, "Job well done." Sheesh.

While I'd been having my internal debate, I'd missed the fact that Jason's hand had stopped moving. Oh, shit! Had he said something? Maybe I missed it. I didn't think so. Since I wasn't planning to spend the night, maybe I should start getting myself together and thank him for a wonderful evening. After all, sex or no sex, we were not ready for the intimacy of sleeping in each other's arms all night. Mornings are a pretty private thing. Morning breath. Drooling on pillows. Morning routines. That's serious relationship territory, and I was pretty sure we weren't ready for that. Were we? It was technically our first date, so of course not. That would be ridiculous. Right?

On top of that, Jason wasn't comfortable being open with me yet, so, yeah, not staying the night. I made the decision to enjoy the cuddles, but also to make sure I didn't fall asleep and I would Uber or ask him to take me back at a reasonable time. While I was busy rambling in my head, I also concluded that it was probably awkward for him too. He'd probably worry about asking me to leave because he wouldn't want me to feel like he was kicking me out, so it was up to me to say something. Right? I was just about to, when he said my name.

"Summer?"

"Yes?"

"Everything okay? You seem, pensive and a little tense. Are you okay with everything we did?"

"Oh, hell yes." I bit on my bottom lip. *Hell yes?* "What I meant is, I really enjoyed tonight. All of it. You?"

"Me too." He wrapped me tightly in his arms. His strong, muscular, sexy-as-hell arms, and I relaxed right into him again. "Jason?"

"Yeah?"

"I'm bad at this."

"What are you talking about? You were phenomenal. I've never come as hard as I did with you."

"Oh." I dug my face into his chest as I felt my cheeks flame. I mumbled into his pec even as I gently hit him with the hand that had been resting there. "I didn't mean about that and you were phenomenal too, by the way. I *meant*, now. This. After. I've had only a couple of boyfriends I've stayed over with because we were together a while. I've had only a few hookups. What I haven't had are a lot of lovers between those two points or in general, really. I'm nervous about what happens now."

"Oh."

"Oh?" I lifted my head and caught a look I could only call smug satisfaction on his face. I rolled my eyes, put my head back down, and said, "Men. Always wanting women to be virgin sex kittens. Down with the patriarchy!"

My world upended and I found myself flipped onto my back. He braced himself on his elbows on either side of my head, and I saw pure sin in his expression this time. "You said you want the patriarchy to go down? Well, I aim to please."

Then, the patriarchy did in fact go down. In fact, it went down kissing. Kissing me all the way down my body and yeah, he totally pleased me. Again. Two more times. As I was coming down from my —What was that, fourth orgasm for the night?—he kissed his way back up my overly sensitive body. Each touch of his lips was like a brand. His passion-filled eyes collided with mine, and after gloving up, he slowly, inch by very slow inch, slid back into my body. He was so hard, and thick, and the feeling of fullness once he was seated completely inside me, was perfection. I was burning up and ready for round two. All thoughts of leaving left somewhere between patriarchy and down.

Now that leaving was off the table, I was seriously considering homicide instead, because he continued to take it slow. Too slow. Painfully slow. He pushed in and out in a lazy rhythm that drove me utterly insane. I was completely lost to sensation. He kept on going, playing with my breasts, with my clit, with my mouth, and my body. Kissing, licking, and sucking until I was one giant throbbing pinpoint of painful need. I couldn't take it anymore, so I begged but in a demanding tone, "Jason. I need, *need*, to come. Oh god! I need it so much. I need you, right now."

It had been the right thing to say, and I whimpered in gratitude, because Jason released his control and his slow relentless pace became pure, aggressive sexual pleasure. As he thrust into me and roughly played with my clit how I liked, I tensed and then shook wildly in orgasm. I couldn't be sure, but I thought I saw stars, rainbows, fireworks, maybe dancing rainbow kittens, as Jason stiffened, thrust one more time, and found his own release. This time, we were a sweaty disaster and everything felt right. Perfect.

Once again, I lost track of time as Jason went to discard the condom. I drifted in a beautiful haze and could swear I saw the Mesopotamian goddess Nanaya from that morning's card high-fiving me. When I'd drawn that card indicating love, I'd assumed we were going to have a great date. I hadn't considered she was also the goddess of eroticism and sensuality. A pleasure goddess. I hadn't mentally prepared for the amount of pleasure I'd experienced. Still in my pleasure fog, the goddess looked at me smug as hell. Clearly this had been Nanaya's plan all along. Sneaky, sneaky, pleasure goddess.

"You *are* a pleasure goddess as far as I'm concerned."

The sound of Jason's voice and his words startled me so completely—*Had I said that last part out loud? Oh shit!*—I reflexively jerked up. Wrong. Very wrong thing to do. But, I realized too late, as a few things happened all at once. Jason had been looming near me, in the process of lifting the sheet to get in, but at my sudden movement, he jerked back, sheet still in hand. I knew this, because that same sheet had been wrapped around me, and since I was already imbalanced mentally and physically, I found myself tumbled onto the floor. That made me exceedingly grateful that Jason had a platform bed, and my fall was only a short distance. My chagrin, on the other hand, was in a free fall. For a few seconds anyway, but since falling through life was now practically a skill set for me, I decided—screw it —and convulsed in laughter instead.

JASON

Summer was laughing her butt off at my feet and I mentally ran through the last few minutes trying to understand what just happened. I'd headed to the bathroom, having left a contented kitten in my bed, lost in my own musings. It both thrilled and scared me that I felt close to her in a way that I couldn't explain and at a speed that I couldn't fathom. It was so new and I tried to remind myself of that fact, unsuccessfully, as I tossed the condom in the trash. A deeper part of me knew there was more to it.

It was the same thing that drove me, and I didn't mean my cock, though it was in full accord. No, it was the inner thing that had always propelled me in my career, in choosing my clients, in finding the right fit, that thing knew that Summer was special whether I wanted her to be or not. Whatever I was feeling didn't feel new at all and that was a very scary thing because, what did I know about caring for someone? *Exactly. You'll have some fun with each other, maybe extra special fun, and eventually she'll get that you're who you are, or you'll get bored and move on. Stop overthinking this.* I took my own advice and stopped thinking about it, period.

When I came back into the bedroom and saw her blissed form sprawled in my bed, I stood back and enjoyed the view. I'd mentally patted myself on the back for being the one to bring her to bone-melting and mind-numbing pleasurable heights. It had been obvious that she wasn't asleep, but... adrift. I'd come over with every intention to join her, lifted the sheet, and heard her mumble something about a pleasure goddess. Since I couldn't agree more, I'd told her so. That's where things went horribly wrong. When all hell broke loose.

What I was left with was part of a sheet still clutched in my hand, the other side of which was completely entangled around my pleasure goddess, and she was rolling around on my floor giggling herself silly. That part put a smile on my own face. "Clearly, my work here is done."

She gasped between giggles, "What?" Chest heaving and eyes watering, she paused long enough to look up at me and damn, she was so beautiful like this. Something in my chest clenched, but I ignored that too.

"After you fell out of bed from the orgasm you gave yourself when we sexted, I vowed I'd bring you enough pleasure one day to get the same result. I'm a man who likes to succeed, Summer. Check." I used my free hand to make a check mark motion.

That sent her into another fit of giggles and I felt her happiness deep down in all those places I was ignoring. I also felt rather silly standing over her holding on to the sheet. Joining her on my floor was an option, but instead, I scooped her up in my arms and sat down on the bed with her in my lap. She attempted to regain her composure as I cuddled her.

When she did, she finally spoke, "You know, I'd been trying to figure out, after round one, what I should say or do. If I'd known you were waiting for me to fall out of your bed, I would have happily accommodated you earlier."

"Ah. But then we would have missed out on round two. This is way better. In all seriousness, though, are you okay? Anything hurt and needing kisses?" I purposefully leered, keeping things in a realm I was comfortable being.

She wrapped her arms loosely around my neck, looked me in the eyes, and gave me a gentle kiss on the lips. I kissed her back in the same exploratory, gentle way despite how conflicted it left me. The kiss felt full of soft promises and intimacy unlike the fiery, hungry kisses we'd shared previously. Just holding her felt good. It felt so damn good. *Of course it feels good. She's fun. She's sexy. You're into her. No big deal.*

My voice came out gruffer than I intended, as unused feelings and status quo thoughts fought within me. They tightened my throat as I made it clear what I wanted any way you sliced it. "Stay the night." It was supposed to be a question not a statement. *Shit.*

She took a few moments before answering me. "Are you sure that's something you want? I was thinking earlier that it was too soon for a sleepover, but I also don't really want to go."

I appreciated her directness since it matched my own. "I hadn't planned to ask you to stay the night either, but, yeah, I'm sure. Nothing would give me more pleasure than to hold you and fall asleep smelling and feeling you tonight."

Summer pushed back some of her tangled, messy, sex hair that had fallen forward and looked back seriously, all giggles forgotten. I prepared myself for her to say no and maybe that would be for the best. Maybe I'd pushed too hard. I was used to going after whatever I wanted, and I wanted her here, all night. I wasn't going to analyze why.

"Jason?"

"Yes?"

"If I stay the night, it'll mean something—" She paused as though looking for the right word, and when it came, it was the same one as earlier in the night, but I knew she meant it in a very different way. "—more."

Apparently, I was going to have to analyze it. I understood what she was saying and for the briefest of moments, my normally commitment-resistant self... panicked. I steadied my features so it wouldn't show, but inside I was grabbing a brown paper bag and breathing as the sign overhead pointed toward the exit. Everything within me was revolting but in different directions. It all released into calm certainty as I looked into Summer's beautiful, languid, and hesitant eyes. Maybe more didn't have to be scary. It felt so dang right to have her in my arms. Whatever this was, Summer was right. It was more. I suppressed my doubts, because that always works, and said, "Yes. This is more. More than I was looking for. More than I expected. But, I can't deny, I want it. I want you. You okay with more?" My inner voice tried to make a comeback but I buried him. I was doing this.

She nodded and gave me the sweetest smile. "Yeah. I want you too. I want more too."

It was probably one of the most profound moments in my life. It was broken seconds later, when a distressed Summer scrambled off my lap and ran from the room. I was rarely dumbfounded, but I was totally dumbfounded. *What the hell?* "Summer?" I was about to run after her when she ran back in. All gloriously nude, flushed, and holding her cell phone? "Are we moving into home pornos, because I'm not totally opposed to the idea, but I think it's a little soon, don't you?"

She looked up distractedly, "What?" I waited. I could tell the moment my question permeated her brain as her eyes twinkled and she mischievously smiled back. "Very funny. No. No home pornos, though I'm filing it in my notes that you're not totally opposed to the idea." She winked, but continued with an explanation. "I promised my roommate, Jessica, that I'd let her know I wasn't dead by an axe murderer. I was supposed to do that by ten-thirty and I've missed that by a decent margin. Hopefully, no SWAT teams will break down your door anytime soon. Jessica is fiercely protective. No joke. I'm texting her to call them off, just in case." Her phone dinged just as she finished talking.

"Has she called them off?"

"Turns out she decided to hold off until midnight. Just under the gun. Whew. Um, are you still sure about the all-nighter?"

She looked unsure, and still deliciously and unabashedly nude. A true pleasure goddess in all her glory. Her confidence was just one more amazing thing to add to the list of all that was Summer, to all that drew me to her. I had only one answer. "I'm sure." I stood and moved behind her, wrapping my body around hers. One arm wrapped around her abdomen with my hand cupping one of her breasts while the other wrapped around her shoulder, across her throat, hugging her to me. Her head tilted, resting into the crook of my elbow. I bent my knees so her butt lined perfectly with my semi-hard groin, thigh to thigh, and felt so damn sure. Every part of me was sure. Almost. I ignored the bag breather part completely. "I want to hold you just like this, but horizontal, all night."

Summer typed out one more text and then gently tossed her phone to the nightstand. "Let's get horizontal then."

"Definitely."

20

PARENTS

Summer

I floated into my apartment, like foam on a latté, Sunday morning. It was hard to believe that I'd ended up spending the whole weekend with Jason. I wasn't irresponsible, I'd come home to check on the café and pack a weekend bag on Friday. There may have been a few seconds or minutes where I reconsidered what I was doing. It felt both unbelievable and inevitable. Inevitable won, though. Who was I to mess with fate?

After making sure that everyone scheduled to cover the café wouldn't need my intervention, I'd met Jason at his home and from there, well, from there we'd had the most amazing few days. He had been everything I could have hoped for in a boyfriend. He'd been fun, exciting, attentive, kind, and if he hadn't totally opened up about whatever caused the shadows I still caught sight of from time to time? I had faith that he would eventually. He was worth my patience.

Midnight, on the other hand, had no patience for me. As soon as I walked in, I felt the soft push of his head against my shins and heard his purr. "Aww. I missed you too, sweetie." I lifted him into my arms, cuddling my face into his silky soft fur and gave him scratches under his chin, eliciting even louder purrs. I was allowed cuddles for only a brief few minutes. Midnight must have remembered that he was mad at me for my disappearance because I felt his displeasure in the squirming of his body and even more so in the nails he dug into my shoulder until I put him down. "Ow!" Utterly unapologetic, he flicked his tail at me and sauntered away. "Well. We'll see if you get any tuna later, buddy," I yelled after him. He was totally going to get tuna later, who was I kidding? And, worse. He knew it too.

I didn't see Jessica, but heard the shower going, so I assumed she was in the process of getting ready for the day. Since I couldn't spew happiness at my friend and my cat wasn't speaking to me, I closed myself in my room. I dropped my purse and keys onto my brown-black Ikea dresser whose drawers I'd decorated with rainbow splatters. The original idea had been to paint flowers, but then Jess, Kevin, and I got into a paint fight and splatters seemed the way to go.

Flopping down on my bed, I placed my phone on my nightstand and smiled as I remembered my own shower that morning. Jason had washed and dirtied and washed every part of me quite thoroughly. It had been decadent and fun and downright delicious. And, even after a weekend full of the hottest sex in the history of sex, somehow I was still turned on just thinking about it. About him. I sighed. Was it just lust? It didn't feel like it, but I'd definitely enjoyed it when he'd woken me up with his mouth trailing kisses down my spine. When he bit my butt and then licke—

I startled out of my sexual musings when I heard my phone make a sound and without looking at it, I already knew who was calling. If the ringtone hadn't given it away, "Respect" by one of Mama's favorite singers, Aretha Franklin, then the timing would have because it was Sunday afternoon in Colorado. That meant Mama Palmer just got out of church and this was our time to talk. I hit the speaker option and answered right away, because no way would I keep Mama waiting. "Hi, Mama! How are you? How was church?"

"I'm doing just fine, baby. Church was pretty uneventful but Reverend Perry gave the most beautiful sermon about the importance of community and holding together through adversity. That man sure has a silver tongue, but you know your pop always has to say something."

I laughed, picturing Pop walking up to Reverend Perry, as he often did since they were good friends, and pulling him aside to discuss some minor point he disagreed with. "Yeah. I know Pop. What was wrong this time?"

Mama huffed. Well, I thought I heard a huff, but it could be that I just knew my mama well enough that I pictured it in my head. Either way, the familiar behavior made me feel close to her, even over the phone. "He thought the reverend did a fine job describing community but that he didn't emphasize the family as a community enough. Not that he hadn't mentioned it for a good fifteen minutes, but that wasn't enough for your father. Oh no. You know he always puts the family first. Anyway, Louise said she agreed with him, your father that is, which I think she did just so she could watch him and the Reverend argue, and of course, that was all he needed to hear before he went righteous with indignation and stomped off."

"And here I thought you said church was uneventful. Sounds pretty eventful to me." Love for my family and their familiar actions warmed me. Just another Sunday with the Palmers. We were all outspoken and uniquely ourselves but also oozed love when it came to family and community. I was one lucky girl to be a part of my family. Losing my mom so young, things could have been infinitely worse, but they definitely couldn't have been better.

Sure, there were inevitable times where I would still feel a little bit like an outsider but through no fault of anyone. All the Palmers helped me to keep my Jewish identity, celebrating my holidays with me even while including me in all of their celebrations if I wanted to participate. And, no one in our immediate community ever dared to make me feel like I wasn't welcome, not with my family. In fact, our church had always been a safe space free from judgement. Somewhere where I got to watch my pop argue with the good reverend, where I ran around with my brother and friends, and where I ate the most amazing home-cooked food at the after-church cookout. When my mom was alive, we often spent Sunday afternoons with the Palmers so it felt so familiar to me. It was an easy transition to being home.

It was always the broader world, like kids at school, who hurt my family with their racism or harassed me for being Jewish. People who shouldn't and didn't matter but who ruined every interaction with their ignorance. We had each other and our family and that was everything.

Mama's comment brought me out of my musings. "Oh, sweetie, I would call that just another Sunday, not eventful at all. Regardless, how's my baby doing?"

I briefly pondered the pros and cons of keeping mum about Jason but knew that wasn't really an option. I never kept anything from Mama. "Well, Mama, I have a boyfriend."

"What do you mean you have a boyfriend?" That's when I realized my mistake. *Oh shit.* Mama continued, "I don't remember hearing about you dating anyone. Have you been keeping secrets from me, Summer Evangeline Harris Palmer?"

Well, shit. Now you've done it. When Mom passed away and I was adopted by Mama and Pop Palmer, I'd added my mom's maiden name as a second middle name. When Mama was really upset with me, she pulled out all four names. "Mama, I have not been holding out on you. It's just new, but it's also more than just casually dating. I would call that a boyfriend, wouldn't you?" I knew as soon as the words left my mouth, I was digging my own grave today.

"Did you just sass me?"

"No! Yes? I didn't mean to?" I took one of my calming breaths and tried to save the conversation. "I'm sorry. I didn't mean to sound like I was sassing, because, believe me, I know better than to sass the sassiest woman I know—"

"Well, now you're just trying to sweet talk me..."

"Is it working?"

"I'll think about it. May depend on what's going on with this boyfriend situation."

"Mama. It's not a situation. I'm seeing someone and it's going really well."

"Uh-huh. How long have you been seeing each other?" I could hear the air quotes around the word *seeing* by the way Mama said the word.

"We've been talking to each other for a couple of weeks, but we went on an official date Thursday night and spent much of the weekend, when neither of us was working, together. It's been wonderful."

"Uh-huh." *Shit!* I knew that if I couldn't change that 'uh-huh' then this was not going to go well. Not at all.

"I promise you'll like him. He's funny, smart, successful, treats me with respect—" Had to give myself a huge thumbs up for throwing Aretha's word in there. "—and he looks like Thor."

"Uh-huh. He wears tights and a cape? What kind of LA-metro boyfriend did you find?"

I groaned. Mama was now just misunderstanding on purpose. "No tights and cape, just tall, blond, and lots of muscles." *Fuck!*

"*Uh-huh.* And tell me, just how do you know about his muscles, young lady?"

That's it. You can do this, Summer. Tell Mama you're an adult, and what you do with a man is none of her business. "He looks amazing in a suit?" *Close enough.*

"I see. Have you introduced him to your brother?"

Well, "I see" was moving in the right direction from "uh-huh," at least. "Not yet. Derek's been out of town for a few weeks. Remember? He had that trip to meet with some screenplay writer in Seattle."

"I see."

Before Mama could say anything else and I could implicate myself any more, I said, "Mama. I really like this one. I know you think it's sudden, but he's special. I can tell. I don't know if he's the one, but he is the makes-me-feel-things-I've-never-felt-before one. I promise to introduce him and Derek at the first opportunity. Think you could be happy for me?"

Long pause. Long, long pause. Finally, Mama spoke, "All we ever want for you is to find happiness, baby. If this man makes you happy, I'll be happy for you, but I also want to make sure you're safe. You promise that you'll contact Derek as soon as he's in town?"

"You do know I can take care of myself, right?"

"Oh, I know. I didn't raise no damsel in distress Disney princess. Honey, I just want to make sure you know you have your family to back you up. You promise?"

"I promise. And, Mama?"

"Yes, baby?"

"I love you."

"I love you too, baby. Now tell me about this man you're, ehem, dating."

So I did. I told Mama everything from the moment I met Jason. Well, almost everything. Of course, it was the PG version. I described the date of a lifetime, minus the extracurricular activities. I told her about us taking walks on the beach, strolling through the local farmer's market, and my introducing him to some of the best pastries in Los Angeles. When I finished, I sat like a defendant waiting to hear judgment.

"I can tell by your voice that he really is making you happy. You know, that's all we want for you, sweetie. Your pop approves on a contingency basis."

"Pop? *Pop?* He's been listening? For how long?" *Oh god!* What had I said? Had I said anything Pop shouldn't have heard? I didn't think so.

"He's been listening since you started telling me about this boyfriend of yours." Once again, I heard the air quotes this time around the word "boyfriend." Mama continued, "He should be aware you're dating someone. Don't you think?"

Hell no. I was NOT falling for that trick question. "Of course. I have nothing to hide. Um, hey, Pop."

"Hey, angel. When do we meet this man?"

"I don't know. Could we give this at least a few weeks before I have to decide on a meet and greet with you guys?"

"Sure. If he hurts you, I'll make him eat his balls. That's all."

I laughed. "Everyone around me is so mercenary. Jessica already promised to remove a certain appendage if he hurts me. Kevin has offered to tie him up for me—"

"How is Kevin?" That came from Mama chiming back in.

"Kevin's wonderful. The café is amazing. Life is good."

"That's what I like to hear. Love you, angel."

I could hear Mama grumbling at Pop in the background, "Really? That's all you've got?"

His response was a cool and collected, "Yep," which drove Mama bonkers. She got back on the line, but all the while mumbling to herself. "That man... I tell you... some days, I wonder...you know you have him wrapped around that little finger, missy."

"Oh hey! What did I do?"

Another long pause. It was obvious from the sounds that Mama had put the phone down. Silence. I waited, knowing how this was going to go from experience. Mama came back on the line and was in a somewhat better mood. "I'm back, baby. Just needed to grab an iced tea." That was what Mama did any time she did something or said something that sat wrong with her or might require an apology. She took a moment to herself and grabbed an iced tea. Everyone in the family knew, though, that what she meant was she was sorry or she was ready to talk. It was just her way of saying it.

"I know, Mama. Are we good?"

"Yes. We're good. You make sure you talk to me about this boy from now on."

"Yes, ma'am."

"And don't forget what I taught you about using protection."

I stared at my phone utterly flabbergasted. I did not just hear that. "Mama, I don't think I heard you right, could you repeat that last part?"

"I said," she sounded frustrated again, *shit*, "you need to remember to use the brain that God gave you and protect yourself."

"Mama! I. We. I—"

"Spit it out, girl. Actually, since I think you're about to lie, maybe don't. I'm not stupid, Summer Evangeline." Still unable to believe my ears, somehow I still processed that Mama only used two names, so not too bad. "With that earlier tone in your voice, you need to be using some protection because as much as I want grandbabies, I want them to come in the appropriate order if possible. And, if you don't need protection and sound like that, we're going to have another talk about the birds and the bees. Now then, sweetie, I have to run, but promise me, I raised you smart."

"Yes, ma'am. Of course. Very smart over here."

"Good."

"I love you both."

"We love you, too. Talk soon."

After hanging up, I stumbled from my bedroom, a bit dazed. I found Jessica in the kitchen and slumped against a cupboard next to her. I was about to say something when I noticed Jessica's shoulders shaking... suspiciously. *No way.* "You heard!"

She couldn't contain her humor anymore and started laughing outright. "Of course I heard. Why are you surprised every... single... time. It's a small apartment. And, I just love Sunday phone calls. It's like Sunday morning cartoons, only live action style and more love and drama than humor. Today's was freaking comedy gold, though, listening to you stumbling around your words when it came to your new man."

I wavered between embarrassment and just saying *fuck it* and moving on, and the latter suited me a lot more. "Well, at least I *am* being smart and using lots and lots of condoms."

Jessica gasped in outrage, clearly having caught on to the zinger about her lack of a recent sex life. She didn't take it well. Since my roomie was all about revenge, I prepped to run or evade. I watched as Jessica took a handful of the flour sitting on the counter and pulled her hand back, ready to launch it at my head. Nice try, but I stopped her in her tracks saying, "You know you don't want to actually launch that. Think about how messy your kitchen will be."

"Dammit!" Her hand went back down and the flour was placed safely in the bowl. Instead, in her best Wizard of Oz witch impersonation, she said, "I'll get you for this, my pretty."

"No doubt you will."

"I'll have you know I met a really nice woman Saturday night."

"Did you get her number? Are you seeing her again? Did you do anything fun that night?"

"We did exchange numbers, so here's to hoping."

"What're you making?"

"While you were busy on the phone, I was trying to do a little writing, but I was stuck at a part I wrote and rewrote, like, thirty-one times. I couldn't get it to work. That had me thinking about that time we were at work together before you opened the café and I had that family of, like, twenty individuals who ordered almost every item on the menu, but then left without much of a tip. And the tip had me thinking about this advice we once got from the lady that lives next door regarding her favorite, and now our favorite, Thai restaurant around the corner. Anyway, one thought led to another and I decided to make a chicken piccata for dinner. That work for you?"

Jessica peered over her shoulder at me and so I nodded. "That sounds divine. You know I'll eat pretty much anything you put in front of me. I would offer to help, but I think I'll just go clean something instead."

"Good call, roomie. And by the way, I'm happy for you. When do I get to meet him?"

I grabbed a dishrag and spray and began wiping things down in the family room, calling back, "I was thinking maybe we could have him over for dinner sometime this week. Maybe Kevin could come too."

"Sure. Name the night and hopefully I'm free to cook, and if not, we can always order something from Casa de Salsa."

"Okay. I'll find out his schedule. Due to mine and Kevin's, we are probably looking at Thursday or Friday."

"I'm early on both those nights, I'll cook."

"Awesome. I'm excited for you all to meet."

"Can't wait. Oh. And, Summer?"

"Yes?"

"Don't forget to use what your mama gave you and stay safe out there."

Grrrr. I was never going to live this down. "You know, I think I've changed my mind about helping out with dinner."

Jessica's contorted-in-horror face was sweet revenge. "Don't you dare. This is now officially a no-fly zone for you!"

"Who needs to fly when you're flying high on orgasms?" I smirked.

"I hate you right now."

"I got nothing but love right now."

With Jessica's heartfelt two-handed flipping of the bird, we both got back to the work we were doing.

21

DISTANCE AND MILKSHAKES

Jason

I clenched my fist in frustration as the flight attendant finished informing us all about the safety measures. I could still hear the disappointment in Summer's voice when I'd called while on the way to the airport and canceled our dinner plans. It was obvious that it meant a lot to her and that she'd been looking forward to it. So had I, but I hadn't had a choice about canceling.

One of my clients, Matthew Prince, was working on a movie being filmed outside of Austin, Texas and he was about to walk out on the whole production. I couldn't quite understand over the phone, as Matthew ranted, what "everything is all fucked up" really included. I even recognized that my client was being ridiculously overdramatic, but I prided myself on the details and it sounded like the details were being mismanaged. So, here I was, utterly frustrated at missing the opportunity to meet Summer's friends and, more importantly, to see Summer again. Instead of holding and kissing a brilliant and funny redhead tonight, I was sitting on a plane heading to Austin, where a cold hotel room awaited me. *Maybe it's for the best. Meeting friends can be a big step. You're not ready for that.* Yeah, that voice was still in lockdown, but his messages somehow snuck out at all sorts of inopportune times.

I didn't even know for sure how long it would take to fix the situation. It better be fucking fast, because I didn't intend to miss the whole weekend with my girl. My girl. I liked the sound of that, but I liked being with her even more, and that meant tying this up as soon as possible. I passed my hand through my hair in agitation and firmed my jaw with conviction. Get to the set outside of Austin, figure out what will calm my client, fix it, head out, get the girl. No problem. *Sure. Keep telling yourself that. No problems, indeed.*

Summer

"Was that Jason again?" Jessica asked while sitting on Elvis with her laptop propped in front of her.

"Yep." I sat cross-legged on a mat on the floor. I'd been trying to meditate my way out of my bad mood, but as soon as my phone dinged, any success I'd been having flew out the window. Instead, I found my frustration multiplying. Not exactly at Jason, but more at the circumstances or even maybe at Matthew Prince, the ass. I flopped back on my mat. "I think I need boxing, not meditation."

"I hear that. There are days I could totally use an aggressive outlet instead of finding my inner peace. You know, I think there's a studio around the corner from the pharmacy down the—"

"I know. I already looked into it yesterday, when I felt like punching something. They're too expensive for me to justify it right now. Know of any fight clubs?"

"If I did, I wouldn't be able to tell you about them, because the first rule of fight club..." Jessica smirked.

"Ha. Ha. Okay, fine. I'll just go into a bar and start a good ole bar brawl." I sat up, waving my fists in front of me, probably looking as pathetic as I felt.

"I don't think spending a night in jail will make spending a night away from Jason any better, though you might get lucky in jail, so who knows, maybe you do want to do that."

I reached for maturity and couldn't quite find it, so I stuck out my tongue at her.

"My mom always said if you stick your tongue out, you'll catch flies… or something like that. Of course, my mom isn't talking to me again since we can't see eye to eye about my life choices, so what does she know? Stick it out far and proud."

I studied her and saw the pain behind the humor. "She still won't talk to you?"

"Nope. She refuses to speak to me until I stop playing games and get serious about my future. Until I show the proper respect to my heritage." As with many immigrant stories, it was hard for Jessica's mom to separate the sacrifices they had made from the life choices of their children. In her third year at Stanford, Jessica dropped everything, took some money, and moved to LA. There was more to the story, but that was the gist of it.

I respected the hell out of her for having the guts and conviction to leave everything behind and pursue her dreams. Unfortunately, as happy as her career choices made her, the gulf between her and her parents had been hurting her ever since. "I'm sorry, Jess." I adjusted to sit on the floor near the couch and said, "Can I hug you?"

She thought about it, but then said, "Yes."

That gave me the go-ahead, so I wrapped my arms around Jessica's middle and felt as her ridged muscles relaxed after a few minutes. Touch was another thing that wasn't prevalent in Jessica's family. It had taken some time, but she'd slowly gotten used to my touchy ways. "I'm here if you need to talk."

"Thank you. I know. There isn't really anything to talk about. I love them. They love me. We don't agree on what I'm doing with my life. I need them to accept my choices. It is what it is."

"Yeah… but sometimes 'it is what it is' really sucks ass." That made Jessica snort.

"Listen. Writing is not happening right now and I could use a break. How about you and your failed attempts at meditation?"

"I think my mat even started to laugh at me."

"I say, in honor of all the sucks ass going on around these parts, we need to go out and get some giant milkshakes."

"Count me in."

Jessica flipped her laptop closed and we made our way to the door, grabbing our purses along the way. Jessica paused and put her hands on my shoulders. "You know he would be here if he could. From all you've told me, it really does sound like he has a situation on his hands."

"I know and I appreciate that you're trying to make me feel better, but..." I paused to think about what I was feeling. "I ninety-nine point nine nine nine percent believe him, but this is all so new, and we were barely getting to know each other, and there is a part of me that feels like he is holding part of himself back, and I admit, there is a small, miniscule, itsy-bitsy insecure part that wonders if he's being honest. What if he isn't as eager to see me again? What if it didn't mean as much to him? You know?"

"I know. It's hard to trust people. It's so easy to get hurt when we do. And I really, really, really hope I'm not wrong about this, but in my gut, I feel like this is legit and you know I wouldn't just say that. I mean, considering how often the man texts and calls you, if he wasn't wishing he was here, he sure is doing a great impression of a person who does. Either way, I'm here."

"And, you're the best."

"You know it."

"Now, didn't you say something about milkshakes..."

"No. I said something about *giant* milkshakes!"

"I can think of a lot of giant things I want and milkshakes is definitely near the top of my list."

"Summer!"

I winked at her. "What?"

"I guess after what you told me about the other night, you've shed any pretense toward prudishness?"

"I guess so." I shrugged.

"I like it. It suits you. So get your butt in gear. I need me some hot fudge, Oreo, and M&M's monstrosity."

"Oh. That does sound good. Make that two." My mood had definitely lifted by the time we were halfway through our respective monstrosities and laughing at some of the stories we hadn't had a chance to share about our weeks. I knew, though, that a small part of Jessica still mourned her family's silent treatment, and a small part of me still thought about Jason and wished he was back and hoped, hoped he wanted to be back. Damn this new relationship angst. I took another giant slurp of my milkshake and set myself straight for the hundredth time. It was only Friday night. Maybe he'd be back by tomorrow night.

22

OH, BROTHER

Jason

Upon landing Wednesday afternoon, I was thrilled to finally be back in LA. I had yet to lose a client, but would it count as losing one if I murdered him? Were there union rules against murdering one's clients? In my current mood, perhaps it was worth researching. What should have been a twenty-four-hour fix had stretched into a full contract negotiation clusterfuck.

Matthew Prince had seemed like a good idea at the time when he signed with Avalanche. The performer had been a low A-list actor, meaning he wouldn't have been able to carry a major franchise, but I saw his potential right away. If Avalanche, meaning me, could get Matthew Prince to reach leading-man, major-franchise level, it would set us up to nab a desirable A-list client like Vanessa. Prince's career had been on the precipice of exploding into obscurity or big budget and I had been just the person who could make sure it happened in the right direction.

That was then. Now that I'd helped make the actor a household name, Prince became a huge pain in my ass. I couldn't believe that this whole fucked-up situation all started because Prince didn't agree with the look the director wanted for his character. Apparently, Prince wanted to look "hotter" and "younger" even though he was playing a middle-aged executive dad. What the fuck did he think a middle-aged dad looked like? Things spiraled from there. Then the actor didn't care for his accommodations—too small—he complained about the catering—too bland—and about the amount of lines he was given in a particular scene among other things. Basically, he was completely unreasonable and threatened to leave mid-production, which would have cost everyone involved a lot of money.

I ended up needing to put a bunch of smaller deals on hold, work on the others I couldn't put on hold remotely from the set, all while trying to talk my client down *and* salvage the relationship with the studio and director on top of renegotiating compromises to fix the situation. Just that was enough to piss me the fuck off, but underlying all of this, I missed Summer something fierce. It made no sense and it didn't matter. It had been a long week and a half since I'd held her and even though we talked constantly, which included another couple sessions of sexting and one super-hot sexy FaceTime—sextime?—I needed the real thing. I needed Summer. There was nothing I could do, of course, because business had to come first—*Didn't it?*—but the ache I felt told me otherwise. Luckily, I wasn't controlled by such aches.

Still, today had been my lucky day, and it was about time. I woke up lamenting that it was going to take at least another twenty-four hours to work out a deal, but everyone involved came through early. Everyone had signed and was happy as of that morning. I'd considered calling Summer and letting her know, but hadn't wanted to get her hopes up, so instead, I'd headed to the airport and jumped on the first flight back to LA. I knew, based on our conversation of the night before that she was working at the café today until closing. It was only three o'clock and I figured I could surprise her and then complete some work from her café until she closed. Then we could grab some food-to-go and head over to my place and reacquaint ourselves. I was in dire need of a long and thorough refresher course on all of Summer's erogenous zones.

After being gone so long, though, I couldn't show up empty-handed, so I stopped at a florist a few storefronts down from The Frisky Bean and bought her a medium bouquet of cream-colored roses with a vase for the café, a small bouquet of purple tulips for her apartment, and an extra bright red rose for her hair. I'm an agent. Basic is not in my vocabulary.

I stroked the red rose, imagining how she might look, red hair splayed across my pillow, with the contrasting red rose behind her ear, and nothing else on. The image had me hustling and hard. Armed with my gift of apology, and aching to hold her, I walked swiftly down to the café. I was looking forward to her reaction to my surprise. Hmm. Maybe I could even convince her into a little quickie in her office or my car...

I halted at a dead stop. Apparently, I was the one who was in for a surprise. As I walked up to the glass door, I saw Summer embracing another man. And dammit, she was beaming. Just fucking glowing. Why was it that every time I showed up to her café, another attractive and successful man was flirting with her. I assumed the ebony, tall man was successful by the cut of his dark gray slacks and his slim-fit, light blue, button-down shirt. The attractive part was not an assumption either. In my career, I had to be able to assess everyone's potential. You didn't want to accidentally pass up a future heartthrob. It wouldn't make me much of an agent if I couldn't assess men and women alike. And the man currently all over Summer was People's-sexiest-man-alive attractive. In other circumstances, I would have signed him right away. Fuck. As the two broke apart from the hug, Summer even kissed him. Sure, it was on the cheek, but since I hadn't had a chance to feel those lips for far too long, I wasn't keen on another person feeling them. Those were my lips. I knew I wasn't behaving very rationally, but forget rational. I wanted my lips back.

I stepped inside the café, which caused Summer and the model jerk to jump apart. Good. When Summer's eyes landed on me, everything else stopped. All my jealousy melted away under the unadul-terated happiness I read on her face. She jumped up and down, screeched, and ran from around the counter. There was no thought or preparing for the ball of energy that was Summer. All I could do was move my arms to the side to avoid destroying the flowers or vase, as she plowed into me. And like the other times, I found myself slammed back into the door with Summer in my arms. As I wrapped my burdened arms carefully around her, I buried my nose in her hair and just allowed my body to process the feel of her pressed against me top to bottom. A person could get used to this kind of reception to come home to. I couldn't remember ever feeling so wanted.

Summer whispered to me in a voice heavy with feeling, "You're back."

I whispered back, "Yes. Happy?"

"Of course. Yes. I missed you!"

"Missed you too, baby girl. I hope it's okay I chose to surprise you at work?"

"Absolutely. I'm so excited that you're home. I mean, um, back." I could somehow tell that if I looked at her, I would see my favorite color was back on her cheeks and it soothed me. She was in my arms. That eased me in ways I didn't yet understand. Also, I couldn't deny, though part of me was trying, that something had tightened around my heart at her use of the term home. I was surprised at how right it sounded. How right it felt.

"Ehem." The model cleared his throat behind us. As far as I was concerned, the guy could wait, or even better, leave.

Summer had other intentions. She pulled back and her blush was definitely in full bloom. As much as I loved seeing her pinken, I found I didn't like someone else putting it there. She indicated the model with one hand and me with the other. "Jason, this is my brother, Derek. Derek, this is my boyfriend, Jason."

It took a few moments for all of her words to sink in. Summer's brother. Well, damn. I was a total ass. I released her and pushed the bouquet under my left elbow with the hand that still held the vase, then reached out to shake Derek Palmer's hand. "I've heard a lot about you. It's a pleasure."

Derek's gaze was assessing me. It was only for the briefest moment but I had the impression that Derek's shrewd eyes worked as quickly as my own. He reached his hand out and we shook. "I've heard about you from Mama more than Summer, but I did get an earful. This is a new relationship, if I heard right."

"New can be such a relative term." I tried to recall what Summer had said about her adopted brother. "If I remember correctly, you own an indie movie production company?"

"That's correct. I've got a small production company, but I'm working on growing it. I hear you're in the industry as well. An agent, I believe?" Derek raised an eyebrow even as he leaned back against the counter and crossed his arms. "You represent anyone I'd know?"

"Perhaps. I just got back from helping one of my clients, Matthew Prince. I also recently signed Vanessa Daring. I'm also working with an up-and-comer named Amber Justice. Heard of her?"

"I know of all three. Perhaps we'll have reason to work together some day."

"Perhaps. Give me a good script and a decent salary to show one of my clients, and I'll be happy to do so. It's always a good career move to work on a well-written indie movie."

Derek looked over my shoulder with amusement and it actually took me a moment to realize that I had tried so hard to impress Summer's brother that I forgot to impress Summer. I turned to find Summer with her hands on her hips and her head quirked to one side. I gave myself a thorough mental thrashing and walked back toward her, holding up all the flowers I'd bought in offering. Feeling utterly contrite, I said, "These are for you. They can't make up for my prolonged absence, but I hope they convey how much I missed you." Silently, I added, and hoped she could see in my expression, "and sorry for botching the return."

Summer came up to me and took the vase from my hands. She

stuck her nose amongst the cream roses and inhaled. "These are so beautiful, and they smell amazing."

"They're for your café." I leaned in and whispered directly into her ear, so Derek wouldn't hear, "I thought cum cream roses would fit right in." Summer's throaty laugh had that tightening effect on my chest again. It was a challenge to breathe. *Isn't that a sign you should get out?* I was still ignoring that small voice, because it was inconvenient for the rest of me to listen.

"They're perfect. Reminds me of the cream my cat likes to lick up." That was what she said out loud. Her eyes said, she was the cat, and she was remembering licking me up like I was cream the other night. If I turned around now, her brother would get quite the eyeful. My thoughts needed redirection. Summer walked past me and I watched her place the vase down near the register as I turned to follow. I used the other flowers to cover up my erection as I walked up to the counter across from her. That happened to put me side by side near her brother. With the counter hindering any visual of my lower region, I lifted the other bouquet and offered it to her. "These are for your apartment." Before she could snatch it away, though, I reached in and grabbed the one red rose from inside the bouquet. "And this one is for your hair."

"They are all so beautiful! Thank you."

"May I?" I wondered at the audacity and stupidity it took to want to put the rose in Summer's hair during my first meeting with any of her family members, but it was too late to back down. Summer leaned forward from behind the counter and offered up her right ear. I carefully pushed the de-thorned, shortened stem through her curls behind that ear until the petals caressed her cheek. My fingers itched to run up and down that same cheek to feel her heat and softness, but that would have been one step too many. Summer smiled at me in return with those intimate fuck-me eyes and damn, I was thankful for the counter.

Wanting to make a semi-decent impression at least, I partially turned toward her brother to diffuse the tension, and asked, "You live in this area?"

I felt Derek's disapproval but didn't get to the position I was in by squirming easily under pressure or scrutiny. I waited. Summer, clearly unaware of our standoff, replied for her brother. "Derek lives in Burbank, but he's always keeping his eyes open for a place to move closer to West Hollywood. He moved out here from Denver a couple of years before I did, and it's been so great to be in the same city again these last few years."

Derek finally spoke to add, "Yes, it has. I missed keeping an eye on you when we were living in separate cities."

Well. That was pretty obviously meant to warn me, and I understood him. If I had a sister like Summer, I might act the same way. Apparently, the only one who didn't understand was Summer. "As though I let you keep an eye on me. Hah! Want me to keep an eye on you?"

Derek responded gruffly, "Sure. What are siblings for?"

"Good point. I'll make sure to intimidate and harass any woman you bring around." Apparently, she was not as unaware of the underlying tension as I'd first thought.

"Summer, don't be like that. Mama mentioned that you two were just moving a bit quickly and we want to make sure you're safe."

"I'm safe." Now she sounded downright irritated. I hadn't heard that tone from her before. "I don't know why everyone insists on treating me like I can't take care of myself. Mama was the one who taught me how to kick a man in the balls—" I couldn't help my internal wince at that thought, "—and you taught me how to defend myself in every other way. I know how to take care of myself when necessary." She seemed to emphasize that last word.

It was probably wrong of me, but I felt a little smug and a lot turned on. I hadn't seen this warrior woman side of Summer before, but I liked it. She was quite formidable, as evidenced by her brother backing down.

"I concede your points." Well, he seemed to back down, until he turned back to me and continued, "But if you hurt her..."

"I won't hurt her." I said it with as much gravity and sincerity as I thought the moment deserved. Her brother needed to back off, but I also understood that he needed to know she was safe with me, and she was. *Keep lying to yourself that you can make her happy.* I could. I would.

23

GNOMES

Summer

I was fuming. I'd had all of seven seconds to be happy at my brother's return and that my lover had come back when my brother decided to throw down gauntlets that Jason seemed all too happy to pick up. Fucking men. Well, I was having none of it. "That's it. Both of you get out of my café until you unlearn some of your toxic traits. I have a café to run and I need to be cheerful. Do I *look* cheerful to you right now?" I looked them both in the eyes and felt like growling. Jason was back and I wanted to celebrate that fact. He even brought me flowers. Three different sets of flowers, and could I have a minute to enjoy it? No. I wanted to enjoy it, dammit!

I kept looking between them, and Jason broke first. Of course, Derek had the advantage on him because we'd been bickering since we were kids, even from before I was adopted into the family. "I'm sorry. You're right. This wasn't the reunion I had planned and I allowed my goals to get derailed." Jason looked like he was going to glare at my brother, but before he had a chance to turn his head, I narrowed my eyes at him, and he snapped his gaze right back to me. I smiled, on the inside for now, knowing he knew there were times I was not to be messed with. Good. I could pull off grumpy like anyone else. I was only mostly happiness and sunshine. Mostly. Then Jason continued, and my heart melted all over again for him. "My negotiations ended earlier than expected and I rushed on the first flight back to surprise you. I can't tell you how happy I am to be back."

"I was perplexed when I pulled the Tibetan goddess Lam Lha's card this morning and, of course, she is the goddess of travel. Last night when we talked it sounded like you weren't going to be able to come back for a couple more days perhaps, so I assumed it meant Derek. When you," I indicated my brother, "showed up, I thought that was that, I couldn't have guessed it would mean the both of you." I beamed at them both.

"Goddess card of travel?" Jason looked perplexed. I hadn't had a chance to share my Goddess Guidance Cards with him yet.

"I'll explain another time. I'm really happy you came early." I glanced back at Derek and saw him reviewing Jason all over again. "And what about you, dear brother?"

Derek turned back to me. From the side of my eye, I saw Jason still only had eyes for me. He could take charge of me in many ways, but I was not going to be a pushover and it's a good thing he learned that earlier than later. Derek said, "I'm sorry if I ruined this for you. Truly, sis. You know I love you and just want you to be happy. I hadn't had a chance to ask, but since I just returned from my trip, I was hoping you'd have dinner with me after you close the café." I was about to protest when he continued, "But, I see that there is another reunion happening today too." Then a gleam entered his eyes, and I grew wary. "Maybe we could all go out to dinner together. It would give me a chance to get to know your man."

I saw the trap and I didn't see any way out of it. Siblings! I was about to ask Jason if he was available and also agreeable to doing that, when he answered, "It sounds like a great idea. I'll meet you back here at closing time?" I adored this man. He read the situation and did what he knew I wanted him to do.

Derek nodded his head in acknowledgment. "Sounds like a plan. I'll see you then. Do you think Kevin will be available?"

"I'm sorry, but no. I know you must miss him too, but Kev has to keep such early hours that a dinner after closing isn't going to work for him today. Knowing him, he'll already be heading off to sleep."

"I forgot about his hours. You're right. I'll contact him and see about getting together with him another time. See you both tonight." My brother walked around the counter and hugged me close. He whispered in my ear, "I'll see you later, squirt. I really am sorry."

"I know. Love you."

"Love you, too."

After walking my brother out, we were finally alone, and I felt almost shy. Kinda awkward. I should have known better. Jason's arms wound around my waist from behind and he nuzzled my ear. "I'm really damn sorry, too." Goosebumps instantly popped out along my neck and down my arms as my body came alive for him. Yes. This was the reunion I wanted.

I spun in his arms and molded my lips to his. Hunger took hold of me from my mouth crashing into his, to my nipples rubbing against his chest, and down into the wet heat of me. We were standing in plain view at the glass front, unlocked door, being horribly unprofessional, but I needed this kiss. Right now. We'd totally lucked out on the privacy side of things this whole time, even though my bottom line would have loved some customers. Knowing that luck couldn't possibly hold, I pulled back and leaned my forehead to his. We were both breathing heavily, and I could feel Jason's erection through his slacks and my loose skirt. "We need to stop. I don't want to stop. But. We need to."

"Are you sure we can't take a few minutes in the back somewhere? I want to take my time, but I know I won't be able to this first time. I missed you too much."

I vibrated with indecision. Every cell in my body wanted to take him up on his offer while my rational mind told me I needed to do the right thing for the café. Sure, our café was doing well, but it needed to grow over the next few years to stay viable in the long run, not to mention the project I was considering, and a reliable reputation was a part of that. At least, it was an important part of it until Jason kissed all the way up my neck and bit my earlobe, hard, and I became a total goner. I flicked the lock on the door, grabbed his hand, and ran him through the café and kitchen to my office saying, "Fast. We have to be fast."

Jason was so clearly on board with fast, because as soon as we entered, he picked me up and placed me on the edge of my desk. Luckily, this was one place I liked to keep completely neat and tidy. He pushed up my skirt with one hand even as his other hand was undoing his pants. I was busy holding on to him and kissing his neck. I heard a snap and realized that Jason had ripped my panties right off of me. That. Was. So. Hot. Just like in the books I liked to read. I hadn't known it was actually a thing and especially not a thing I would get to experience. On the heels of thinking it was hot, I tried to remember if I liked that pair, but all thoughts fled again, when I caught sight of his beautiful cock popping out from behind his open pants. *I need that inside me, right fucking now.*

"I agree. Inside now sounds good to me too." Apparently, I'd said the last part out loud. My personal conversations could not be trusted while I was aroused around him. Jason paused long enough to pull out his wallet from which he drew out a condom. He swiftly rolled it on, and then he was right back to me. One hand stroking my folds, feeling for himself how wet I was. And yeah, I was ready-to-go wet. I wished we had more time to explore, but that would have to come later.

He wasn't done positioning me, though. He pushed my shoulders back until I was propped up on my elbows and then pushed my knees up until my feet were up on the edge of the desk opening me completely to him. I felt, since I could no longer see, the head of his cock at my entrance, and tried to push down with my hips to take him in. He grabbed onto my hips and stopped me from moving so he could push only the tip in and out, over and over again. He played his thumb across my clit and I thought I might lose my mind. "Jason! Please. I need you inside me even more than I need to come." I looked up into his face and saw something raw and needy pass over his features, but it was fleeting and I was no longer thinking about anything because he had gone balls deep with one firm thrust and it felt like heaven. The slight discomfort adding to the sensations. "Yes!"

I dropped back to the desk, my back arched over something mildly uncomfortable, but I couldn't bring myself to care. The only thing I truly felt right then were Jason's relentless thrusts. Rough. Hard. His thumb rubbing harder and harder at my clit exactly how I wanted. I was pushed swiftly to ecstasy until my reality fractured and I shook, gutturally yelling his name.

He looked like a man possessed as he took his own pleasure, his cock hitting just the right place to cause me an aftershock orgasm. When he came, he growled my name, too. I felt a tug on my arms and then I was sitting again on the edge of the desk, with him still buried inside of me, as he claimed my mouth once more. The kiss eventually lost its heat and turned more sensual, and then languid and intimate, and finally we just snuggled together. Jason even reached up and righted the rose that he had skewered behind my ear. "I needed that. You. So damn bad, baby girl."

"Ditto." That was when a few different realities hit me all at once. First, I was horrified to realize I was going to have to sit through dinner, with my brother, wearing no underwear. Second, I realized my back was mildly sore and wondered what I could have possibly been laying on. Jason pulled out of me and was disposing of the condom along with tidying himself when I turned to look behind me on the desk to see what I could find. Then I laughed. A full, deep, belly laugh, with snorts, of course.

"Should I be offended?"

"No. But we weren't the only ones getting busy." I pointed at the desk and sitting there, well, laying there, where my back had been, were my desk gnomes. Jessica had given them to me a couple of months before saying, "If you ever have a customer troll, just come back to your office and squeeze the shit out of these trolls. They'll make you feel better." I wasn't sure if I would ever be able to look at my trolls the same way again. They must have toppled over when I was toppled over and my boy gnome had his face firmly smooshed between my girl gnomes legs. "Lucky girl."

Clearly Jason understood too because he laughed along with me. Then, he wrapped an arm around my middle, pushing my back against his front, and whispered into my ear, "Don't be jealous, sweetheart, I plan to make you equally lucky later tonight."

His warm breath brushing against my skin, along with his words melted my insides like butter on toast. That would explain why my next words were, "I can't believe we just had an orgy with my gnomes."

That was the moment he must have realized that I'd actually been laying on them, because I felt the back of my shirt lifting. "Damn. Why didn't you say anything? I didn't mean to hurt you. You should tell me to stop next time." Jason actually sounded angry at me. The men in my life needed to stop treating me like I was a wilting flower. Well. All the men but Kevin. At least he knew I was made of sterner stuff.

"If I'd been able to say anything except "yes," "harder," or "Jason" I would deserve a freaking medal. I was quite lost in the moment and guess what? I'm okay. Somehow I'll survive the gnome sexcapades that were going on under my back." He did *not* seem mollified. "Jason, really. I'm okay. That hickey you left on my thigh last time was more painful than this."

Now he gave me an arrogant smirk. "But that had pleasure mixed with any pain. This was unintentional. Please tell me the next time anything hurts."

"I'll try. How about that? It's not my fault if my mental faculties are completely compromised by you."

"Perhaps the next time we use a desk, I should be the one laying down and you can ride me."

"Mmm. Can I bring along my cowgirl hat and boots? Dress-up sounds like fun!"

"Maybe you should close your café early and come home with me now," he said as his hand started sliding down to cup my sex through my skirt.

I slapped at his hand. "Nope. No. No can do. I'm a working girl." I continued in my best impersonation of a New York accent, "I gotta earn a livin' selling smutty co-ffee and pastries. You need to come back later. Now, get outta here!" He conceded and released me so we could reassemble our clothes. He ran his fingers through my hair and repositioned the rose back over my ear. We both tried, but also both still looked rather ruffled as we headed back to the front of the café. "Jason?"

"Yes, sweetheart?"

"I'm really glad you're home. Thank you for my flowers."

"You're very welcome." He pulled me in for another brief, blazing kiss and then released me breathless. I stumbled my way to the door and only then took note of who was on the other side. Embarrassed to my core, I nonetheless turned the lock and opened the door. "Um. Sorry to keep you waiting, ladies."

In walked Camila and Lisa with giant, knowing smiles on their faces. Camila spoke first, "Oh. No trouble. None at all. Nice rose, Summer," she teased. "Hello, again," she directed at Jason.

"Hi, ladies." Jason smoothly walked around them toward the door. "Nice to see you again. I'll see you later, Summer."

"Yep. Later." That was about all I could get from my brain to my mouth in my mortified state. As soon as the door closed, Lisa spoke up.

"Oh. My. God. Tell me you just did what I think you just did, because if you didn't then you're a fool, and I never took you for a fool. Please don't be a fool."

I saw nothing but admiration and inquiry in their gazes. No condemnation. I loved my regulars so much. It put me at ease enough to respond, "I'm definitely no fool." The ladies giggled along with me and besides some gentle teasing and coaxing for some dirty details, they moved on to settling in for an hour of afternoon CRT, as they called it, coffee recovery time.

Even with the trepidation of how our dinner might play out later, I had a smile plastered to my face the rest of the day. I attached my phone to the café sound system and played "Walking on Sunshine" by Katrina and the Waves amongst a bunch of other cheery tunes. As long as I didn't think about the dinner, I could stay in my happy place, so that was what I did.

24

I'LL HAVE WHAT SHE'S HAVING

Summer

I should have listened to my trepidation. It obviously came from a superior part of my anatomy, namely my brain, while my happy-go-lucky, Little Miss Sunshine personality came from the enthusiastic unplugger of logic. This was made clear because dinner so far was, well, the emotional equivalent of clashing weather fronts. Anger earthquakes and lust hurricanes were buffeting through me with equal intensity and if I couldn't find some equilibrium, everybody would get to view a Summer tornado pop up in my favorite Thai restaurant. Some might say I was being overly dramatic. Of course, some are also sitting there eating popcorn waiting for the drama to happen so...

We'd settled on eating at this restaurant because it was just a few blocks over from the café. The walk over seemed benign enough, and I was lulled into a false sense of ease. When we sat down in our booth, ugh, my brother on one side of the table and Jason next to me on the other side, all bets were apparently off. The casual tone of the walk was their way of sizing each other up in preparation for the main event of rather impressive, while utterly annoying, verbal sparring.

Turned out, Derek hadn't actually agreed with anything I'd said earlier, despite saying he would back down. Instead, throughout our meal, he'd thrown sly verbal attacks, as if they were darts, at my man. For his part, Jason did a masterful job of deflecting them. For my part, I found his cool and collected demeanor in the face of the attacks kinda hot. Like Magneto turning away bullets. Yeah. Magneto was hot too.

As frustrated as I was with Derek, though, he wasn't the real problem. Nope. The real problem was that I couldn't think clearly enough to do anything about anything because Jason decided to secretly pull out my torn underwear from earlier, which he'd clearly stolen, and lay it between us on the booth seat. Every time I looked down, despite supposedly focusing on Derek, I found Jason's finger stroking the material as though he were stroking me. And, oh god, I wanted it to be me. Fucking craved it. Our quickie had been an appetizer, much like my spring rolls, and now I wanted the full meal, dammit, and I wasn't talking about my chicken pad Thai.

And. even worse, I had no underwear on, only my thin, flimsy excuse for a skirt. He needed to stop for my sanity's sake, but he didn't. When I tried to stop him by reaching over to cover his hand, he would start stroking my hand instead. He rubbed his finger along my palm, as if along my breast, only to pinch the end of my finger. So fucking hot. Lesson learned, I kept my hands to myself for the rest of the meal, but, really, how much visual stimuli was a girl supposed to handle? And for his part, Jason was an amazing multitasker, because he kept up his verbal Olympic games with Derek, ate his shaking beef, and continued tormenting me with his sensual underwear foreplay. All while appearing as though he was expending no effort at all.

I tried to distract myself multiple times so I wouldn't strangle Derek or fuck Jason and be forever evicted. I couldn't let that happen. I loved this place because it had great food, but also because of the ambiance. The stunning décor in bold colors of red, black, and white, with lovely bamboo accents. In the center of the room stood a black pebble fountain half-wall. The sound coming off the water running over the pebbles was used to create a soothing, somewhat meditative space. Perhaps it would work if I walked over to it and splashed the cold water on my face first. But, I would never know, because it reminded me of being wet with Jason in his shower, and yeah, it was time to stop looking at the fountain too.

The seat began to vibrate in some new rhythm and my brain tried once again to send "don't look" messages like flashing neon signs. I shouldn't look. Like, I really, really should not look. It was a bad idea. The fountain was probably a safer look, but the unplugger of logic was still in control. Maybe, I was a glutton for punishment, because, of course, I looked... and damn the man and his creativity. He was rubbing his thumb back and forth in a fast clit pleasing, orgasm inducing type of way, and I was melting right into the seat. I was going to end up coming like Meg Ryan in *When Harry Met Sally* and the little old lady sitting next to us would be asking for one of whatever I was having. I snuck a peek at the little old lady, but so far, it didn't appear she was noticing my near-orgasmic situation. Good.

I looked back up in time to hear my brother grill Jason about his family background and that was it. I'd had enough! This had to stop, and I was the one who was going to stop it. I opened my mouth to speak, and nothing came out. Nothing at all. That may have had something to do with the fact that Jason gripped the inside of my thigh with his strong, warm hand. So damn close to where I wanted it. To where I was beginning to need it. Just a little bit higher and all my tension could be released because, really, after everything, it wouldn't take much. What the hell was I even thinking? I didn't want his hand there. My *brother* was sitting right across from us. *I'm mad at my brother right now! Stick with mad. Mad is safer. Forget my cunt and just be blunt. Did I really just use the word cunt to argue with myself in rhyme? Just go with it and stop talking to yourself. Oh yeah. Right.*

I cleared my throat in an attempt to find my voice, and this time, I was going to fight fire with fire with *both* of them. *You can do it. You bet your ass I can.* I casually moved my hand to rest on Jason's cock under the tablecloth while at the same time, waving my other hand in the air to indicate my need for a check, all while saying to my brother, "Derek, you've had enough time to grill my boyfriend and I've been patient, but I'm done. I hope you got it out of your system so the next time we do a meal together, it can be all movies, sports, and favorite pastimes."

Though I'd used my most stern sounding voice, Derek just smiled back at me. "Honestly, sis, I was surprised you let me go on this long. Your boy there can hold his own, though. I can respect that."

Jason nodded but didn't say a word in response. That might have been because I was now stroking him up and down through his slacks and he was hard as granite beneath my fingers.

I decided to speak for him. "With you and Pop around as my examples, did you really think I would fall for someone who couldn't match my family?"

"Touché, little sis. Touché. Since I was being a bit of a dick, this meal's on me. Why don't you two go on ahead? I'm actually parked near here, and I'll catch up with you sometime this weekend."

"Sounds good." I really was lucky. "I love you, you jackass." I released Jason's cock and heard the groan hidden behind his sudden coughing fit.

"Love you, too, squirt. Be good to my sister, Jason, and we're cool."

Jason reached over the table and offered his not-underwear-busy hand for a shake. "I only want to make her happy and thank you for dinner. It was very... invigorating."

They shook hands and then Jason scooted out of the booth, offering me his hand to help me out. I couldn't help but notice that he held my light sweater in his other hand in front of his crotch and that my underwear was nowhere in sight. I leaned down and gave Derek a kiss on the cheek. "Thanks for dinner. I'll see you this weekend."

The check arrived just as we walked out.

25

ELVIS AND MIDNIGHT

Jason

I couldn't believe that Summer had ultimately bested me at dinner. Even as I verbally fenced with Derek, I could tell that she'd been strung tight. Real tight. Thighs clenched together and ready to jump me in the middle of a restaurant tight. With one move, she'd disarmed me completely. I'd already been sporting a semi-boner as I visualized doing to her body everything I'd done to her underwear, but when her hand gripped my cock and started rubbing, I actually had concerns that I might shoot off right there in my pants, across from her brother, and wouldn't that have made a great impression? "I'm your sister's new boyfriend, and now you both know what I look like when I come. Blame her and her dirty, dirty but amazing hand." Nope. Definitely *not* a very positive impression.

I followed her out of the restaurant, grabbing her hand as we fell into step together. It already felt so natural to lace our fingers together and I loved the feel of her hand completely entangled in mine. She was being a lot quieter than usual, which left me wondering about what she might be thinking. Since I didn't plan to wonder for long, I commented and inquired, "Well, that wasn't completely painful.

What do you think? Good first impression? Do I have an in with your brother?"

Summer tapped the index finger of her free hand on her chin, as if she needed to ponder my questions quite heavily. "Hmm..."

"Hmm?"

"Hmm..." She suddenly stopped walking, threw her body flush against mine, wrapping her free arm around my neck, and whispered in my ear, "Somehow you managed to get in with my brother, food into you, and lust into me all at the same time. That takes some serious skill, Mr. Winter. Do you think you could take some time to get your cock inside me instead?"

My hand tightened a fraction on hers. I wanted exactly what she wanted, considering the giant physical and mental hard-ons I was sporting. "I could pick you up right here, lift your skirt, wrap your gorgeous legs around my hips, and take you within seconds on this sidewalk. Public indecency be damned." I felt the quake that ran down her spine at my words. She was so wonderfully responsive. Public indecency charges or getting caught by her brother were most definitely not ways to make a good impression, though. "I would give anything to be inside you right this second, but I still need to be able to get you to my home safely and all this is making that a near impossibility."

"That's because I don't think I can wait until we get to your home."

"The café then? My car? You don't actually intend for me to take you in the street, so—"

"No. Definitely not the street. Nor the car. And, not the café either."

"Then where? Because I'm dying to be inside you too."

"My place. It's not much to look at compared to where you live, and the walls are thin, buuttt it's also currently empty, and it's only about a ten-minute walk from the café."

"I hadn't realized you lived that close."

"I do. Now—" She ran her hand down the front of my shirt and undid the top button. "—are you coming over?"

I was most definitely coming over to her place, but first, I lifted her up and claimed her mouth with a kiss. When we broke apart, I left my mouth hovering less than a hairsbreadth from hers, and groaned, "Now... I'm ready to go. Take me to your home so we can properly celebrate my return." She gave me a swift kiss as I placed her back on her feet and then I followed her down the street.

Walking nearly fully erect was just plain physically uncomfortable. My dick was still on full alert when we stopped in front of a set of duplex-style apartments. We walked up to the first building past the parking spaces where an older model silver Prius sat.

The entry had a black wrought-iron locked door. Summer let my hand go to search through her purse for her keys and with a loud jingle, pulled out a monstrosity of keychains, fobs, and keys. Locating the appropriate key after a surprisingly short expedition into the mess, she unlocked the iron door and then the wooden door beyond.

As we stepped in, my first impression was eclectic. But, I wasn't here for a tour. Not of the house, anyway. I had one goal and its name was Summer. I needed it... her, and from every hot look she sent me on the way there, she needed it... me, too. I wasn't a total animal, though. I gave her enough time to lock the door and put her purse down before I pounced. Grabbing her arm, I swung her to me, and took up the kiss we'd interrupted earlier near the restaurant.

It was good. Really good. She responded instantly and I growled in satisfaction. Summer was busy undoing more of my buttons as our lips feasted and my hands found the hem of her formfitting, red, cotton shirt and yanked it up over her head, sealing our mouths together again as soon as it was off. I hadn't even taken the time to see what her bra looked like. I didn't care. It was just the thing keeping me from full contact with her breasts, so it had to go. I was able to undo it after a few tries and threw it to the ground. Both hands cupped her breasts and I sighed. It was as though her breasts were made for my hands and they'd felt empty until that moment.

Some part of my subconscious registered the sound of purring. Was Summer purring? Oh, I would love to make her purr, and bite, and scratch, and... it was coming from the floor, though. I broke off the kiss and looked down. There, rubbing against my leg, was a fairly grumpy-looking black cat that was purring. To my understanding, cats were supposed to purr when they were happy, but this cat looked like it was plotting world domination, someone's demise, and to knock all the things off all the counters and was quite pleased about it all. I was about to ask Summer about him, but then realized that my hands, with a mind of their own, had been playing and pinching and plumping Summer's breasts the whole time I was distracted by the evil cat.

Summer

I was quite sure I no longer had Jason's attention. How? I'm pretty sure when they are no longer looking at you, their attention is elsewhere and Jason was most definitely looking at Midnight, my jealous feline. I always knew he was an accomplished lover, but this took things to a whole new realm. Being distracted wasn't a problem for him. He was doing an exemplary job in the fondling breasts department, no thoughts required. It was fascinating to watch and feel what his strong hands and fingers could do to me all on their own. How they plucked at my nipples and squeezed my whole breast as if they were trying to remember the weight and firmness of them. All of this, while their owner was staring down at my cat as though Midnight was a mystery. When he glanced back at me, I was breathless and I saw the second he realized what he'd been doing during the kitty sabotage attempt.

"Summer's breasts, one. Feline distraction, zero." I wondered briefly about giving my girls an award, but nah. That would be weird. And, who needed an award when I had Jason's mouth take my nipple in his mouth and suck? Hard. *Oh, yeah.*

"Definitely, your breasts will win every time. If I could keep them attached to my hands or mouth all day long, I would, but I think it would be confusing for the other people around me. Don't you?"

A nearly inaudible, "Yeah," escaped my mouth as he bit down on my rigid peak. Fire raced along every nerve ending from my breast to my pussy. I lost track of time as he moved from breast to breast, worshipping and punishing them in turn. His hands finally dislodged from them, and I whimpered in protest until he turned me so my back was up against his front and he cupped them again.

"These beautiful tits are really demanding."

"Yes. They're very high maintenance. You should make sure to stay attentive— Oh!" I squeaked as he pinched even harder than before.

"I'll do my best. I'm struggling to decide if I want you totally naked right the fuck now or if even that will take too long and I just want to flip this skirt up again. Do you have a preference?" he asked, as he rubbed his nose along my neck and hair.

"Whatever gets your cock inside me the swiftest works... for... me."

"Done." Where before he seemed to be exploring me, now, he pushed me forward, tugging at my nipples while using his body on my back to apply forward pressure until we were behind Elvis. It was evident that he was in the mood for control, and I was happy to hand the reins over as long as he continued to make me feel this delicious. Desirable. Needy.

My hips hit the back of Elvis and before I could even wonder what he had planned, I found myself bent over with my face in the cushions. He had one hand resting on the curve of my back while the other lifted my skirt up over my ass and was busy running along my inner thigh. "So fucking beautiful. Your back, your ass, and I love the feel of your soft skin. My hand is practically shaking from a desire to feel your wet pussy. Almost there."

Yeah, he was. I was quivering with anticipation as well. When he cupped me finally, I was surprised I didn't come right then and there.

"Oh, honey, you are very, very wet."

I might have mumbled a "yes" into the couch, but who could be sure anymore what came out and what was in my head when I was this lost in desire?

"Tell me, honey, were you wet throughout dinner? Your poor pussy having no cloth to stop it from soaking your skirt?"

"Yes!" He slowly rubbed his fingers through my folds. Leisurely. Then it hit me, he was moving just like what he had been doing to my underwear at the restaurant. "You are cruel. Especially doing it in front of my brother, but now too?"

"Your brother was too distracted with me, I made sure of it, for him to notice what was happening between us, baby girl. Dinner was only excruciating for the two of us. Of course, you did have a bit of a flush on your cheeks throughout. It was lovely but could easily be attributed to how frustrated you were with us. And, regarding now? I was desperate until I got you in this position and now I find I want to torture you and taste you and only then, fuck you. Is that okay? I know how eager you were as well."

He was moving around behind me, spreading my legs wide. I forgot to answer as I wondered what he was up to now. Then I felt his face pressed into my wetness. His tongue licking me like he was eating ice cream and I whimpered. "Oh god. Please." I automatically pumped my hips against his face and was rewarded when his tongue went a little bit deeper.

It was brief, though, as he moved again, his hair brushing along the inside of both thighs. His arms wound from between my legs, over my ass, to grip my hips as he pulled me down until his face was buried in my sex. He licked deeply into my cunt and then nipped and licked at my clit and my whole body was a quivering mess.

"Yes! Just like that. Ow!" He'd slapped my ass with one of his hands. It wasn't actually that hard, considering our positions, but stung enough to catch my attention.

"How quickly you forgot. You know what I want to hear."

Of course I knew. But, in all honesty, I kinda liked the feeling of having him spank me. A new sensation I'd read about but never experienced. So, instead of giving us both what we wanted, my playful spirit took control of my tongue. "I think I need a refresher course. Was it, do me?"

Three more slaps in quick succession switching between my butt cheeks landed. I could barely catch my breath before the next hit and then he stopped, and heat rolled through my entire body, starting with my stinging butt cheeks. My insides had clenched and my wetness dripped from my pussy, and his tongue was there, lapping it up. "Somebody liked her spanking. Want to try again?"

Orgasm? Spanking? Orgasm? Play? Decisions. Decisions. "Oh! I remember now. Hammer me, Thor!" I giggled, but it didn't last long as another five slaps burned my backside. This time, he left his hand on my ass and massaged the heat into my skin. It felt divinely painful. Not hurt, just really, really sensitive. I wondered what it would feel like to get a real, hard spanking and hoped we would explore that someday.

He chuckled, lips pressed against my lower lips and said, "I have a funny girl. I'm more than happy to keep this going as long as you wish." He sucked my clit hard as he moved his hand off my ass and delved two fingers deep into my wetness. "Is that what you want?" His magic fingers fucked me and found that sensitive spot inside and I was right back to needy, only the need felt intensified. Necessary.

"Please, Jason. I want to come. I need you!"

"You've got me." His teeth rasped against my clit while his fingers delved faster and faster in and out of me. My quivers became quakes and it wasn't long before I splintered apart. I was very thankful that the couch was there holding me up because my legs were jelly, and there was no way I could hold myself up at that time.

Jason was moving behind me again. I heard the sound of a zipper and a wrapper and then he was there, his erection hard against my ass. One hand grabbed a fistful of my hair, pulling me up by it. My scalp came alive from the slight pain, and I arched my back to accommodate the position he was putting me in. His hand turned my head so he could claim my lips in a deep, dirty kiss that tasted of my arousal. When he broke the kiss, he pushed me back down over the couch. I was so completely his at that moment. He was dishing out pleasure and I wanted to experience his all-you-can-eat buffet. Every moment. Every sensation. I was all in. "Fuck me. Please."

The tip of his cock was right where I'd needed him all night. He began pressing in, firm, and thick, and perfect. He pressed in slowly at first, but with me being soaked from my orgasm and his mouth, the glide was super smooth. He must have realized that, too, since he slammed the rest of the way in with one thrust. It was heaven even as I flinched just a little when his hips hit the sensitive skin of my ass.

"You feel so good, sweetheart. All hot and wet, just for me. I love the feel of your hungry cunt clenching my dick." He lifted my left leg onto the back of Elvis, opening me up even more to him. When he began thrusting, I saw stars and felt, well, everything. Jason's rough possession, the rasp of Elvis's soft suede along my nipples, stomach, and thighs, the pull of Jason's hand gripping my hair again, and then the fingers Jason moved to play at my hypersensitive clit. The pleasure was so intense it bordered on pain, but I welcomed it because I was already so close and wanted to come again. Needed to come with him.

"Please! Jason, I need... I need to come! Please." And then I was. It was so intense I came on a gasp instead of a scream. One minute wound so tight, filled with kinetic energy, like a firework, and then I just exploded in all directions in a blaze of light and color. Jason was right there, thrusting hard a few more times and then buried as deep as he could, shuddering as his cock pulsed inside me. One day, I wanted to feel it all, no barriers between us. He slumped over my back, panting and nuzzling my ear. His hand still tangled in my locks as his other hand wrapped around my middle. I was engulfed in him and felt... utter contentment.

"Welcome home."

"Fuck yeah."

I chuckled. "A poet, you're not."

"If you were looking for a poet, you'd have found someone else. I'm just here to give it to you raw and unfiltered."

"I like you raw and unfiltered."

"Good. Because I don't plan on letting you go anytime soon."

"Neither do I. I guess we're both—" I couldn't help that my silly side always found its way to the surface. "—literally stuck together."

"Sorry to disappoint you in any way, but I do have to get rid of this condom," he apologized as he pulled his softening cock out of my body. I always hated that empty feeling I got right after the good stuff ended.

I leaned up to stand behind Elvis as I pointed Jason toward the bathroom. "Elvis finally got some action."

He called back from the bathroom, "What? Elvis? Like the singer? Please tell me that you're not one of those Elvis-is-alive people." He walked, naked from the waist down and stunningly gorgeous, toward me.

I indicated the couch with a flourish of my hand, "Jason, meet Elvis."

"And it all makes sense. Then, yes, I thoroughly enjoyed giving Elvis some action tonight." He rubbed the back of his knuckles down the line of my throat to my breast and over my nipple still hard from all the earlier action. I could have sworn I was completely sated, but my breath hitched anyway. Heat still shown in his eyes, too. *You wanted passion and you've definitely found that.* There was a shower in our very near future but it was obvious that we were not done for the night. In fact, if I was a betting woman, I would say, not by a long shot and I couldn't wait to experience every minute of it, with him.

At least, that was going to be true after I fed Midnight, who had left us alone while we got busy, but was impatiently winding between our legs looking for his reward, no doubt. Feline distraction, one.

26

GRUMPY? SUNSHINE?

Jason

Life couldn't get any better than this. Really. I was one lucky SOB. Things with Matthew Prince had smoothed out completely after my visit, working with Vanessa Daring was fantastic and seemed to be on course for a more permanent arrangement, my other clients were satisfied, and I even had a new potential client who was subtly watching to see what Vanessa would do. Then, there was Summer. I hadn't been looking for a relationship but now that I had her, I couldn't imagine not having her with me.

The last two months were full of romantic dinners, cozy WebShowz binge-watching, and the hottest sex of my life. She didn't give me a hard time when I had to cancel our plans last minute due to a surprise work conflict. She was understanding and supportive in a way my parents never were. In a way I never expected. Sending me with gift pastries to some of my meetings and showing up with dinner on nights I couldn't get away from the office.

Even her brother was a pleasure to get to know now that we understood each other. We both had a love for working in the entertainment industry and were actively looking for the right project to work on together.

I'd finally had a chance to meet her friends, Kevin and Jessica and gotten their nod of approval as well. Since I didn't really have many friends, I enjoyed the times we would spend with them. Jessica was a tough nut to crack; clearly deep waters ran through her. Kevin was so funny and personable I couldn't imagine anyone not liking that man. It was all so new but also wonderful getting to be a part of their circle. I did have one person I felt close to, or as close as I ever got to before now, so I made sure to introduce Summer to Janet. The two hit it off like they'd been friends for years.

If there was a part of me that was waiting for the other shoe to drop, for Summer to disappoint, disapprove, or leave me, well, it was a part that was losing strength every day. *Or maybe you've just gotten better at muzzling it.* In fact, it was now such a small part, that I could bury it under all the awesome in my life. *My very awesome life.*

I'd figured out that as long as I could compartmentalize, to keep my business and my personal life separate, then I could keep a firm grasp on them both. I didn't think it would go well for my career nor my relationship for Summer to be a part of my Hollywood dealings. She wasn't the Hollywood, money, and power type, which could make her feel uncomfortable. *Or so you think.* On top of that, she was way too distracting for me to include her in my work life. When I was working, I needed to stay focused. When I left work, I was all in with her. It was perfect that way. I could stay in control and make sure everything and everyone was happy that way. *How long do you really think you can keep this up?*

Yep. Life was great and it was about to get even better. There was a week and a half left to go and Vanessa would be under a long-term contract. We had an announcement planned in a few days regarding her new project with WebShowz called *Sharing Spaces.* At the beginning of next week, there was a premiere party planned for her latest movie release. I carefully crafted it that way, because having those two events in close proximity would only intensify the amount of media coverage she'd receive and it was immensely gratifying that all of my plans were finally going to pay off. This series of events would skyrocket Avalanche into a top-tier agency, and it was everything I'd ever wanted.

I couldn't wait to see Summer later to celebrate. She wasn't available until after closing, but we had plans for a late dinner with Jessica, Kevin, and Derek at The Seafood Cabana. I checked my watch, and I still had an hour before I was supposed to leave.

Janet walked into my office with her purse in hand. "I'm heading out. How about you?"

"Not yet. I'm meeting Summer and her friends for a late dinner, speaking of which, any chance you would change your mind and be able to come?"

Janet looked like she would like to say yes, but her answer was, "No. My mom's been watching Evan a lot lately since we've been working overtime organizing next week. I would have loved to come, but I really want to spend some time with my baby."

"I'm sorry if it has been too much wo—"

Janet rushed in, "Oh. No. It's not too much. I knew what I was getting into when I took the job. I enjoyed putting the announcement and the launch party together. I can put in whatever time is needed. I wasn't complaini—"

"Janet." It was my turn to interrupt because Janet was obviously misconstruing my comment, and I wanted to set her mind at ease. "I have no concerns over your ability to do the job. I know you weren't complaining and please never worry that I plan to replace you because there is no way you are going anywhere. I think you're the best and I wouldn't be here without you. I was concerned as your friend and your boss that you might not have enough time with Evan."

I grew up with distant parents and I wouldn't want that for her kid. It was one of the reasons I never planned to have any of my own. An image of Summer popped into my head, and I grimaced wondering if she wanted kids and what it meant for our relationship.

Nope. I was not marring my current state of perfection worrying about it. That was Future Me problems. We would figure it out, eventually. Today Me was not letting anything get in my way of enjoying tonight and celebrating over the course of the next week.

Summer

I looked down at the note again and rolled my eyes. The people that had been protesting the theme of our café had started leaving notes for us to find. Our café wasn't for everyone, and that was fine, because we had a steady flow of regulars and were growing in popularity. If people didn't like us, that was okay with me, they could always go to one of the chain coffee shops.

It was tiring. Why do these puritans have to stick their noses in spaces not meant for them? You don't want sexy food, go buy unsexy food then. End of story. Nope. They seemed to enjoy telling the rest of the world what kind of food they were allowed to eat.

I didn't play that way. I wasn't going to fold to that kind of intimidation and pressure. In fact, my little idea of expansion I wasn't so sure about before, yeah, these notes were giving me the fire I needed to make it work sooner rather than later. That and my relationship with Jason.

The way that man went after what he wanted was inspiring. Watching him work. Seeing him take big risks for big rewards. It was rubbing off on me and I was so thankful for it. *That's not the only thing I was thankful for. Last night I was thankful that we pulled out one of my toys and we found a way for both of us to enjoy—*

I jumped back, slamming into the back counter, and yelped as I felt a big hand land on my forearm. "Fuck!" My hand with the note shot up to my chest, and I found myself staring at a concerned Shane Paxton.

"Are you okay?" he asked softly.

"Oh god. I'm sorry." I wondered if he would be able to read the lascivious thoughts in the blush I was surely sporting. "I... I guess I was a little distracted, I didn't hear you come in."

"No. I'm sorry for startling you. You looked, well, doesn't matter how you looked," he smirked, "but I didn't mean for you to hurt yourself. Are you okay?" he asked again.

"Yeah. I'm okay. I'm so used to running into things, that barely registered. How are you?"

He studied me and I tried to maintain my happy-go-lucky cover under scrutiny. He finally answered, "I'm fine." I thought I'd succeeded in getting past the moment, but for only a heartbeat, because then he continued, "Anything you want to tell me about that note you're grasping to your chest?" He leaned casually against the counter and crossed his tattooed arms over his chest.

Oh! He thought I'd been thinking about this note. I guess that's as good a cove- up as any. "Um. No?" I hadn't meant to make it a question, but it was, because Shane seemed like he was not in the mood to let anything go. But, that didn't mean that I was in the mood to be easily pushed. If Shane and Jason hadn't taken an instant dislike to each other, they'd probably be friends instead of barely tolerating each other. They had a lot in common. Or, maybe their strong personalities was exactly why they didn't like each other.

Sounding much friendlier and less demanding, Shane asked, "Summer? As your friend, I'm curious. Why don't you tell me what's in the note?" *I guess he'd decided to change tactics.*

"Fine. It's not as exciting as you think. Just some people in the neighborhood leaving notes to tell us how pure they are and how we are all sinners blah, blah, blah. Like we didn't already know that?" We both laughed and that was all those notes deserved. I threw it in the little trash can I kept under the register and addressed Shane again. "Ready to place an order, *friend*?"

"We are friends."

"Ohhhh. I know. I still can't believe the way you behaved that night when you first met Jason."

He had the decency to look at least a tiny bit abashed. "It was fun to see how he reacted to me checking you out. What can I say? You looked particularly lovely that night."

"But, we are just friends."

"Sometimes, I sleep with my friends." He winked at me, playful playboy puppy that he was.

"Whatever. I'm just glad you guys have made your peace with each other since then, mostly. Now... are you ever going to place an order?" He made the hand-to-heart you wounded me motion, so I rolled my eyes.

Shane finally placed an order, and it was for his whole office. If his orders were anything to go by, he seemed like a good boss. He was often bringing back coffee and treats for his employees when he stopped by. "I'm going to throw in some samples of our newest product. We just started including it today. I'm sure at least some of your employees will appreciate it."

"What's it called?"

"We called it Naughty Neapolitan. It's a play on the flavors of a Neapolitan ice cream but made into a moist dessert bread. When eaten in-house, we warm it up and put a scoop of vanilla ice scream with a dash of cinnamon on top. But it's good on its own as well."

"That sounds delicious." He tried to snatch a bite as I packed up his order, but I swiftly closed the lid.

"You have no idea, but you'll have to wait until you get to your office to find out."

"How very cruel of you."

"Yes. I'm known for my cruelty. Speaking of which, could I also give you some scones and waters to hand out to our homeless friends on your way? I promised Benny I'd be by today and—"

"Absolutely. In fact, double the amount and add it to my bill."

"Thanks! I appreciate that."

After he left, I realized what was bothering me about the notes we were getting. With my thoughts on expansion, there was a part of me concerned that, with people like the note-writers out there, I was deluding myself thinking that our theme could be anything but local and niche. If this was how we were received here, it was hard to justify more. I moved past my doubts because tonight was for celebrating and that was what I planned to do. I would find a way to shake off my mood entirely by the time I met up with Jason and the others for dinner.

―――――

Summer

We'd all met at the cabana approximately forty minutes earlier, and the conversation hadn't stopped flowing. Jason had gotten to know my friends and family, and they him, over the last couple of months and now everyone seemed so much more relaxed during group get-togethers. That meant the world to me. I couldn't imagine being with someone who couldn't get along with the people who mattered to me most. He was swiftly becoming one of those important people in my life, so it meant that much more to watch him enjoy these get-togethers.

Having finished our main courses, Derek and Kevin decided to regale Jessica and Jason with hilarious and often embarrassing stories from our shared childhoods. Even though it had been hard to lose my mother at such a young age, and it definitely left me with some scars, overall, I knew I'd had a wonderful childhood.

Before she passed, even though we didn't have much money, and because my mother worked so hard, time was a limited commodity, but the quality of my time with her couldn't have been better. We enjoyed a very close relationship and shared everything with each other. Often, we could be found singing off-key and way too loud to songs from the radio in our ancient, broken-AC Subaru Forester with the windows down and annoying the people around us. Other times, we'd curl up on the couch with popcorn and chocolate, watching a barely age-appropriate romantic drama or spy flick, crying, laughing, or screaming and sometimes all of the above. Tears briefly swam before my eyes as I recalled those precious moments, but I blinked them back and refocused on the story at hand.

Oh lord! They were telling the story surrounding me and Kevin planning a double date for the Sadie Hawkins dance.

"Our dates were coming from farther away. We all decided that it made the most sense if they would meet us at the fancy restaurant we'd chosen. Summer and I went and waited. And waited. And waited. We were both stood up." Kevin smiled sadly at me like we were both still those kids and still experiencing that sad moment of realization.

"I'm over it!"

"Speak for yourself, sister." He turned to his rapt audience of two and continued, "You see, we found out later that our guys decided they had something better to do but never bothered telling us."

Jason gave my hand a gentle squeeze. Yeah, okay. That was not a funny part of the story. It had hurt and I appreciated that he was offering me what comfort he could since it happened so long ago. I knew what was coming next, though, and squeezed him back to assure him I was okay.

Kevin continued, "So there we were at this posh restaurant, dressed all fancy, and feeling like kicked puppies. I rang Derek from my phone because he'd been wrangled into chauffeuring us from the restaurant to the dance but we figured he could come early and take us home so we could lick our wounds. Meanwhile, Summer and I fed our feelings with dessert for dinner while waiting for big bro to arrive."

"And those were some amazing desserts. May have been worth the abandonment," I chimed in.

"You know they were." He reached across the table, and so did I so we could high-five. "We ordered every dessert they had. Next thing we know, big bro arrives like an avenging angel ready to kick some serious butt. He was sure he would find us both depressed and crying and was ready to take out a hit on our missing dates."

"And I really wish I had kicked their asses," Derek added in a grumble.

"Mama would have skinned you if you had."

Derek shuddered, "Too true. Near miss."

"Soooo... What happened?" Jessica inquired.

Kevin winked at me and continued the tale, "So, Derek arrives and finds Summer and I having a full-on taste testing session with the pastry chef who'd come out of the kitchen to answer all of our questions and even brought out a couple of new desserts he was working on. In fact, we were so busy with our dessert-a-palooza, we kept poor Derek there for an extra hour and a half."

Derek chimed in, "What I've never told them before is they actually saved me that night."

"What?" I sat up a little taller and leaned in. This was new news to me.

Derek continued, "Do you guys remember what else happened of note that night?"

Everyone grew silent. I looked over at Kevin and saw that he, too, was filing through his memories to see if he could remember. Then inspiration hit me. "Are you talking about the seniors who were arrested for defacing the school that night?" Based on Derek's face, I knew I'd hit the nail on the head. "Holy shit! You *are* talking about that."

Kevin looked stunned but chimed in, "Derek! You have me utterly shocked. How is this the first time we're hearing about this?"

"Yeah. I don't like to think about what could've happened," Derek affirmed. "I was with the group, planning our senior prank. Initially, it wasn't supposed to be so destructive. When we were wrapping up our planning session and were about to head to the school, I got your call. I stepped away to come get you, and, well, considering I was eighteen already, it would have been really, really bad for me if I had stayed."

Kevin shook his head and waggled his finger at Derek.

"I suppose we really did save your ass. Happy to be of service. I can't even imagine what Mama and Pop would have done if they'd been called to the police station that night."

I couldn't help the shudder that went through me even thinking about such an incident.

"Getting back to our story, one senior-prank-gone-wrong attempt foiled and a few hours of dessert buffet later, we arrived back home. Of course, when we walked in the door, we were flying high on sugar. Lots and lots of sugar."

I picked up the storytelling torch, "At first, we received a lot of sympathy for our story of being stood up. That was until we got to the part about our dinner." I used my free hand to indicate air quotes around dinner. I continued, "Even as we explained, our extreme high precipitated our extreme crash with the kill-me-now worst stomach aches ever. My stomach clenches just thinking about it. Anyway, there we were all curled up in balls of pain and Mama just looked on and tsked her tongue."

Mimicking an older woman's voice, Kevin continued, "One dessert is nice, two indulgence, three greed, and more than four... have you lost your damn minds?" In his normal voice he said, "Then she stomped off to get an iced tea, or so she said."

"Pop, all the while just stood there, harassing us. He kept offering us chocolate bars, donuts, and ice cream with this mischievous evil gleam in his eyes. That man has a sadistic side." As everyone laughed, I looked over at Jason and grew a little concerned. He was laughing along, but underneath I thought I glimpsed something else. Was that sadness? Jealousy? I couldn't quite place it, but I took note to ask him about it later.

The evening continued with more stories coming from Kevin, Derek, and myself. Jessica threw in stories from her early years as well, but Jason barely spoke about his childhood. Over the last two months as we'd dated, I'd noticed that even as we got closer, he seemed to always maintain some sort of distance, a bit of a shield between us. I really hoped that one day, he would feel comfortable enough to open up in every way. Sadly, I was honest enough with myself to note that my hope was growing perilous. I was growing impatient. Not because he wasn't an open book yet, but because I didn't feel the distance had changed in any meaningful way in all this time. Not even a little, if I was brutally honest.

Not tonight. Not yet. I shook off my dark thoughts because I wasn't going to ruin tonight. There was time enough soon to bring all of this up, and I would. On top of having a fun evening, we'd both been looking forward to later when we could be alone. After using a condom all this time alongside my IUD, we'd both gotten tested and our results had come back yesterday. Satisfied with both of our outcomes, tonight, we were going to be intimate with nothing between us and I couldn't wait to feel all of Jason with nothing at all between us. To feel connected to him in every way he would let me, anyway. *Ugh! Stop it!* Good advice. I squeezed his hand and vowed to myself that I was going to try really, really hard to stay in the moment. I didn't think I had much of a choice, anyway, because even as I grew more impatient with the distance, I also grew more certain that I was falling in love with him. Heck. What I really thought? I already had.

27

WHAT WILL THE NEIGHBORS THINK?

Jason

The ride back to my home was silent, but also uncomfortably loud with sexual tension. I couldn't wait to get Summer over, under, and basically all around me tonight. I thought about playing with her in the car, like we had after our first date, but I was enjoying the edge we were both teetering on too much. Every moment that passed it felt like that tension ratcheted up another notch. Arousal permeated the air in the cabin, and I could see in my peripheral vision every time Summer clamped her thighs together to deal with her own desire. Personally, I was rock hard. Painfully so.

I thought about the game plan I'd made coming into our evening and reviewed everything I wanted to do to her and with her for our first time bareback. It had been a good plan. Now that we were pulling up to my house and I watched Summer clamp and hold her thighs together again, I was ready to throw that plan out the proverbial window and just sink balls deep into her. And, yep, that was starting to sound like the perfect plan, and I was all about implementation. Hard, deep, and thorough implementation.

I swiftly parked the car, jumped out of the driver's seat, and uncomfortably walked around to the passenger-side door, yanking it open. Summer was spilling out at me as usual, but I was ready for her. After months of practice catching this woman, I scooped her right up into my arms. Her legs wrapped around my waist and, yep, plan B was definitely a go.

With one hand supporting her ass, my other hand reached up and tugged at her hair. She'd worn it loose today and I wrapped my fingers deep into her curls. I pulled gently, but a whimper still escaped her lips, as her head tilted back. I kissed the column of her throat down toward her collarbone. Luckily, she'd worn a wide scoop neck black shirt, which gave me access to all of the soft, creamy skin of her throat. When I reached the juncture where her throat and shoulder met, I sucked, hard, really fucking hard. I sucked hard enough to release some of my tension with a mark on her skin. Over the last couple of months, we'd established the places she was okay with me marking since we both enjoyed it. This was one of them, but definitely one of the ones that made her life harder picking out shirts to cover it.

Summer groaned my name. "Jason."

"Yeah, baby girl?" I carried her through my gate and over to the doorway, but when I thought about trying to figure out my keys, I realized I was on to plan C, because fuck it. I was done. Luckily, Summer had worn one of her beautiful and functionally perfect loose skirts. I pushed her up against the door and released her hair long enough to pull up the material of her skirt trapped between our bodies.

"Aren't we going inside?" Summer asked, but there wasn't much conviction behind her question.

"I'm going to fuck you right here. Right up against my door, on the outside of my house, unless you tell me to stop." I took a moment to absorb how beautiful she looked. Flushed, head thrown back, hard distended nipples pressing through the material of her bra and shirt, and all mine. Totally fucking mine. "You want me to stop? Take you inside and lay you on the bed or across the couch?"

"No. Do it. Fuck me. Right here. Right now."

Finally managing to bunch the rest of her skirt between us, I felt her wet heat through her panties. We were both hot for this moment. I swiftly unzipped my pants and pushed them and my boxer briefs down just enough to release my aching erection. With swift fingers, I pushed her underwear to the side for expediency, because time was up. Then I thrust home with one hard flex of my hips. Her tight pussy was absolute heaven with no barriers. I groaned in fevered ecstasy, "Fucking perfect. You feel fucking perfect."

Once again, I grabbed onto her hair, this time bringing her mouth to mine in a possessive kiss as I surged in with my tongue and my cock relentlessly. Summer panted into my mouth as I took full control of her body and our pleasure. The door rattled on its hinges from the force of our lovemaking. All the tension of the evening coalesced into a need so exquisite, so engulfing, that I couldn't remember any plans at all. Just Summer.

"Jesus, Summer, you've always felt amazing, but feeling you like this... fuck! So hot, and wet. I want to feel you coming all over my cock. Come for me." I'd never felt deeper. Summer shifted her legs to ride me at a slightly different angle and then she went over the edge.

The walls of her pussy clamped around me even as she yelled out. "Yes! Jason! Oh god, yes!" I held her tight as my balls drew up and tingles ran along my lower back and then I, too, was coming.

"Fuck." Flying high on the best orgasm of my life, it took me longer than usual to return to coherent thought. When I did, I was still in mental ecstasy as the results of our combined orgasms made a mess of us both. I loved it. My pants and boxers were probably a disaster, but I didn't care. "Feeling you dripping with my cum is so fucking hot and I love being able to just stay inside you. No bathroom disposal run needed. I can now take you anywhere, at any time."

"I didn't know how hot I would find it until now and I love that you can stay where you are too."

I wrapped both arms around her and held her close, enjoying the satiation coursing through me. Yep. One lucky SOB.

Summer

I had never felt so close to anyone before. Even standing up, fucking against his house fully clothed, this was the best sex and most intimate feeling I'd ever dreamed of having. And there was no longer any doubt, I knew. I knew the reason it was so right, so... everything, was because I loved him. I'd fallen and I could only hope that he felt the same way. *Not tonight. Soon. Enjoy tonight.* That sounded like a good plan.

With humor lacing my voice, I said, "Whether inside or out, this wall is getting an awful lot of action from us."

"I'm sorry. I seem to lose my control around you." Jason touched his forehead to mine.

"Don't apologize. I love knowing that you want me so much you can't always wait. That this door and wall are about as far as you can make it, because, baby, I feel the same way. If it means getting orgasms like this last one, count me in twice." I kissed him gently on his lips to show him how I felt without the words. "FYI, have I mentioned how much I love it when you talk dirty to me?"

"I don't think you have, but that doesn't mean I haven't observed and taken notes." He smirked.

"Keep it up and you may just get lucky."

I gulped as he flexed his hips and his newly hardening cock moved inside me. "I think that's proof I'm definitely keeping it up and I'm ready to give it to you twice, but, Summer, I'm already feeling lucky, sweetheart."

"Me too, Jason." I wrapped my arms more completely around his neck and squeezed him to me. "Are we going to make it inside, you think?" I whispered in his ear.

"Plan on it. I just can't bring myself to let go of your luscious body long enough to fiddle with my keys."

"Hand them to me."

He pulled back and looked at me in horror.

"What?" I asked in confusion.

"You're kidding right?"

I grimaced. "You really going to hold our first meeting and keys against me? You dropped them the first time we came here, if you recall."

"Oh. I definitely recall. I recall that while I may have dropped them then, you've dropped your keys on at least five separate occasions. Once, you said that you had butter fingers from the popcorn. Another time, you complained that you'd been working with icing, which, by the way, is considered sticky, not slippery. Then—"

I tried hard to maintain an affronted look on my face, but I was going to fail, so instead, I clamped my thighs on his torso and started moving my hips, interrupting his recitation, "I have something sticky and slippery for you right here. You sure you want to keep talking?"

"You make a great point. You never drop your keys, honey. I have no idea what I was thinking. Now do that again." I did. He fumbled his way with the keys, but somehow maintained a hold of them, and managed to get the door open. Eventually, I found myself carried through his house as I slowly rode his newly hardened cock. I thought he was going to take us to his bedroom, but instead, he sat and then laid down with me straddling him on the couch in front of the sliding glass door to his deck. "Ride me, Summer, use my cock for your pleasure and let me watch you come apart for me."

"Okay, but I want your hands on me." I reached down and pulled my shirt over my head. My bra followed it to the floor, and I sighed in contentment as his hands found my breasts. I ground my hips on him teasingly slow. I also placed my hand over his on my breast. It was an interesting sensation to feel his hand from above with mine and from below with my breast as he played. It was as though we were a team working toward my pleasure in that moment. "Yes! Squeeze harder. Please, Jason. I want to come, for you."

He did as I asked, giving my hard points a twist and then the bite of his nail scraping over them, and I was completely lost to sensations, as usual with him. So lost, my eyes had drifted shut and I didn't notice when he shifted us both. Even his words barely penetrated my lustful haze. "You do that. Come for *me*. Fall apart for *me*." I only realized the shift when I felt him take my nipple into his mouth. He bit down then licked gently, soothingly before moving on to my other breast.

"Oh my god!" I moved my hips faster after that, pumping up and down and then grinding, feeling the erotic scrape of his cock on my inner walls. "Yes! Oh, yes! You feel amazing everywhere."

"So do you. Fuck, so do you. Now do it. Come for me." When he sucked on the plump part of my right breast, leaving another mark, the thought of that, the feel of his mouth, and the length of his cock impaling me all became too much. I gasped in a breath, like the quiet before the storm, and then I began to shake all over, inside and out as pleasure permeated every pore of my body. I had enough clarity to feel Jason's hot cum fill me again.

Satisfaction. Joy. Love. All filled me along with his orgasm.

I couldn't imagine anything better than being with this man. He was smart, funny, kind, and so very passionate. My dream man come to life and I wanted to float here, joined with him, forever. As I lay there recovering, I thought about the Goddess card I'd pulled that morning, the Hindu goddess Lakshmi. The goddess of wealth and good fortune. Thinking back over my day, the puritanical note was but a nuisance in the abundance I had in my life. I was fortunate, indeed. My gratitude was immense for all my blessings. I held on to Jason a little bit tighter and hoped that he felt the same about me. That we could get past whatever was holding him back.

28

PLAN A

Jason

It took me a few good minutes to get any willpower to move after the couch, but I was determined to revisit plan A. I wanted to let Summer know how much I cared for her and while I probably didn't have the right words, I could show her. When I was finally able to move, I stripped us both of our clothes and carried her to my shower so we could rinse off before moving forward with my plan. While toweling partly dry, I playfully tackled her, and she ran and fought back. Many giggles later, and Summer was on my back as I gave her a naked piggyback ride down the stairs and out the sliding back door.

"What are you doing? Why are we out here? Nude, no less," she exclaimed while slapping me on the arm and wiggling on my back.

"Stop wiggling. My neighbors can't see us, and even if they could, I don't care, do you? I want you in the hot tub. Doesn't that sound good?" I turned and pushed the button that lifted the cover off the tub. I carefully placed her bottom on the edge of the tub and then spun around while still between her thighs to face her. "Get in."

"Why?"

I saw the stubborn gleam in her eyes. Perhaps I'd given her one command too many tonight. I chose a different approach. In my most regal voice I said, "Summer, will you please do me the honor of turning your gorgeous body around and climbing into the hot tub so I can make you feel good all over?" Okay. Perhaps sarcasm wasn't the most romantic approach, but I liked the one where I issued orders so she would just have to deal.

"Well. When you put it that way. How can a girl refuse?"

I may have mumbled under my breath, "Oh. I know one that would try." I realized my mistake as her mouth dropped open, gaping at me. At least I also saw humor in her eyes. I hadn't royally fucked this up yet. "Please?" It should have been a plea but came out as a question. I really did like the part where I issued orders. Much simpler.

I waited for an answer, and I wasn't sure what I received was exactly an answer but it was definitely, um, something. Summer reached out and palmed my semi-hard cock. I would have thought that two orgasms later, and I would be unable to get it up for a while, but my cock had other plans, as evidenced by my current state. "What are you doing?"

"You don't like it?"

"I wouldn't say that exactly."

"You did mention 'good all over,' didn't you? I'm just checking the validity of that statement."

"Minx."

"I try."

I groaned. "Stop that. Get in the damn tub."

She gave a big, dramatic sigh. "Okay. Fine. See you there." She spun around before I could recover from the loss of her hot palm around me, and all thoughts of sex fled to be replaced with concern as she slid unceremoniously into the center of the giant tub because her foot slipped. I watched her head go under and reached to try to save her and missed. *What were you thinking? See? You can't even get through one simple plan.*

I hadn't heard that voice in my head for a while, but I completely ignored it. I didn't have time right then for any annoying doubts. I quickly scrambled up the side stairs and was ready to be a knight in shining nudity when her head cleared the surface of the water with an explosion of laughs. "Graceful, I am not. My muscles can't decide if they want to thank me for the wonderful heat or if they want to protest me for the abuse they just experienced. Between your love bites and my natural problems navigating the world, I'm going to be black and blue."

She made her way to one of the seating areas and I relaxed. I finally climbed in myself, and made my way to where she sat, kneeling in front of her. "I sometimes feel like I should just pad you in gauze so that I can keep you. Otherwise, I may lose you to a pebble on the sidewalk or a wobbly chair."

Her arms wound around my neck, and she looked into my eyes as she answered me solemnly, "You aren't going to lose me, Jason. I'm like Arya from *Game of Thrones*."

I narrowed my eyes at her. "A murderer? She killed everyone on her list."

"Only if they deserved it. Otherwise, she's shown the ability to always come back from anything bad that happens to her and to stay devoted. I can stay devoted and make a comeback. Just don't get on my list." She smirked.

I had to laugh. In fact, I hadn't laughed so much in my life like I had since Summer entered it. "Touché, sweetheart. You should know, I'm not going anywhere either. I've never wanted a serious relationship and then you dropped into my life. I think you're amazing and I hope you know that." I was actually a little impressed with myself for being able to get that many emotional words out. I honestly hadn't believed that I had it in me. I attempted a few more. "I enjoy how you tease, how you do what you want, how you treat the people around you, and how you share so much with me."

There were tears swimming in her eyes, but I'd grown to recognize her happy tears. "I love you, Jason."

Oh damn! Exactly. What are you going to do with that?

At my dumbfounded silence, Summer rushed in with more words, "I know it's quick, and I don't expect you to say it back. You'll say it if and when you feel it, but I wanted you to know."

I heard her, but I was still a little lost. Love? What did I know about love? My parents never said they loved me. They never even said they loved each other. They were all mutually emotionally defunct. I continued to struggle with what to say, but I needed to say something. "Summer, I'm not sure I even know what love is. I know I have very strong feelings for you. I want to see you all the time. I like making you happy. I definitely can't get enough of your body, but I also can't wait to talk to you whether by text or phone or in person. Do you think that can be enough for now?" *Damn! What if she says no?*

She didn't answer me right away and I was about ready to scramble to say more, to salvage this, us. How could I save us? I couldn't lose her. I may not know anything about love, but I knew I wanted her in my life. When she smiled at me, finally, I relaxed the littlest bit and continued to wait for her answer.

"It's enough for now, Jason. Love is freely given. It's not something you can demand from someone. When I gave you mine, it was not an attempt to demand more from you than you're ready to give. It was just a declaration of my own feelings. I love you regardless of whether you love me back."

I may not know anything about love, but I knew I adored this woman. I swooped her into my arms, switched our positions so I sat in the hot tub, and settled her in my lap. "Thank you for loving me." I began to massage her shoulders and down her arms, hoping every touch told her how I felt. *Whatever that is. You understand that she won't stay when she realizes you can't love her back.*

"You're welcome. Now. I do believe you promised to make me feel good."

"That's the plan." I turned her so her back was to me and began to massage her with firm strokes from neck to lower back. She moaned as I pushed and kneaded her muscles. "Actually, you feel rather stiff, baby. Something going on at work?"

"There are some annoying notes lately, but I don't want to ruin tonight by discussing them. We can always talk about them another time." She turned her head to look back at me with a saucy smile flitting across her lips. "You know, you promised to make me feel good, everywhere."

"Mmhmm."

"Well—" Now she looked downright devilish. "—I think your mission has been accomplished. Now, I want to play."

I was intrigued, and also couldn't resist teasing her. "Chess? Risk? Pacman?"

"Har, har. Keep that up, and I may just take you up on one of those. First, though, I want you sitting on the ledge." She wiggled off my lap.

I was game, so I sat on the ledge with my legs dangling into the enticingly warm water as the warm breeze cooled me. I watched as the droplets clung to Summer's skin as she stood in the water. One droplet rolled from the mark I gave her on her shoulder, down her chest, over her nipple, and off the second mark I left on the underside of her breast. My mouth watered. Summer, the picture of a water nymph, slid her hands from my knees up my inner thighs and situated herself between them while kneeling on the seat I'd just vacated. Her hands kept exploring higher until one was cupping my balls and the other gripped my erection. "What are you up to, sweetheart?" I growled.

I could never claim that my girl was subtle. Instead of answering me, she licked me from balls to tip like a Popsicle, only stopping at the tip where she grabbed the bit of precum that escaped on her tongue. "You are so fucking hot. I want to feel your mouth on me, sweetness."

She smiled up through her lashes and said, "I'm playing. You'll get what you want... soon."

I groaned. My fingers itched to grab her hair and direct her movements, but I also enjoyed seeing her pleasure at exploring me. Ultimately, it was her choice right then and she had chosen playing with me. I'd try to be patient. Well, I thought I was going to be patient, but then Summer took my balls in her mouth, rolling them with her tongue while pumping her hand along my length. "Dear God, woman. I may not survive your playtime."

I had a hard time concentrating on the details for a while as I was too swamped with sensation. One of her hands ended up resting on my abdomen and I think occasionally tweaked my nipples. The other continued its motion but at some point her mouth covered as much of my length as she could. She worked both together and I did everything I could not to let go too soon. To give us both a chance to enjoy the moment. "You're killing me."

She must have liked that because she took me impossibly deeper down her throat. My words fled. Well. All except, "Fuck!" and "Deeper!" and "Take all of me." Those flew out of my mouth like alphabet soup in some random order and I only hoped they made sense.

Summer got my message as she moved her other hand out of the way and onto my abdomen as well. She practically impaled herself on my cock and it was one of the hottest things I'd ever seen. That was it. That was me losing the fight. She moaned around me and I lost all control. As I came, she swallowed as quickly as she could. "Fuck!" She swallowed every drop. When she lifted her head, I stared in awe at her beautiful face, still a bit dazed.

"I really enjoyed that," she said with a satisfied smile.

"I'm pretty sure that I'm the one that enjoyed the hell out of that."

"You say tomayto, I say tomahto."

"No. I say thank you, and you get up here on my face." Summer enthusiastically jumped up, nearly falling over again, but I caught her this time. I pulled her up on the ledge as I lay back and she was once again straddling me. My face this time. I was in pussy heaven. Licking, nipping, sucking, smelling her arousal, and listening for every little sound she made. I couldn't help but think, once again, that I was one lucky SOB.

29

SURPRISES

Summer

The next night, I stood awkwardly in the bright green, knee-length, satin monstrosity of a dress waiting for Jason to open his door. We'd made a plan for me to come over today, but before I did, I received a package by courier with a note that just said, 'Wear me tonight. Jason.' I'd done as he requested, putting on a set of black pumps that seemed like a good fit with the wild dress. *Were we going to a costume party? An Eighties or Nineties themed party? What the hell was going on?* I hadn't been this nervous with him for quite some time.

The door opened and I had to blink twice at what I saw there. Jason, usually dressed in some sort of expensive, hot-looking suit, was wearing a suit that matched my dress in the throwback look and feel. Yet, in all that is unfair, he looked like a sexy Nineties rock star. He'd even put some sort of product in his hair to get it to do that messy but organized thing guys did back then. He had an appreciative smile on his face and a mischievous look in his eyes. "You made it. I was worried you'd stand me up once you saw the dress."

"I would never stand you up, handsome. I am curious as to what you're up to, though." I walked right up to him and pretended to adjust his tie. "Are we going to a theme party you forgot to tell me about?"

His lips lightly descended to mine, just gracing them, and then he pulled back. Now I was growing a bit concerned. Since when did he kiss me like that? Normally, we could barely draw air from the crazy lip-locks we found ourselves in.

"I'm so honored you asked me to come with you tonight, Summer. Shall we go sit down?" He appeared to be on his best behavior. He even wrapped my hand into the crook of his arm as he walked me farther into his home.

When we arrived at the dining room, kitchen, living area, I saw that it, too, was transformed. The furniture in the living room had been moved to the walls of the room, leaving an open space in the middle. There was a disco ball hanging from his ceiling fan and the soft, sexy melodic voices of Boys II Men was playing in the background. There were some streamers decorating various shelves, lamps, and other furniture strewn around like a snake can popped open. The dining room had candles on the table and the light above had been dimmed. Two places were laid out with formal silverware, awaiting them to sit, and from the kitchen, an amazing aroma was permeating the whole room.

"What is all this?"

"I'm taking you to your Sadie Hawkins dance."

My jaw dropped so far, I was worried it became unhinged. "Did I hear you right?"

"If you heard that we are having dinner and going to the dance—" He winked at me. "—then you heard correctly."

"Is this because of the story from last night?"

"Of course."

"You know I'm okay. Right? That I'm not still upset about this?"

"Yes. I know. That doesn't change the fact that standing you up was a shit thing for some asshole to do, and I wanted to give this to you." He rushed on before I could say another word. "Now, please come have a seat." I allowed him to guide me to my seat at the table.

"How did you find out it was a throwback to the nineties theme party?"

"I have my ways."

I sat down and noticed a clear box sitting to the side of my plate. Inside, I saw lovely red roses bunched with baby's breath and a dark green leaf plant.

Jason opened the box and pulled out the beautiful floral arrangement. He lifted one of my hands and carefully slid the elastic band onto my wrist. "You bought me a corsage?"

"Of course. What kind of date would I be if I didn't?"

"But I didn't—"

He tapped a finger on the lapel of his jacket, even as he lifted a smaller, matching arrangement I hadn't noticed sitting there from the box. He kneeled down on one knee so we were at the same height and handed me the small arrangement. "As you can see, you did." That up-to-something gleam was still in his eyes, but I found I kinda loved it. Jason was amazing, but it was rare for him to be truly relaxed and playful, and I was enjoying this side of him, thoroughly.

"This has to be one of the most romantic, nicest things anyone has ever done for anyone."

He turned a little serious as he answered me, "Baby, I may not understand love, but I know that I want to make you smile. I hoped this would do the trick."

I couldn't help beaming at him. "I love you and the ways in which you find to put a smile on my face, regularly." I leaned forward to claim his lips in a kiss, but, once again, he barely touched mine with his and then was gone. Apparently, we were playing at being awkward teenagers to the letter. Okay. I was game. "What are we ordering for dinner?"

"I've already ordered for us. We're having a caprese salad followed by lasagna. We're also having blackberry Italian sodas. All of that work for you?"

"Sounds delicious, but not wine?"

"Wine is for adult functions not high school dances."

"I see." I now sounded just like Mama.

Jason wandered into the kitchen and came out holding two plates decorated beautifully with fresh mozzarella, fresh basil, tomatoes, and drizzled with olive oil. He placed one in front of me and took the other to his seat. He left again, but came back quickly, setting a fizzy drink in front of me. He went and sat down with his and we both started eating. We chatted casually about our days as we ate. When we finished, I began to stand so I could clear the plates, but he was faster and told me to stay seated. So I did, waiting. My heart was cheerleading and forming pyramid formations.

He disappeared into the kitchen again. When he came back out this time, he had two plates that held ceramic bowls on top of them. He once again placed one in front of me and took his seat with the other. The lasagna was individually cooked inside each of the ceramic bowls. "This is definitely restaurant-quality work. Did you cook all this?"

"The chef will be happy to hear it. I'll make sure he knows." The look in his eyes said that, yes, he had cooked all the food himself and he was continuing to play along with his dance date evening charade. "Dig in. We don't want to arrive late to the dance."

"Of course not. It feels like I've been looking forward to this dance for forever."

"Me too."

I took my first bite and the cheesy, meaty goodness had me moaning. Conversation slowed as we continued to enjoy the delicious meal. I couldn't finish my bowl, though I made a valiant effort. "I can't eat another bite, even though my taste buds want to revolt against my stomach and dive right in."

"We also have dessert ordered. You sure you can't eat another bite?"

"Oh. My dessert stomach is totally empty. No worries there."

He laughed. He may love to make me smile, but I equally loved to make him laugh. Tonight, my hope for a future together was back in full force. He had to love me, even if he didn't understand it. No one would put this much effort into such an amazing evening, unless they cared very deeply. It was probably going to take him some extra time, but we'd get there. I was sure of it.

Jason once again disappeared with our plates into the kitchen. This time he came out bearing two perfect slices of tiramisu. Jason was a fantastic cook, but I also knew that he didn't do desserts. "Should I send my compliments to the chef for this too?" I fished.

He grinned and replied, "The chef may have had help with this particular dish."

I took a bite and knew. "From someone I know?"

He snorted. "I should have known you'd recognize his handy work. Yes, someone close to you."

"He really does make the best desserts and pastries."

"I'm a total convert."

I was going to have to thank Kev later in between giving him a hard time for keeping this surprise from me today.

I ate every bite and so did Jason. He cleared everything from the table, came up to me offering one of his hands, and said, "Shall we dance?"

"Yes. I'd love that."

I put my hand in his and he lifted me from my seat. I almost tumbled into him, but his hand helped me to stay upright. He knew me so well, now, and that thought made me smile. Jason smiled back as he led me into the living room. He picked up a remote from the bookshelves and clicked on a button that started the disco ball spinning. He clicked another button and the music changed to the sultry sounds of Seal's "Kiss from a Rose." Jason held me close and we began to sway. I was sure that the love I felt coursing through every inch of my body had to be glowing at him from my eyes.

"I like holding you in my arms."

"Me too. I've had a wonderful evening."

"It's not over yet."

"True."

The next song started playing and it was Alanis Morissette's "Head over Feet." We continued to sway together as I put my head on his shoulder. I loved his strong shoulders. His arms tightened around my middle. I was left speechless by all the effort he went through for tonight and so I just let myself feel the moment. Then another song began to play, and it was Luther Vandross singing "Here and Now."

"Did you make this music mix?"

"I was wondering if you would notice." Humor laced his voice. "I made you an actual mix CD." I leaned back in shock, but he just stared back in all seriousness. I broke up laughing and snorting so hard, we had to stop dancing. "Should I be offended?"

I gulped in air to catch my breath and answered, "Not at all! I'm not laughing at the gesture. I think it was my totally inappropriate reaction to being overwhelmed. You really thought of everything. You made me a freaking mix CD!"

Jason ran his hand over my hair while his other hand cupped my cheek. It felt wonderful. Electric. "For you, anything."

I huskily replied, "I think that you, sir, are going to be getting lucky tonight."

"God, I hope so."

"Jason. I love dancing with you, but I want to do a different kind of rocking with you now."

"Hallelujah! It's been so hard to keep my hands to myself. As soon as I saw you in that dress, I began imagining stripping you right out of it. I deserve an award for keeping my hands off you all night."

"You'll get a reward, because this dress has definitely got to go in more ways than one." I jumped and wrapped my legs around his waist as he supported me in his arms. "Jason, you big stud. Take me to bed or lose me forever!"

"Did you just *Top Gun* reference me?"

"Maybe."

"Well, show me the way home, honey!" Then he kissed me.

Reeaallly kissed me. Finally. The night was still young, but we weren't, at least not teenager young, and it was far past time for us to get to enjoy being the adults we were.

The next morning, I didn't much like the adults we were. It had started out as all sleepover mornings did with us, deep kisses, intimate sex, and intense cuddles. All of it came to an abrupt end after we showered and dressed and I asked Jason about the announcement event scheduled for the next day. I wanted to know where to meet him and what to wear.

He just looked at me as his eyes grew distant. Then he responded, "Summer, this is my work. It's no big deal, really. I hadn't planned on having you there."

"I guess I assumed since this is one of the biggest events happening for you right now, I would be joining you. To support you. I've seen announcements like this before. People do often show up with their significant others." I looked at his firm jaw, his still distant eyes, and the tension in his stance and knew that I had gotten it all wrong. "But, you don't want me there."

"I just like to keep my work and my personal life separate. That's all. It has nothing to do with you. With us. I enjoy my work and I enjoy our time together. It's really not a big deal." His voice even sounded different. Remote.

He may say it wasn't a big deal, but it was to me. Not because of the event itself but because of the logic he was using to keep me away. Just in case I was reading him wrong, though, I asked, "Are you planning on having me come with you to the premiere?"

He looked thoroughly agitated, but he still answered with a firm, "No."

I couldn't help the gasp of indrawn breath that escaped in my shock. "You do realize that work is a part of life and when you are with someone you share your lives. The good and the bad?"

"That was never my plan."

"So you've never brought anyone to an event, ever?"

I saw the answer on his face.

"You have." Direct hit to the heart. I suddenly found it hard to breathe.

He rushed to answer the question I hadn't asked, "They were people I met in the line of my work. Hollywood types who live in that world. It's different."

"So what you're saying is that you're embarrassed of me?"

His features finally softened and even looked mildly horrified. "No. I would never be embarrassed to be with you."

"Then... I don't get it." My heart was in so much pain trying to reason through this. I even tried putting my therapist hat on to see if something made sense.

"They were already a part of that world. It didn't make sense for them not to come, but you are not. I think that part of my life could potentially hurt you or make you feel like you don't belong, and I am worried that you will need more of my attention than I will want to give you when I am working. It works better for me to have all of my attention on work when I work and all of my attention on you when I'm with you."

"You really think I'd be a detriment to your work or that your work would be a detriment to me." I knew, *knew,* that this probably made sense to him based on what little family history I was able to get from him. Business was everything and he had no basis on how to handle relationships with true connections, but, but, *but* it didn't matter. I didn't know if I could be with someone who only wanted to give me a part of himself. I'd always felt that he held back, but I hadn't realized just how much he planned to hold back indefinitely. Not wanting to delve into your past traumas is reasonable and we could have worked on that over time, but to want to keep me completely separate from such a huge part of his life, his aspirations, his successes and failures... I couldn't do that. I couldn't live like that. Tears burned at the backs of my eyes. "I see." There I went, being Mama again, but that woman might be on to something.

"I don't understand why this is such a big deal. What am I not giving you? We have fascinating conversations. We go on amazing dates. We have great sex. I made you a mix CD, for fuck's sake. What is missing in what we have?" He threw his arms out and I could read his frustration because clearly, in his eyes, he was giving this relationship his all. His best. All he knew how to give. I wasn't sure that was going to be enough for me.

"I never asked for you to try to give me fairy tales. All I ever wanted was all of you."

"You have all of me. All of me that is not my work. Why is that not enough?" He looked desperate to make me understand, and it was breaking my heart that this was going to hurt us both because I would not be able to live like this even if I tried. This would eventually be the end of us anyway. Now. Later. It wouldn't matter.

"I need some time to think." I blinked rapidly to keep my tears at bay. I was happy that I'd driven to his place by myself last night because it would allow me to make a clean exit. I swiped my keys, purse, and phone and turned back to face him. His demeanor was guarded. His eyes were bleak. "I understand your position and I even understand why you feel it's enough. I just don't think that it's enough for *me*, Jason. I don't need extravagant dates, but I do need to feel like I am a full partner, not just a partial one. In an effort not to make rash decisions, I'm not making one now, but I need some time to think," I repeated. "I'll be in touch with you soon, but probably not tonight and probably not tomorrow. Maybe the day after or by the end of the week."

I was ready to bolt, but I looked into those bleak eyes and knew I couldn't leave like this. I slowly walked up to him, went on my tiptoes, and pressed my lips to his. I dropped back down before he could hold me or deepen the kiss. Tension was thick, choking, leaden between us. I looked him right in the eyes. "I love you. Good luck tomorrow." That was that, then. I turned swiftly and walked away. Out the door to a different day, a different life, than the one I thought I had when I first woke up.

30

FALLOUT

Jason

I stood frozen to the spot for a long time. Or maybe it just felt like it. Who knew? Everything inside me hurt. Why couldn't she understand? What did she expect from me? I was rooted to the spot, vacillating between righteous indignation and despair. I treated her like a queen. I opened myself to her in ways I hadn't even known I could be open. What more did she want? Why was it so wrong for me to want to keep this one thing for myself? *You knew this was always going to end this way. Damn you. Shut the fuck up.*

I had so few answers. The most important question I needed an answer for was, what did she mean "she needed time to think"? Would she leave me for good over this? I couldn't imagine not having her in my life after all we'd shared. What was I supposed to do? I couldn't lose her. But this is exactly why I wanted to keep everything separate, isn't it? I have an event I need to focus on and as long as I compartmentalize, I'm able to do that. I'll come back to my love life problems later. Maybe in the meantime, she will reconsider everything and realize what a good thing we have. *Keep telling yourself that. You know you don't believe it.*

My day went by in a blur of activity in preparation for the big event the next day. Keeping busy helped, but I'd be lying if I said I hadn't checked my phone at least four times an hour. She hadn't called or texted.

The next morning had me going through the motions after a sleepless night. I was once again so busy with making sure it would all run smoothly that I didn't have a lot of time to think about anything but work. As the time neared for the announcement, I headed in to see how Vanessa was doing. She was stunning in a white pantsuit with nothing under the jacket except a slew of thin gold chains. The world wasn't ready for the way she was going to dominate both big and small screens over her next few years signed with me.

She looked up from her latest book when I walked in and the first thing she said was, "You look like shit."

I plastered on my warmest smile and said, "With such an important client, I've been working extra hard to make sure everything goes smoothly today."

She stared me up and down, scrutinizing me in a way that made me want to squirm, but of course I didn't. I don't squirm. "Vanessa—"

"Don't you Vanessa me. This is the first time in these last few months that has me regretting choosing to sign with you. Don't try to schmooze me, Mr. Winter. People who have been in this game a lot longer than you have tried to sell me some bullshit. I can read a bullshitter a mile away. You... until today, were not a bullshitter. What has changed? Is something wrong with the announcement? With the movie? With you? Ah... by the way you tensed, it's you. Want to tell me about it?"

"Not particularly. It's not work-related, so it shouldn't impact anything here." I shrugged in nonchalance.

"You do realize that a private life, even one that influences your work, is okay to have. Right?" She raised an eyebrow expectantly at me.

"No. I don't. Why would you want to let the mess of your private life spill into your work?"

"Because, Jason, you are a whole person. You don't think my acting is at times changed by my mood based on things going on in other aspects of my life? That's life. Want to tell me why you're so out of sorts?"

At this point, I couldn't see what I had to lose except her respect and potentially her as a client if I kept trying to, as she put it, bullshit her. I could be real with her without diving into my private life if I wanted, but seeing as how I didn't have a lot of places to go for advice I thought, what the hell? "I was seeing someone and I think it might be over."

There was no misinterpreting the look she gave me as anything other than, 'No shit, Sherlock.'

"Okay. Fine. We've been together for a few months, and they've been the best months of my life. When she asked me yesterday about attending this event, I told her I didn't plan for her to come with me."

"Why not?"

"Why would I?"

"Because she was important to you."

I jumped to correct her phrasing without thinking about it, "She *is* important to me."

"Yes. Okay. *Is.* And this announcement is also important to you?"

"Of course. I'm very excited to sign you and to help you forge this new path for your career." She put up a hand to stop me. I stopped.

"Not the tagline. I don't need to hear what you're going to tell the crowd of reporters. I want to know if you are excited about today. Is this an important day to you?"

I had to think about the distinction she was making. "Yes. It is. You are my first A-lister, my first deal with WebShowz, and my first announcement of this size. It's everything I've been working toward from when I started Avalanche."

"And you don't think someone who you find special, and I assume therefore also finds you special, would want to share in such a momentous moment for you? Right. So... Why don't you let that sink in for a bit. We need to get going. Let's get this show started."

She was right. We needed to get going. The rest of what she said I'd consider after we were finished here. For now, the only way forward would be the one I was used to. I was Jason Winter and I needed no one. It sounded like bullshit to me too, but the show must go on, and it did. And, it was everything I'd wanted. The buzz was everything I could have hoped for. So... why hadn't I been able to enjoy it? Janet kept giving me strange looks when no one was looking. Vanessa was more sly about it, but she looked like she pitied me, or maybe that was me pitying myself.

I had so many damn questions and so few actual answers. Maybe it was time to get some help in finding those answers.

Summer

Present Me is asking Past Me why she thought it was a good idea to watch his announcement. Did Past Me have a masochistic side that had bigger consequences than Present Me wished to deal with? That bitch had some 'splaining to do. He looked as handsome as always standing center stage, all eyes on him. Everyone seemed to enjoy the news and Vanessa was such a stunner. He seemed so unaffected by my absence. I was an unhappy Elvis potato and he was successfully pulling things like that off while looking and sounding like a total professional. This separating his work self from his romance self might really work for him. The announcement from start to finish was over within a half hour. That was the length of time between us together and us apart.

It wasn't just those thirty minutes, though, was it? It was a lifetime of watching from home as he celebrated or lost. Feeling on the outside of a big chunk of who he was. I asked for time so I wouldn't make a rash decision, but even then I'd known that there was no decision to be made. I deserved all of him, just as he had all of me. I wasn't sure why he felt the need to keep me and his work so separate, and maybe he didn't know either. Didn't matter. If that was how he felt, then I had to honor that, but I couldn't stay. I had to honor me too.

I wished I could drift off to sleep, because really, I was so damn tired, but I couldn't run away from my feelings of loss any longer. Not when I accepted the truth that meant the end of us. I covered myself in multiple blankets as I shivered in reaction to my pain and grief.

I tried so hard to stay quiet, but Jessica must have heard something, just like she always did, because my door opened, and then my friend crawled under all the covers with me and held me from behind. I also felt a tiny dip in the blanket, and then Midnight was curled up against my front. I was cocooned between them. Safe in their hold, I fell to pieces. Jessica said nothing, she just stayed and continued to hold me together until I finally fell asleep.

I woke up a couple of mornings later, feeling like roadkill. I wasn't exactly the epitome of hygiene and I was pretty sure Midnight stopped sleeping with me because of the smell. I sniffed at my underarms and confirmed that probability for myself. Yep. I'd been a miserable, ice cream eating, lumpy blanket wearing cautionary tale of love. Derek, Kevin, and, of course, Jessica each took turns eating, watching movies, or threatening all manner of bodily harm on Jason.

I kept trying to explain that I'm just as responsible as him for us not working out, but the good friends they were, they only saw it in one direction. I gave up trying. Derek was so supportive, he promised me he wouldn't spill the beans to Mama and Pop until I spoke to them about it first. I wanted to have that conversation after it was officially over. Jason and I hadn't made it official yet, seeing as how we hadn't talked since I walked out. I was being a coward, but today I was going to suck it up and end our relationship like an adult.

But first, I needed a shower and to probably change my sheets. As I rolled out of bed, I pulled the sheets with me and threw them in the hamper. I stared at the bed where we'd shared so many intimate moments and I missed him all over again. Nothing changed, though; I could never be happy in the relationship he wanted. Perhaps even needed. I turned my back on the bed because some things were unfixable, unlike new sheets, which I would fix later.

I stumbled across the small space between my room and the bathroom and didn't see Jessica on the couch. She must have actually used her bed last night. Nice. After a hot, rejuvenating, and freshening shower where I only dropped the soap once, I felt a little bit more myself. I stared at my steam-blurred image in the mirror and grinned saying, "Nice hair," since it was sticking out in every direction. It felt good to get up and feel capable of smiling, especially when it was just me there to see it. This was authentically me. While my heart was still broken, I was not.

I looked over at my Goddess cards. It had been a few days since I'd sought them out, but I was ready to believe again. Or maybe I needed to believe again. Either way, I finished drying off, especially my hands, and then picked up the deck. I shuffled them, set them down, and drew the top one.

Fuck! That had been a shitastic idea. "What the fuck, Goddess cards? Are you mocking me? Seriously." I was tempted to rip it into pieces when the door to the bathroom opened.

Jessica stood there looking like she was ready to do battle. "Are you okay? What's wrong?" She seemed to assess what was in my hand and added, "Are you yelling at your Goddess card?"

"Yes! Look." I shoved the card into Jessica's hand like it was disgusting, but the kind of disgusting you insist your best friend had to try too.

Jessica stared down at the card and her face went blank. What was that supposed to mean? She just kept looking at it for a while, but I got the impression that she was trying to come up with the right thing to say. "Well. This card could mean different things, right? I mean, I don't follow or believe in these, but from all you've taught me, they can be interpreted in many ways."

"Okay. Yes. That's true, but it does seem a little like it's taunting me. Don't you think?"

Once again, it felt as though Jessica chose her words carefully. "The goddess Eos may have played a part in your relationship with Jason, but she also did with you opening your café. No? Maybe today you'll have a great day strategizing your expansion."

I didn't want to, but I had to admit that Jessica was right and I took the card back from her. "Since when am I the doom and gloom girl and you're the everything is sunny girl?"

Jessica faux shivered. "Don't tell anyone we switched bodies for a while. I'll be back to my normal 'it's all going to hell in a handbasket' soon enough. In fact, I was just on my way out. You're going to the café after you get ready, right?" She walked out of the bathroom.

To keep up our conversation, I leaned out the doorway. "No. I'm going to see Jason this morning."

Jessica was grabbing her purse and keys but paused when she registered what I'd said. "Oh. That's what had you so freaked out over Eos. Will you be okay? Want me to come to be your emotional support getaway car friend?"

"No. I got this. And, Jessica, thank you for everything the last few days."

"You're welcome. I've always got your back, you know."

"Same here."

"I know." She winked, smiled, and was gone.

I stared down at the goddess again and could swear she had a self-satisfied look on her face. "Whatever you mean for my day, it better be good, because I will come back and rip you up if you try anything." Did the goddess's expression become a little bit wary? Well, good. I tossed the card on the deck and finished getting ready.

I'd texted Jason the night before. Simple texts establishing a time, which was soon, I needed to go, and a place, his for privacy. We were going to talk, but in my heart, I knew there was nothing that could be said to make this situation okay for me. We both knew this talk had only one conclusion, assuming all things stayed the same. I grabbed my purse and keys and was on the move, heading somewhere all too familiar with a destination that wasn't familiar at all.

31

TALK TO ME

Jason

It was hard sitting around waiting for Summer to arrive, so I didn't. By the time her car pulled into my driveway, I had rearranged my kitchen cabinets and cleaned them out of any old nonperishables that had perished. I had so much to say, but where to start? *You can't salvage this.* I was scared that voice was right. Had been silencing it again and again out of fear that it knew better than me what I was capable of.

She was at the door. Even this felt wrong. After a month we had taken to having me leave the door unlocked when I knew she was coming over and she would just walk in. She knocked. I hated it.

I opened the door and she looked so grim. Like I'd stolen all of her shine. "Come in."

"Thank you."

We walked into the dining area with the family room couch beyond and I was rooted in place. Was the place we made love in so many times a bad idea for a discussion of one's relationship? Would it be better to stay in the dining area with separate seating and a table if needed? *Jesus. You can't even decide on where to have a talk. What makes you think you'll be able to convince this amazing woman to stay?*

"Where would you like to sit?" I left it in her court to see where she felt most comfortable.

She'd chosen the living room. Right. That made sense. We sat across from each other, as she chose one of the lounging chairs and perched on the edge, while I sat similarly perched on the couch. We both rushed to speak...

"How are you?

"How are you doing?"

At least that helped break the tension as we both chuckled. "I'm not great. I have a lot I want to say. How about you?"

Summer nodded. "I have things I want to say as well and yeah, the last few days have sucked. A lot."

Her eyes had been so sad as she'd said the last part, and I was the cause. *You were always going to eventually make her feel this way.*

"Do you mind if I start?" she asked, but then quickly added, "Actually, it's not so much a question. I would like to start so I can get this out."

I wasn't sure we were going in the correct order, but I wanted to respect her wishes, so I agreed with a nod.

"I watched it, you know... the announcement. It looked like it was a resounding success. Congratulations. I was so very proud of you. I know how hard you worked to achieve it. You looked so confident and handsome talking to everyone. I realized some things while watching you. The first is that even when you aren't getting enough sleep—yes, I could tell that too—" She gave me a wry grin. "—you were able to pull yourself together and get the job done. This brings me to my second realization. Perhaps you were right and this works for you. And this leads to my third realization. I love you and want you happy and if this works for you and makes you happy, then that's what I want for you."

Was I hearing what I thought I was hearing? She wouldn't meet my eyes so it was hard to tell. In fact, she was staring at the floor so it was not looking good.

"With all of that in mind, and nothing but love from me to you, I'm walking away. I can't live the life you want. It has nothing to do with Hollywood. In fact, after all these months together, your drive and passion to grow your business inspired me to pursue the expansion of The Frisky Bean into catering with a focus on movie sets. I'd been thinking about it and was too worried to rock our little boat, but you always pursued each new step with all the gusto and confidence of a conqueror, and I guess I needed to see that to remind me that I don't have to stop with my first big accomplishment. That I'm allowed to keep chasing even bigger dreams. I don't think I've thanked you for that, so, thank you."

She looked me in the eyes when she thanked me, and it actually helped with what I was going to have to say when it was my turn to talk. "You're welcome, but I have every faith that you would have gotten there on your own eventually."

"Eventually. You're right, but I wanted to pursue it now and since the café is still pretty new, it felt like wanting too much. I won't think that way again. Anyway, I think that's it from me. I appreciate that what you want in a relationship works for you, but I can't be a part of a relationship like that. I need all of the person I'm going to be with. I give all of me and need that same openness returned to me. I love you. I really hope you find what you need." A lone tear trailed down her cheek before she swiped it away with the back of her hand. "I guess it's your turn with the talking stick."

I gave her a small smile at her attempt to lighten the mood. After taking a couple of deep breaths, fortifying myself with the knowledge that the decision I came to in the last couple of days was the right one for me, and I was hoping for us both.

"I'm going to start by telling you a little bit more about my family. I hope that's okay."

"Yes. Go on."

"My example of a relationship was not good. I've told you a little about it, but I don't think I've ever painted the full picture. My parents barely looked at one another. They never delved into each other's lives and barely did into mine, either. They made sure my basic needs were met, usually by staff. They made sure I attended school and that my grades matched their expectations of me. When we had dinner together, they would be silent dinners. Everyone was busy engaging in their own lives. The only form of affection I got was praise for my accomplishments. For going above and beyond and getting recognized for it."

"I'm sorry you didn't get the love you deserved." Her eyes were tearing up and I knew those tears were for the little boy I'd been, not for the man I was now.

"My grandparents weren't like them, especially my grandmothers. I hadn't thought about them for a while, since I lost them when I was pretty young, but when I think back to visits with them, I remember playing and hugs. They would enquire about my day, my thoughts. And they would cheer my successes but from a place of mutual joy and not a judgement on my value for being successful."

"They sound wonderful."

"They were, as far as I can remember."

"Thank you for sharing all of this with me."

I turned to face her fully because the next part was the most important and the hardest. "I'm sharing all of this with you because I want you to understand why I'm about to say what I'm about to say. I agree with your decision." She paled so I rushed to say more, "Not because I don't want you, God, I've missed you so much the last couple of days. I don't want you to ever think that is the case, because it couldn't be further from the truth. I... I reached out to a therapist yesterday. We talked and we are going to continue to talk. Turns out... I have unresolved mommy *and* daddy issues." I smirked and winked at her. "It's a mystery, I know."

She smiled and it was like the sun for me.

"There was this voice I never told you about that hung around during our whole relationship. The louder it got, the more sure it was that I was going to fuck up our relationship, the harder I tried to win you. I used my skills from being an agent, skills I probably got because of my childhood trauma, to be the perfect boyfriend. As hard as I fought for that to be true, I fought equally hard to keep you separate from my work, so when things didn't work out, I would still be okay going back to solely focusing on Avalanche."

"You got all of that from one session? That was one hell of a therapy session."

I chuckled. "No. I got reading material that I devoured overnight from one therapy session. I recognized so much of myself in the stories I was reading. It's going to take so many more sessions to untangle what's been going on in my head and to stop looking for ways to maximize one part of your affection while keeping away other parts. The therapist assures me this will take time and I hate it, but I think back to my grandparents and I think I knew love once, so why not again? Right?"

Summer moved to the couch next to me and held my hand. Feeling her skin on mine was a balm to my soul. I missed her so, so much and I was about to miss her even more. "You deserve love, Jason, no doubt about it, and it's not because of all you do for me, it's because of who you are."

"Thank you for opening my eyes to wanting more for myself than what was comfortable and safe. I guess we're even. Both driven to want more."

"And you wanting more is wanting us to be over? I just want to understand fully what you are saying."

"No. Me wanting more means taking the time to grow into the person I want to be for you. I think for at least the first few weeks of therapy, I will need to focus on, well, me. If we are together, I'm worried that I'll be tempted to follow some unhealthy patterns that won't let me grow."

"That makes sense." Tears were freely falling down her beautiful face now and I wanted to make it better so badly. "The gnomes and I will miss you."

"Hopefully, if all goes well, not for too long. And I'll miss you too. In fact, I miss you already."

There really wasn't anything left to say. We hugged and held on for probably too long, and then she was gone. I only hoped that one day in the near future, I could have her back. For now, I figured my linen closet needed some organization.

32

GROWTH

Summer

I walked past my café, enjoying the California sun on my skin. I paused to look up with my eyes closed and let the warmth soothe me. *You can do this. You can make this a reality. You are doing just fine without Jason.* I knew that two out of the three of those were truths and one was a lie. I shook the melancholic feelings off. Not today. The nights, well, those I couldn't control, they were hard, but I wasn't going to lose this opportunity to grow my café. Not a chance.

I continued on, seeing one of the signs we recently put up on a bus station stop. It read:

Operation Romance and Roasting: Please join The Ripped Bodice as they present a signing of the recently released book-to-movie, Catering Love. The author, Cathy Benét, and the lead actress, Vanessa Daring, will both be signing books for your donation. Fun-draising is the name of the game, so come have a blast as we raise funds for our local coffee shop, The Frisky Bean, to expand into catering big events.

Location: Bowltime, a generous contributor

Time: 9AM to 3PM

Date: Today

I arrived at the bowling alley, hopeful that there would be at least a few people there. Kevin had arrived early to set things up and I was going to stay late to do cleanup. When I stepped inside, I couldn't believe my eyes. There were so many people. I saw a line of people to my left, a bunch of people bowling, and others milling about chatting and eating baked goods they'd made the day before.

Sitting at the head of the line, at a table, with stacks of books, were Vanessa and Cathy smiling and signing books. Next to them, sat a jar full of money as well as checks. *Holy shit!*

I surveyed the crowd and saw Camila and Lisa among some of our other regulars. Shane was there talking to a few of the other employees I recognized from his company. He didn't seem to be paying attention to his circle, though, and when I followed his gaze, I saw that standing a little off to the side, were Derek, Kevin, and Jessica. Who was Shane looking at? Just then, Jessica looked up and caught my eye, and a huge smile broke out across her face. She yelled, "You're here. Look what a success your idea is." She rushed forward and gave me a giant hug even as cheers went up all around her.

I was utterly flabbergasted. "I can't believe it. It's just the morning."

Jessica leaned back while Kevin and Derek surrounded us.

"Isn't it amazing?" Kevin asked.

"It really is. It's like everybody in the neighborhood is rallying together for us." Tears of joy pricked my eyes. "After some of those notes we'd been getting, I admit I had a few itsy-bitsy doubts."

Derek spoke up this time. "So proud of you, squirt and Kevin. You've really made something awesome from that dream you used to bore me with."

"Hey." I nudged him. "You didn't find it boring to be our test subject for new recipes."

Kevin nudged me. "Ain't that the truth. The book signing has been a huge success. I still can't believe that Revi is Vanessa's cousin. What a coup that they were able to convince her to do this."

"According to Revi, Vanessa has some selfish reasons for helping.

She wants us to be able to cater the shows and movies that she is working on."

Jessica put her arms around me again and pulled Kevin in too, saying, "You are an unstoppable duo."

Kevin squeezed. "Yes, we are."

I could feel my eyes swimming with unshed tears. Dammit. I was not going to cry. I'd cried enough lately. "I want to check in with Vanessa and Cathy myself. Now, stop making me sappy." I hugged each of them and walked to where the signing was happening.

The owners of The Ripped Bodice caught me before I made it. They'd heard about our café, loved the premise, and were happy we reached out to get their help. I told them about the bookshelf addition and we agreed to discuss how we could work together to stock and sell books as a joint venture. They also wanted to talk about getting their book club meetings catered by the café. That was just, wow. Our potential first client before we'd even launched. Looking around at the exceedingly successful fundraiser, I reaffirmed that I could trust my instincts on this. My voice came out steady and full of confidence when I said, "I would love that and I'm sure my partner, Kevin, will feel the same way."

If my time with Jason taught me anything, it was that sometimes you lost, but if you didn't try, you lost by default. Taking a risk on expanding was worth it. Taking a risk on Jason had also been worth it, no matter what happened next. I could not regret our time together.

"Great. We should set up a meeting to discuss the details as soon as you're ready."

"I look forward to it." I would squeal in delight if I could, but that would probably be considered totally unprofessional. "It was a pleasure talking to you and once again, thank you for your help in pulling this together."

"It was a pleasure talking to you as well."

"I'm off to say hi to Vanessa and Cathy and to make sure they don't need anything."

"We'll talk soon."

I politely excused myself and continued toward my destination. Of course, just as I was coming up alongside Vanessa, my foot snagged on, well, who the hell cared, and I flew forward right into the Hollywood actress, who had some surprisingly good reflexes. Before I could body slam her, Vanessa gripped my shoulders and held me on my feet. "Oh my god. I am so sorry." I was definitely blushing. *Great first impression. Gah.* "I am so embarrassed. I wish I could tell you that was a fluke, but honestly, I should have totally prepared for that to happen. Lately, I've been saved from myself, because—" I caught myself when I realized whose name I was about to say. I stopped talking instead. "Um, anyway, I guess I've become too complacent and need to watch where I'm going."

Vanessa just gave me a gentle and all too stunning smile. "You know, I heard how you two met. I know all about your stellar ability to fall. I was just happy I was here to catch you. How are you, dear?"

She'd heard about how we met? What? From Revi? From Jason? What else did she know? "I'm fine. I can't thank you enough for doing this."

"No need. I'm happy to help and on a selfish note, my cousin loves working there, and I love my coffee and pastries. Now, about being fine..." Vanessa leaned in to whisper to me, "Are you sure you're okay?"

I whispered back, "Yes. I take it you heard something since you're asking me all sly and secretively?"

A snorting laugh escaped from Vanessa and then she continued whispering, "Yes. I heard. Revi told me some of it. Jason a bit more. And I'm good at piecing puzzles together. I have a feeling, based on all the stories about you, that you and I could be good friends."

"I have no doubt, but it may get awkward since you'll be working with Jason and I'll be—well—not with Jason."

"Yes. Well. I just know that he'll come around. You'll see."

"Regardless, I want to thank you so much for today." I looked up and caught Cathy's eyes as she looked over at us and I spoke louder. "Thank you both."

Cathy just mouthed "you're welcome" and went back to talking to her fans.

"I need to get back to signing these books, go enjoy your success." With that, Vanessa sat back down at the table.

I felt a small stab at what she said. I was enjoying the success of our hard work, but I wished he was with me, too. I whispered to her, "I'll see you later."

"Definitely. We need to get together again soon, but socially."

I walked away and wanted some time to process, so I headed to the arcade to hide out. I sat in one of the haunted house shoot 'em up machines where, I was hidden completely from sight, and let my mind wander over some of the things I missed about him. It was a little masochistic, but it also always brought me a smile and made me feel we might still be able to come together again someday.

My spot was perfect for contemplation, except only a few minutes went by when I heard Jessica's voice. I originally thought Jess was looking for me, but then I realized Jess wasn't talking to me. She was talking to—Was that Shane's voice? I was torn. On the one hand, it was weird and a little creepy to be eavesdropping, but on the other hand, I really didn't want to interrupt them and considering all the things Jessica had overheard in our apartment, it can't be all creepy. Right? Then it was too late to make any other choice but to pull out my proverbial popcorn and wait.

Shane was saying, in what I had to assume was his most seductive voice, because damn, he suddenly sounded deep, "Come on, sugar, one game."

Jessica sounded irritated when she responded, "Does that really work? Listen, I'm not your sugar and I don't play with giant man-babies. Weren't you just hitting on my best friend a few months ago?" Yep, definitely Jessica. I could have warned Shane that talking like that to her was a surefire way to get a one-way ticket to hell-no-ville.

"There is absolutely nothing baby about me, honey. Perhaps instead of a game, you'd prefer dinner? Tonight? Who's your friend?"

Well, I had to hand it to him, he didn't take offense easily. That would definitely play in his favor.

"I'm not your honey either, and clearly you can't take a hint. For your information, my friend is Summer. You think I don't know your reputation, Mr. Paxton? Perhaps you would prefer man-whore to man-baby?" I had to assume that one hit its mark.

Nope. Apparently not, because Shane responded, confidence dripping from his voice still, "Nothing with Summer, we've always been just friends, and I'd prefer you call me Shane. How about you call me Shane, and I'll call you, I think I heard your friend Kevin say, Jess?" Oh dear.

"Only my friends call me that, and you have not earned that right." Yeah, I saw that coming from a mile away.

"Then let me take you to dinner so that I can earn that right." I thought he actually sounded quite sincere that time.

"Hmm. Let me think on it. You see, I once had a test where I was aiming to get a perfect score, because of course, that's what was expected of me. That test reminds me of the guy I thought was perfect in high school. Unfortunately, that reminds me of the very bad relationships I've had throughout my years at university because most people suck. And you see, one thought leads to another, as they do, and my answer is still no. Now, I'm going to go. Have a good life." I heard movement, then Shane curse under his breath, and then silence. I was pretty sure they'd both exited her spot in the arcade.

Hmm. I actually wished Jessica would give Shane a chance. Yes, he was a tiny bit of a man-whore, but he was also a really nice, genuine guy. I was totally team Jesane. Or Shassica.

I was startled out of coming up with better name combinations when "Respect" started playing from my pocket. I hesitated for a few seconds because I wasn't sure if I was ready to do this, but maybe talking to Mama was exactly what I needed. I answered the call.

"Hey, Mama."

"How's my sweet child doing?"

"It's been busy, but I'm doing okay." I silently added, 'I think.'

"Derek's filled us in on all that's been happening over the last few days. I'm so proud of you all."

"Me too, Mama."

"Well, from everything I've heard, the good Lord is providing you abundance today."

"Yes, Mama. Sure is. From the looks of today's fundraiser, we should be able to start our expansion into catering within a month."

"That's wonderful news. How are things with Jason?"

"Still at a standstill. I know he's still going to therapy; he's let me know that during one of our brief text messages. I'm not sure if things will ever happen for me and Jason again. At what point do I move on?"

"We'll see. Give it a bit more time if you still love him."

"You know I do. Wait." I didn't mean to ask, but it just slipped out, "What do you mean, we'll see, in regards to Jason?"

"It means that men can be dumbasses when they fall in love. Especially if they have never experienced it before."

"But..." I felt the tears threatening, my throat was beginning to constrict, and I knew why. I was talking to Mama, and she was my most important safe space. The person who helped me out of the dark place I went when my mom died. Who was there for every pain. For every difficult decision. I felt like a lost little girl again as I broke down and started to babble. "What do you see, Mama, that I can't because I feel so lost. So fucking—"

"Language!"

"Seriously? Okay. Fine. So *darn* lost. I love him. I love him, Mama, and I was so sure he loved me. I was probably being so arrogant. He kept telling me he didn't know how to love. That his parents, well, you remember me telling you what he told me about his family. And, well, I've been patient because I want him to have the space to heal, but I miss him so much. I wish I could share the success of today with him and he's not here. I don't know how long I should wait. I don't know if I should reach out just to let him know I still love him or give him total space."

"Oh, baby. I'm so sorry you're hurting right now. I wish I was there to give you some lovin'."

"Me too. I miss him, Mama. I don't want to, but I miss him."

"I know, honey. I know you do. Are you ready for me to lay some truth on you, or do you need some more time?"

Uh-oh. When Mama laid down some truth, she told you what you needed to hear, not what you wanted to hear. She always checked that you were ready to hear what she had to say first, though. "I'm ready." I braced myself.

"So, you're hearing me?"

"I'm hearing you."

"So here is what you need to consider. You've been through some things, no doubt, baby, but you've always had a family to turn to. Jason grew up without any of that. No one to turn to and no one to lay some life lessons on him, like I'm doing for you right now. Independent to the core because that was all he had—"

I got a bit defensive. "You think I don't know all that?"

"Excuse me? Is that how I raised you? You may have your therapist degree, but I'm giving you what life teaches you right now."

Shit. Double shit. "No ma'am. I'm sorry. I'm listening."

"Good. Some people who grow up like that will never be able to move beyond their upbringing, and they will repeat the relationships of their parents every time. I have not met this young man, so I can't tell you if he falls into that category. And I would never tell you to accept less than you deserve. What I am telling you is that there are others who want, crave, will do anything, especially once they taste the other side, to have the exact opposite of their upbringing in their lives. They are so starved for it, and they don't even know what they're hungry for. Then they get a bite and they become voracious and scared. Only you will be able to decide what you've got in Jason."

"I..."

"I'm not done."

"Oh. Um. Okay."

"If your man falls into the category worth fighting for, then the next step is recognizing that relationships take work and even more importantly, forgiveness. If you think that your pop and I didn't need forgiveness many, many times over the years, you'd be wrong. People make mistakes. People hurt people. If you want a real chance, and this is true with anyone, forgiveness is key. If the person you love is open to learn. Open to change. Shows real remorse. Makes real amends. Forgiveness. Let his actions tell you whether he's worth it. Now, why don't you go enjoy the fundraiser, and give all of this some thought? Let it marinate. Then figure out what you've got in front of you and what you want. Then as Pop always says, take action. In this case, action might be something small, something to let him know if he reaches out, he'd still be welcome."

"Thank you, Mama. That helped."

"Of course it did. I don't lay down the truth for nothin'."

I laughed. "No. I suppose you don't. I appreciate it and I love you."

"Love you too, baby. Why don't you plan a trip out here soon?"

"I'll look at tickets and talk to you again in a few days."

"Sounds good. Call if you need anything else. You know I'm always here. Bye, baby."

"Bye, Mama."

I reviewed everything Mama said again and again and came to some conclusions. First, Jason definitely fell into the second category. Every sign pointed to him wanting to be in a different relationship than his parents. Second, he also showed every sign of wanting love and some signs of giving love. I wondered where he was on his healing journey. Third, I missed him. So, what was something small that I could do that wouldn't impinge on his request for time but would let him know that I still loved him and was waiting, for now? I knew exactly what I needed to do. I only hoped it brought him some comfort knowing that he was loved, if nothing else.

33

SUMMER, WINTER, AND THE LIMO

Jason

Sweating in a tux was not a good look, but I was anxiety personified. I hoped that what I'd sent had been enough. I hoped Summer understood the significance. I hoped she still wanted me. Fuck. I hoped she showed up. I waited in the limo in front of her apartment, and then waited some more.

The day before, I'd sent over an invitation to the premiere. It wasn't Vanessa's premiere, that had been a few months ago. No. It was the Matthew Prince movie I'd worked so hard on early in our relationship. I'd addressed the invitation, "To the woman who holds my heart and the key to my success." I also included a handwritten note saying, "Your presence is necessary for this premiere to feel like a success. If you are interested and willing, I'll be waiting in front of your apartment at four o'clock tomorrow. All my love."

Soooo... I waited. She was worth every minute.

I had heard about the success of her fundraising a few months ago and couldn't have been prouder of her. It physically hurt not to be there supporting her, but I knew if I saw her I would focus all my energy on getting her back instead of my personal growth. If I wanted the long term, I was going to have to play the long game and hope it all worked out.

That's not to say I didn't have doubts. At least, I did until I received the Spotify mix link she sent that was just for me. So many love songs and they all had two themes. Either that I was worthy of love or that she was waiting for me. That link helped me keep the course and she was right, I learned I was worthy of love, but even more, I learned that I could give love too. Healthy love. Not I'm trying to impress you so you love me, but genuine I want you to know me love. It was going to take work, for sure, to keep reminding myself of those things, but I'm not planning on letting go of my therapist anytime soon.

I looked out the open door, so hopeful I'd get to see her, and then, there she was.

Summer walked out of her apartment and for a moment I forgot to breathe. She was absolutely stunning. She wore an ankle-length sheath dress in a deep, dark forest green that set off her hair and eye colors perfectly. That hair I loved so much was up in an elaborate twist that looked both artful and purposefully messy. Some of her curls "escaped" in ways that highlighted her cheeks, eyes, and neck. She twirled for me and the simple, classic design of the dress took a turn for the wicked. The back plunged to just above her gorgeous butt and had crystals in crossing, hanging chains from butt to shoulders. I imagined licking my way up the curve of her back along every chain and needed to shut that thought down unless I wanted to greet her with a boner. I wondered, would there be any leftover trepidation at including her on a work function? Nope. All I felt was a ridiculous amount of pride, knowing that she would be on my arm tonight. The organ that swelled the most, though, was my heart. Cheesy as fuck, but true. She came, and that meant everything. It meant we still had a chance.

She spun back around to face me and stuck out one leg, which is when I noticed the slit running up one side. I was in so much trouble tonight. How was I supposed to concentrate with this walking aphrodisiac at my side? Hell if I knew. On her feet she wore crystal-decorated sandal stilettos. Upon seeing those, I wondered how I would keep her from falling over the whole night. That thought was fleeting as my gaze traveled up her leg, over her curves, and finally to meet her eyes, which now had an arched brow over one of them in question.

"You look absolutely gorgeous. I'm not even sure I want to share you with the way you look." Joy suffused her face even as her stunning blush appeared and I felt like the luckiest man alive. "I've…I've missed you."

"I've missed you too, and thank you. I don't know how to do the Hollywood thing, but I wanted to try. I hope I've done you proud."

"I wouldn't want you to change to conform to some Hollywood cookie-cutter standard. I hope you know that."

"I do. I'm just nervous."

"You look amazing, sweetheart, and you have nothing to be nervous about. Everyone will love you because you're you."

"The question is, do you love me because I'm me?"

"I do. I love you, Summer." I thought when the moment came, it would be so hard to say those words and, instead, with Summer, it was the easiest thing in the world.

"I love you too, Jason."

I walked up and wrapped my hand around her neck. Trembling just a bit at touching her again when I thought perhaps I'd pushed her away forever. "Thank you."

Her palm cupped my cheek, and I couldn't help leaning into her touch even as a soul-satisfied sigh escaped me. Everything righted in my world. I gently brushed my lips over hers and felt her pulse start to race under my hand. I was about ready to scrap the premiere to get close to her again in all ways, but she pulled back.

"Later. Let's go celebrate."

I nodded and pulled back. Then I purposefully put my hand along her lower back, feeling the soft material of the dress, the hard crystals, and the warmth of her soft skin. It was definitely going to be a long, hard night. But, I had her at my side, and I was finally looking forward to the event again.

———

Summer

Hours later, and I was ready to get out of these torture heels. Why do we do this to ourselves? Jason had been amazing to watch as he worked the room. And Janet was like his perfect client wingman. One minute she's talking to someone, the next they were somehow handed off to Jason. He was definitely in his element. At times I was right there next to him, but others, I enjoyed hanging back and people watching.

I also had an opportunity to reconnect with Vanessa, who had been invited to the premiere. A surprising amount of people started up random conversations with me and I had a good time basically shooting the shit with some of them. There were a few that had actually heard of The Frisky Bean and when they learned we were beginning to cater, they all took my card to give to their coordinators.

It was getting late when Jason came over and pulled me tight to his side. He turned his head and his breath caressed my ear, causing tingles down my back as he whispered, "You are everything I could ever want in my life. You complete me in every way. You make the successes in my work sweeter. Please tell me you're mine again."

I looked into his beloved face and had only one answer. "Yes."

The most beautiful smile I'd ever seen transformed his features. "I love you. Give me another hour, and I can show you just how much."

"You better—" I leaned into him and whispered for his ears alone. "—because I'm not wearing any underwear."

His voice husky with need, he grumbled, "Minx. Make it thirty minutes."

For a moment, I worried that he would be upset that my actions were doing the very thing he'd worried about—keeping him from his work. I looked into his eyes for recriminations or resentment, but all I saw looking back at me was heat and love. "Deal."

Twenty-four minutes later, but who's counting, we were in the limo again, alone. The limo was heading to Jason's office so we could grab his car. Jason hit a button, which raised the partition separating us from the driver.

"Come here." It had been too long since I'd heard his voice with that deep, sexual quality to it.

I moved closer to him. My skin tingled with anticipation. When I was within arm's reach, he grabbed onto my wrist and tugged. I couldn't control my tumble into his lap. "What the..."

"I missed catching you the last few months."

A soft sigh escaped my lips because I'd missed it too. I licked my lips before asking, "Now that you've caught me, what do you plan to do with me?"

"I'm glad you asked." His hand snaked around my throat as he claimed my lips. He kissed me deeply, thoroughly, and with great fervor. My insides sizzled and I thought I might combust from his kiss alone. "Summer, I don't want another day to go by without waking up next to you. How would you feel about coming to live with me?" He said that even as he pulled me up to straddle his hips.

The slit in my dress opened wide and rode up on my thighs, revealing my drenched pussy. "I'm going to make a mess of your pants."

"I don't care. Are you ignoring what I asked?"

"Yes."

"Why?"

"I don't think I'm in the right condition to answer you."

He smirked. *Bastard.*

"Why is that?" His hand around my throat tightened just a little even as his free hand trailed up my inner thigh.

"Because I can't think right now."

"Should I stop then?"

I rushed a response. "No!"

He chuckled. I didn't care because his hand kept climbing ever so slowly closer. Closer. Closer. Just at the juncture of my thigh and my hip, he paused. "I really think I need an answer."

"Oh, god. Please don't stop."

"I won't, but first, I think we should discuss this."

"Not a chance. Now move your hand or I'll be forced to take things into mine."

"What does that mean?"

Okay, fine. I rubbed the palm of one hand up and down the hard length of him, clearly outlined through his pants. My other hand moved to my wet folds and I began to play with myself. "You talk, I'm busy."

"Fuck me."

"That was the plan, but apparently you're feeling chatty. I'm not."

"You are the hottest thing I've ever seen."

"And you're still talking."

JASON

Did I want to keep watching her or undo my pants and impale her? She was so beautiful in her abandon. In her wantonness. In her ability to go after exactly what she wanted, no holds barred. I decided on the first.

I used the hand around her neck to pull her face close to mine and spoke low against her lips. "Then go ahead and pleasure yourself. I want to watch you come all over my lap before I fuck you."

Then I claimed her lips, again, delving my tongue in and out like the sexual act I was delaying. I pushed her back up and using my thumb, tilted her head up. I licked a line up her neck and whispered to her, "Fuck your fingers into your pussy for me."

I looked down and got a little light-headed. She was my goddess. Venus in full bloom. I moved my hand from her juncture and delved my finger in along hers. Together they plunged in and out as I held her head up so she couldn't move. Couldn't see. This was mine. She was mine. "Can you feel how hot and wet you are as we both fuck you? Our fingers working together to give you pleasure?"

The word was a bare whisper. "Yes."

"Play with your clit."

She did and then she gasped because I'd driven two of my fingers hard and deep into her.

"Make yourself come for me, Summer."

I held her firm and pumped my fingers hard. Her fingers on her clit moved with speedy flicks back and forth until she stiffened and moaned through her orgasm. I stuck my fingers coated in her juices into her mouth and she moaned again. My woman was amazing.

"Beautiful." I released her throat and wrapped both my arms around her body. I held her to me as she came down from her pleasure. "I'm not sure how I thought I could possibly not be in love with you. It's so clear I've been head over heels for you for so long. I need you so much."

She wrapped her arms around my neck and held on tight as well. "I need you too. And right now, I need you inside me."

"Whatever the lady wants."

"Always keep that in mind."

I felt her smile along my neck. She trailed her hands down my torso between until she reached my belt. She pushed her hips back, giving her hands room to undo it, and then she opened the button and tugged down my zipper. She stopped suddenly.

"Wait. How much time do we have before we reach your office?"

I gave her a sly smile. "As much time as we want. I told the driver to take a very long route there and then circle until further notice."

"Smart. I knew there was something I liked about you besides your dick."

"Baby girl. I don't care if all you want is my dick, as long as my dick gets inside you soon and never has to leave."

"That could get weird."

"Now who's chatty?"

"Touché."

No more words needed to be said. We made quick work of my pants and briefs until my cock sprang free. I was so fucking hard.

I grabbed her on both sides of her hips and lifted her up over my erection until the tip entered her. I thought about going slow, but Summer slammed her hips all the way down in one go. Fully engulfed in her body, I couldn't think of anything else but friction. I needed a lot of hot wet friction and, by the way her hips were grinding on me, so did she.

We worked together to achieve a quick rhythm. One we hadn't felt in too long. I missed this so much on top of everything else. She felt amazing. She felt like heaven. She felt like home. I wasn't going to be able to hold out.

I growled, "Play with your clit. Make yourself come again, sweetheart."

She did and I followed her soon after. The walls of her vagina clenched as her body writhed in my arms and my cock jerked as I came so fucking hard it hurt. She fell forward into me and once again, I wrapped my arms around her, holding her as close as I could while still letting her breathe. Her weight pressed to my body felt like she belonged there forever.

Minutes ticked by and we stayed that way even as I softened inside her. We were a mess and that brought a satisfied, smug smile to my heart and face.

"Now, about moving in..."

"Oh my god. Really?" She leaned up and smacked my shoulder.

I hmphed even as I grabbed both her wrists and pulled them behind her back. "I'm quite serious about this."

"And I'm quite serious that I can't discuss this with your cock in my pussy."

"Seems the perfect time. He's ready to move into you permanently too."

"I see."

"I'm starting to worry every time I hear 'I see' from you."

She gave him an impertinent look. "I see."

Summer

We'd been reacquainting our bodies in the limo, in his car, and definitely ever since we got back to Jason's home. And he was still asking me to move in. I wasn't ready but I understood why he was asking. Being apart was so hard. I bit my lip before speaking. "How about I give you a counteroffer?"

"I'm all ears."

"I like living where I do because it's so close to the café. You are welcome to stay over anytime. I will spend the nights before my non-work days at your place if I have no other commitments. Almost like living together but this will give us a chance to figure out us and also how to handle living accommodations for my work days. Does that work for you?"

He didn't answer right away. His face finally softened and he answered, "Yeah. That works for me. For now."

"Yeah. For now. And now that we've had your talk, how do you feel about reacquainting me with your hot tub?"

"I can definitely do that. It's been mad at me for quite a while."

My heart had never felt bigger but lighter too. Like a hot air balloon. I was giddy with it and I was ready to have some fun. I dashed into his backyard with plans for a grand evasion. It was a great idea, except it turned out Jason had some panther ancestor or something because before I even registered his pursuit, he had me in his clutches. I yelped and laughter cascaded through my whole being. He spun me to face him near the outdoor couch and I was momentarily dizzy. Joyously, recklessly dizzy. I beamed up at him as I walked backward, holding onto his arms so he would follow. I gauged the patio couch was not too far behind and when I felt it hit the back of my calf, I fell backward. Before he could stop it, he lost his footing, too, and fell on top of me.

He leaned up on his elbows, looking very concerned. "Are you okay? I'm so sorry I didn't catch you this time."

I giggled up into his concerned face. "This time the tumble was completely on purpose and I'm more than fine, but now, I want you to fuck the fine right out of me until I'm destroyed in your arms because I want *more*."

"Holy fuck, Summer. I love your dirty mouth. Your wish is my command."

"Make it so."

I nodded as he shook his head at my *Star Trek* Captain Picard reference. I figured if he was going to love me, he was going to have to love my references. Then I figured nothing at all as his mouth claimed mine in a searing, all-encompassing, your-mouth-is-all-I-know kind of kiss. My world tilted. I thought it was all mental, but then I realized that Jason had stood with me wrapped around him. "Where are you going?"

"I'm going to make love to the woman I adore, and I plan to take hours to satisfy my need for her. There's no way that's going to happen on the patio."

"I endorse this new plan of yours." We kissed the whole way up to his bedroom. I couldn't wait to feel him again. My appetite for him left me insatiable. "Love me."

"That's the plan, sweetheart."

I bounced on the bed as Jason threw me down. His hands were on my hips, inching my dress up, up, up until he carefully pulled it over my head. I lay completely bare to him. His gaze raked down my body.

"Open for me."

I would deny him—us—nothing, so I bent my knees and opened my legs wide. For the rest of the night, open to each other was exactly what we did.

The next morning, I stumbled into the kitchen to find Jason

putting the final touches to breakfast. He had two plates covered in eggs and bacon. He handed me a mug of coffee as he kissed me along my forehead. "Good morning, baby."

"Good morning. How did I sleep through all this?"

He winked. "I take full responsibility."

"Clearly, you should."

"Gladly."

"Thank you. This looks amazing and I'm famished."

"Shall we eat on the deck?"

"That sounds lovely."

He turned toward the counter to grab our plates and I couldn't help myself. Really, what self-respecting, modern woman could? I smacked his hard ass.

He looked over his shoulder grinning. Grinning! "Hmm. If you really wanted to try that, I would oblige you and see how we both like it."

"Oh. I just meant it as a smack the chef kinda thing, but now that you mentioned it, it might be fun sometime, but I think I like being smacked more than smacking and did I really just admit that?" I grimaced.

"Yep. You sure did. I am still taking diligent notes."

"Okay. Well. Breakfast?"

"Grab my coffee?"

"On it."

We made our way to the picnic table out back and looked out at the misty morning view. It was so peaceful, I was a little startled when he started talking.

"Summer, I feel I should be totally honest about my intentions here."

I felt every nerve come to attention with concern. I even sounded nervous when I replied, "Okay."

"I plan to marry you, sweetheart. Now that I have you back, I don't plan to ever let you go nor give you a reason to leave me."

"Did you just propose to me?"

"Uh. I guess I did? I hadn't meant to, um, that sounded wrong. What I meant to say was that I hadn't prepared to do it today. I don't have a ring or anything. I mean every word of it, though. You don't have to answer me now. Clearly, we haven't even decided on the moving in together part, but this is my bumbling way of saying I love you and my intentions are... forever."

"Duly noted. Just so you know, when it's right, and if things continue like this, my answer will be yes, and I hope in my heart that I get to give you that yes someday. This will give us a chance to also figure something else out."

"What's that?" He raised a brow in question.

"We have come full circle, have we not? We still need to figure out what to do about names, because just like I told you, upon our second meeting, I will *not* be Summer Winter." I waggled my bacon at him for emphasis.

"I don't feel either of us has to change our last names. If you wanted to, I wouldn't object or anything, but it's definitely not necessary. I could too, but would rather not. Look. It's solved."

"Fancy that. Seems like it was almost too easy."

"Oh. I plan to definitely be too easy. The easiest." He stood, and pulled me out of my seat still nibbling the last of my bacon.

"Hey!"

"Easy. I hope you take advantage of just how easy I plan to be, at every opportunity."

"Mmmm." I was enjoying the bacon, but that sound of enjoyment was all for the feel of Jason's hard cock pressed along my belly. Then he lifted me into the air, legs wrapped around his waist, the t-shirt I had thrown on pulled up, and his cock inside me. How and when had he removed his boxers? The man was truly magic, but I couldn't really think of anything else except the feel of him, easy and hard and all mine.

Back at my house, all my Goddess cards were probably rejoicing that we finally got it right.

EPILOGUE

Jason

I was usually unflappable, but fuck if I wasn't nervous about our upcoming trip. I'd known it was inevitable, but I was not ready. Summer kept trying to reassure me that it would be fine, but I knew nothing about handling this kind of situation. Talk about a fish out of water.

"Are you still on the verge of canceling our trip over there?" Summer's voice was humorous but I wasn't sure there was anything funny about this.

"Maybe it's too soon? Couldn't we delay this by say, a month? A year?" I was definitely being ridiculous but my fight or flight was in full effect and I was ready to flight hard.

Summer walked up to me and wrapped her arms around my waist, offering me comfort. I tried to let her warmth settle into me, but I was strung too tight to succeed. "Jason, ever since you told me about your parents, a lot of things have become clear, and I understand why this is so hard for you, but I promise you, my parents will love you. You've talked to them on the phone. They've already welcomed you."

"I know." And I did, but I still couldn't help the wild anxiety gripping me. What did I know about dealing with parents. It actually would have been easier if her parents had been standoffish or cold, like mine, but they were so wonderful, so welcoming, so loving, and I knew nothing about how to behave with them. Needless to say, I'd been talking about nothing else with my therapist the last few sessions.

"I see. Jason, first take a deep breath for me." So I did. "Great. Now kiss me." Okay. I was usually the one giving the orders about such things, but I could roll with it, especially now. So I did. "Now look at me, baby." I did. "You are so fucking lovable it hurts. I know your parents didn't know how to love you, and you're worried about not knowing what to do when mine do, but, baby..." She cupped my cheek and continued, "...you just need to open yourself up like you have with my friends, with Derek, with Janet, and most importantly, with me. They're just people, and given time, you'll be ready to take the dive with them too. It doesn't have to be on day one. Take your time."

"Right."

"That didn't help," she stated with concern.

Had it helped? Yeah, it had. I took another deep and slightly shuddering breath as I released my anxiety. "I needed that. Thank you."

"Of course. Love you. Now give me a minute to review with Jessica everything she'll need to know to run the café with Kevin while we're gone, and I'll be ready to head to the airport. Denver, here we come."

My woman might find guidance from her Goddess cards, but she was all the guidance that I needed.

STAY TUNED *for Jessica and Shane to return in Frisky Business.*

ABOUT THE AUTHOR

Michelle Mars has an unhealthy obsession with coffee, caramel, and funny t-shirts. This single mom of two amazing, kind, and creative dragons/children has naturally purple hair and loves nothing more than talking books, kids, and living your best life. She enjoys reading romance, traveling, and writing stories that make her readers laugh, sweat, and swoon.

Author of the steamy, paranormal, sci-fi, romcom Love Wars Series; Moving Jack, Chasing Rory, and Embracing Irina out now, and Claiming Jill, coming soon.

And, the contemporary romcom series, The Frisky Bean; Frisky Intentions, the short story prequel, Frisky Connections, and Frisky Business coming 2023.

Michelle's truth: Humor is a turn-on!

For updates go to www.michellemars.com and register to her newsletter.

facebook.com/michellemarsbooks
twitter.com/MichelleMarsHEA
instagram.com/michellemarsbooks

ALSO BY MICHELLE MARS

Frisky Connections - A prequel, Hanukkah short story in The Frisky Bean universe.

Other Work:

Moving Jack, Love Wars Book 1

You can buy both covers in print signed by me from my website www.michellemars.com. Illustrated cover available in ebook and audiobook as well.

Chasing Rory, Love Wars Book 2

You can buy both covers in print signed by me from my website www. michellemars.com. Illustrated cover available in ebook and audiobook as well.

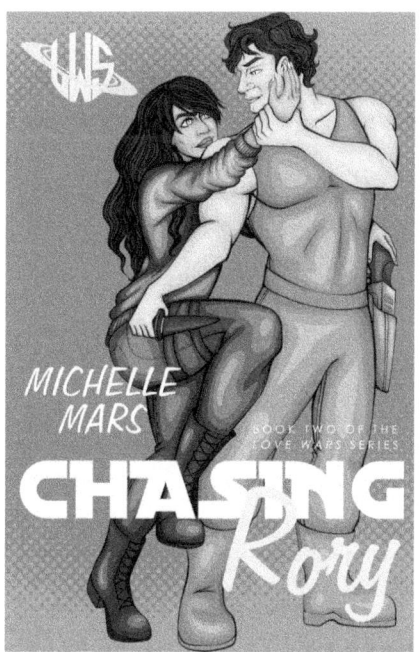

Embracing Irina, Love Wars Book 0.5 Prequel

You can buy both covers in print signed by me from my website www. michellemars.com. Illustrated cover available in ebook and audiobook as well.

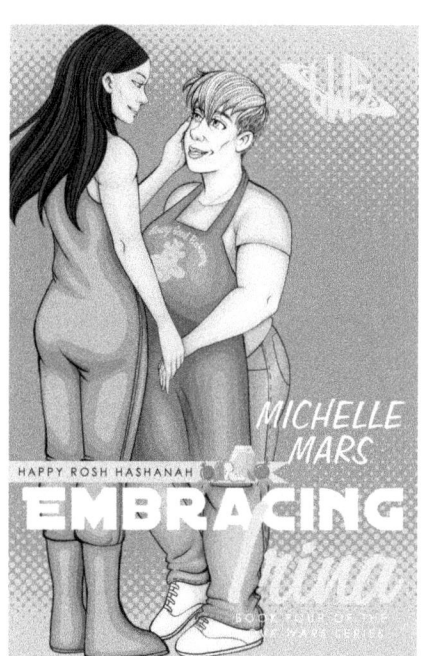

HAPPY ROSH HASHANAH

MICHELLE MARS

EMBRACING *Trina*

BOOK FOUR OF THE MARS SERIES

Printed in the USA
CPSIA information can be obtained
at www.ICGtesting.com
LVHW012128080424
776770LV00003B/415